# Ordinary Saints

# Praise for *Ordinary Saints*

'Beautifully written and brilliant on grief, love and family expectations. Wonderful'
*Daily Mail*

'This debut is pretty perfect. It's informative, original, heartfelt, very real, and stunningly written'
*Irish Examiner*

'Stunning. A beautiful story about the awkward, often painful silences around dinner tables. A fresh, funny, honest portrayal of familial love. I adored it'
Louise Nealon, international bestselling author of *Snowflake*

'Mesmerising and original, *Ordinary Saints* is quite a novel: an empathetic, heart-felt and nuanced exploration of the Catholic church in modern Ireland, queer identity, family and so much more. I absolutely loved it'
Victoria MacKenzie, award-winning author of *For Thy Great Pain Have Mercy on My Little Pain*

'[An] inventive exploration of identity, faith and family'
*Irish Times*

'Funny and deeply moving. I adored it'
Chloe Michelle Howarth, author of *Sunburn*

'A truly extraordinary exploration of relationships, grief, queerness, and its relationship with the Catholic church in Ireland ... fuelled by such complex emotions which are unpicked so delicately and fully ... so deeply worth reading and impossible to not feel some emotional connection towards'
*NB* Magazine

'An exciting new voice on the Irish literary scene'
*Image*

'A clever, emotionally complex, and unfailingly generous debut, I found *Ordinary Saints* both deeply moving and utterly gripping'
Kate Young, author of *Experienced*

'An engrossing and absorbing read . . . Uplifting and absolutely gripping'
Rachel Dawson, author of *Neon Roses*

'*Ordinary Saints* is the best debut novel I've read in a long time. Niamh Ní Mhaoileoin is a writer of immense delicacy, perception and heart, drilling deep into questions of faith, family and love. A beautiful novel and a huge talent'
Jessica Moor, author of *Hold Back the Night*

'Niamh Ní Mhaoileoin's writing has a real magic to it that hits you right from the first sentence'
Okechukwu Nzelu, award-winning author of *The Private Joys of Nnenna Maloney*

'I both learnt – and felt – a lot reading *Ordinary Saints*. An intriguing, compelling and deeply original debut'
Roxy Dunn, author of *As Young as This*

'An outstanding debut. Delicately woven through with the threads of modern Irishness. Emotionally intelligent, hilarious, superb'
Soula Emmanuel, award-winning author of *Wild Geese*

'Deeply emotionally engaging and profoundly thought provoking. A world I knew nothing about was opened up to me. A cracking great read; and one that stays with you long after you turn the last page'
Sui Annukka, winner of the Women's Discoveries Prize

'A fascinating exploration of religion, family dynamics and love in all its forms told in exquisite, crystalline prose'
Angela Chadwick, author of *Xx*

'A moving novel about love, loss and life's mysteries. As someone who isn't religious, I found the exploration of canonisation in the modern age fascinating and I think this will have wide appeal'
*The Bookseller* – Editor's Pick

Niamh Ní Mhaoileoin is an Irish writer living and working in Edinburgh. In 2022, she won the PFD Queer Fiction Prize and was shortlisted for the Women's Prize Discoveries award. Her work has appeared in *Gutter, The New Statesman, The Irish Times*, the *Fierce Salvage* anthology and elsewhere. *Ordinary Saints* is her debut novel.

# Niamh Ní Mhaoileoin
# Ordinary Saints

**MANILLA PRESS**

First published in the UK in 2025
This paperback edition published in the UK in 2026 by
MANILLA PRESS
An imprint of Bonnier Books UK
5th Floor, HYLO, 105 Bunhill Row, London, EC1Y 8LZ

Copyright © Niamh Ní Mhaoileoin, 2025

"The Summer Day" by Mary Oliver
Reprinted by the permission of The Charlotte Sheedy Literary Agency as
agent for the author. Copyright © 1990, 2006, 2008, 2017 by
Mary Oliver with permission of Bill Reichblum

All rights reserved.
No part of this publication may be reproduced,
stored or transmitted in any form or by any means, electronic,
mechanical, photocopying or otherwise, without the
prior written permission of the publisher.

The right of Niamh Ní Mhaoileoin to be identified as Author of this
work has been asserted by her in accordance with the
Copyright, Designs and Patents Act, 1988.

This is a work of fiction. Names, places, events and
incidents are either the products of the author's
imagination or used fictitiously. Any resemblance to
actual persons, living or dead, or actual
events is purely coincidental.

A CIP catalogue record for this book is
available from the British Library.

Paperback ISBN: 978-1-78658-425-0

*Also available as an ebook and an audiobook*

1 3 5 7 9 10 8 6 4 2

Typeset by IDSUK (Data Connection) Ltd
Printed and bound by CPI (UK) Ltd, Croydon CR0 4YY

The authorised representative in the EEA is
Bonnier Books UK (Ireland) Limited.
Registered office address: Block B, The Crescent Building
Northwood, Santry, Dublin 9, D09 C6X8, Ireland
compliance@bonnierbooks.ie
www.bonnierbooks.co.uk

*For my mother, Thecla*

#  Part One

# Chapter One

THE FIRST TIME I KISSED a girl my brother died. I was sixteen and at a party in a big house overlooking Dublin Bay. My brother was in Rome, studying to be a priest. For most of the evening, though it was only Saint Patrick's Day and still cold, I sat alone on an elaborate wooden patio chair, getting drunk and staring at the glimmer of the coastline, following the slow ferry's lights as it pulled out to sea.

'Do you mind if I sit with you? I've brought supplies.'

It's Aisling, a friend of a friend from the Irish-speaking school across town.

'Oh yeah, yeah, of course.'

The words gurgle a little in my throat so I gesture at the other chair in the set to confirm. Aisling, carrying a bottle of wine in one hand and a small basket of garlic bread in the other, lowers herself down.

'It's so sweaty inside,' she says. 'And loud. I was looking for somewhere I could rest for a minute and then I saw you out here.'

'I'm being pretty anti-social,' I say, which is true. I realised too late that I was in no mood for Síofra's house party, with all its shouting and spilling drinks and close, hot breath. My humour was all right when I left home in the afternoon but around seven or half seven something shifted. I felt myself hating every new face that came through the crystal-paned front door. Later, after I find out, I try to track my movements against my brother's, to figure out if this abrupt emotional unmooring is a telepathic reaction to his energy being suddenly and improbably sucked from the universe. But the timings don't match up. I'm just in a mood.

'Fair enough,' Aisling says, pouring wine into the mug I've balanced on the arm of the chair. Lady Golfers Have More Drive, it reads in cartoon letters. She looks up and smiles, her teeth so straight and white that they catch the moonlight. 'Though I have been wondering why you never talk to me.'

I don't know what to say. It's never occurred to me to speak to Aisling, who's a year and a half older than me and half a foot taller, plays football for Dublin and looks like a warrior queen from ancient mythology: big joints, pale skin, a tumble of reddish hair.

I smile back. 'I'm shy.'

Inside, there's the sudden sound of girls screaming and we both turn, thinking something's happened. But then someone turns the music up and they all shriek again, the noise breaking through the patio doors and spilling across the lawn.

'Jesus Christ,' murmurs Aisling. 'If I never hear "Mr Brightside" again in my life it'll be too soon.'

I laugh, a bit too loud. 'I hate them too.'

'Yeah? What kind of music do you like?'

The garlic bread becomes very dry in my mouth and I have to force a scratchy swallow. 'Oh, a bit of everything.'

Aisling raises a fair, almost invisible eyebrow. 'Cool. I love everything too.'

'Nick Cave!' I nearly shout, though I've only heard one of his songs – last week, on the radio in my father's car – and can't even remember what it was called.

'Hmm, OK. That is cool.' Relief floods my body, so powerful that I think it might knock me out. 'It's a bit rubbish though, isn't it, liking different music to everyone else? It kind of makes you feel like an outsider.'

I say nothing. We watch two trains curve silently along the bay, their lights getting closer and closer, looking like they might crash.

'You know, any time I see a train, even if I know it's only going to Bray or whatever, it makes me jealous of the people on it. That they're going somewhere and I'm not.'

It sounds stupid as I say it, but Aisling doesn't laugh. Instead, she reaches out and takes my hand, dreamily, sympathetically, like other girls sometimes do when they talk. The world begins spinning faster then, the stars and the darkness of the sea and the sounds of the party all swirling together, catching fire and extinguishing from one moment to the next so that the two small islands of our patio chairs are the only points of stillness in the universe and our hands the bridge between them. I wonder if this is what a mystical experience would feel like. I wonder if I'm being called by God.

We stay there talking in the darkness for hours until Aisling says that she's sorry but she absolutely has to go to the bathroom.

'But please don't leave,' she says and I shake my head, even though I'm freezing, my lips so numb they're slurring over words.

Once she's gone, the silence and intensity of my feelings are too much to cope with. I look at my phone. Four missed calls, two from each of my parents. My chest tightens. How do they know? A text appears from my father:

*Please call us back as soon as you see this. We urgently need to speak to you.*

Perfectly punctuated, no text talk. They've clearly realised somehow that Síofra is hosting a party and not – as I've told them – a movie night with a few of the girls. But what can I do about that now? To call back when I've been drinking will only make things worse. And worse again, it might break the thread with Aisling, pull me back into my life of a few hours ago. No, I decide, they'll have to wait until morning.

I find out later that my father called the landline too but Síofra – just as drunk and panicked as I was, the party having grown far beyond her expectations – banned anyone from answering it. And so I had my night in the starlight, at the same time my brother's curly head was being sawed open by the surgeons and my parents were packing their bags, ready for the first flight the following morning. When she came back from the house, Aisling suggested we go for a walk around the vast garden and we did, murmuring and laughing, shouldering each other gently into flowerbeds until eventually, in the pitch dark of a small thicket of trees, she caught me by the waist and kissed me, a long wet teenage kiss – and a revelation. Her mouth tasted funny, like a sweet you've eaten too soon after brushing your teeth, and I realised that she had taken a swig of mouthwash from the bottle in Síofra's bathroom cupboard. That meant a lot to me, that Aisling had made a plan. It made me think that maybe it was all being planned somewhere, by someone, the life I was meant to have.

I went to sleep that night, alone in a huge spare room, beatifically drunk and assured that everything was, and would be, as it should be.

# Chapter Two

ANOTHER SUNDAY MORNING, thirteen years later. I'm on the Piccadilly Line, on a long journey east from Ealing Common, where the woman I'm seeing has a flat. We were out in central last night and it may have been unwise to go home with her when I knew she was working this morning. But she had taken my hand, had traced her lips across my cheek and asked me to go with her in a hot whisper that clouded the night air. And, yes, I'd said. Yes to the rowdy night tube and the weight of her head on my shoulder, yes to the hot tea and sleepy sex we had when we got there, and yes to this return train, stuffy with tourists heading for the museums.

I don't know where they all came from; the carriage was empty when I got on and I'd dropped into an end seat, cradling myself between the cushion and the plastic partition, slipping in and out of vertiginous half dreams: a sickening misstep, a failed alightment, my whole body disappearing between the train and the platform like a sheet of paper sucked into a shredder.

I shake myself awake. We're pulling into Barons Court, where the train takes its last gasp of open air before diving under central London – and everyone checks their phones.

My hangover swells when I see my father's name onscreen. I've missed his call. I think I might vomit.

*Could you give me a ring when you see this, please?*

I press the icon and lift the phone to my ear, my hand starting to tremble. But we've pulled out of the station and into the tunnel now and my reception is gone.

This is how life changes, our old selves ripped away quickly, like skin from a wound. I didn't understand that the night I kissed Aisling so I woke up the next morning unprepared, when I finally called my father, for the background noise of Rome Ciampino and the news that my brother was brain dead, soon to be dead dead. But I understand it now, and there's a slide deck of horrors shuffling through my mind as the train rattles under Kensington: my mother in intensive care, my aunt Breda crushed by a lorry, my father himself diagnosed with terminal cancer. I bend over, wrapping my arms around my knees.

'Excuse me, are you OK?'

An American woman is leaning towards me. She got on with her family a few stations back, all in baseball caps and cargo shorts, the children trailing Subway sandwich fillings after them, the father bellowing about the number of stops. I'd rolled my eyes and she'd noticed, tried to hush them. Now they're all gathered around me, hats pecking like worried birds.

'Oh yeah, I'm fine, thank you. Just a little dizzy. Fine.'

She frowns, reaches into her striped canvas bag and lifts out a cold can of Coke. I take it, feeling ashamed. The sugar helps, eases the trembling in my arms and legs.

'Can I give you some money for this?'

'Oh no, sweetheart, of course not. But are you sure you'll be able to get home OK?'

I assure her that I will, that I'm feeling much better.

'Thank you so much,' I say as they pick up their backpacks and sandwich wrappers. 'I hope you have a lovely day.'

The two children keep shooting me nervous glances as they wait inside the doors. I smile and wave. As the train pulls away they're navigating the platform with small serious steps, their parents' smiles spread over them like parasols.

By Leicester Square I can't stand it anymore, the not knowing is like a hot stone in my gut. It drives me out of my seat, through the slow, heaving crowds of the station and on to the chaos of Charing Cross Road. I cut down a side street and crouch in a doorway to make the call, shivering as I wait for my father to answer, the sweat from the packed station going cold under my jumper and coat. The tone sounds six times, seven, eight.

'Pick up the fucking phone,' I murmur.

'He-l-lo.'

'Dad. Hi. It's me.'

'Ah, hello! How's it going?'

His voice sounds strange to me, strong and upbeat. I can't remember when I last spoke to him.

'Yeah, all fine thanks. What's up?'

'Does now suit to talk? Are you out someplace?'

'I'm just on my way home.'

'Well, I can call you later if that'd be better?'

'No, that's fine.'

'Have you been doing something nice?'

'Dad, please. Just tell me what's going on.'

There's a pause.

'Sorry, Jacinta,' he says quietly. 'There's nothing at all the matter. Everyone's fine.'

All the held breath slides out of me in a rush.

'Jay,' I say.

'What?'

'You know I prefer to go by Jay.'

He laughs softly, says he prefers to call me by the name I was given. I sink my forehead into the knuckles of my right hand.

'Whatever. Can you please tell me why you're calling?'

He coughs. 'Well, it's actually a bit of good news. It might get some media attention so your mother and I wanted to make sure you heard it from us.'

I snort. 'Have you won Euromillions?'

'It's about Ferdia.'

Gravity shifts, my head feels light and my legs heavy. I slide off my hunkers and on to the ground.

'For some time, as you know, we've been working to build recognition of his life and his, ah, his legacy.' It sounds as though my father is reciting a prepared speech. I can tell that my mother is there too, can picture her sitting on the arm of his chair, neck craned so she can listen in.

'OK,' I say.

'And this week we've heard that the Archbishop of Dublin has –' he coughs, a moped rattles by and I press my fingertips hard against my left ear '– has informed us that he now intends to open a cause for canonisation.'

'I'm sorry?' I say, though I know what he's said. My hands and feet feel very cold. I can hear my mother's laugh ringing in the background and the next voice on the line is hers.

'Your brother is going to be a saint!'

I lean back against the concrete, flooded with the kind of complete astonishment that comes when something you've always known might happen eventually – the end of a holiday, say, or a long-threatened war – is actually happening, now, to you, in real life. It must be about five years since my parents posted me a thick packet of laminated prayer cards, with a picture of my brother and a prayer. *Heavenly Father,* it read. *For Your glory, that of Your Beloved Son, that of the Holy Spirit, and that of Our Blessed Mother, we ask that You grant the favours we ask, as a sign that the life of our brother Ferdia Devane has been pleasing to You on this earth and that he is now rejoicing with You in Heaven.* I still have them, stashed in the suitcase under my bed with all the other things I have no use for but feel it would be wrong to throw away: filled moleskine notebooks, old laptops, expensive pairs of heels. It seems strange now that I didn't take the arrival of the cards as a prompt to learn how canonisations actually happen, but I didn't. All I can dig up is a memory of the morning Padre Pio became a saint and we all drew pictures of him in the children's chapel: black eyes, grey beard, cascades of red crayon pouring from his hands.

'Are you still there?' My father's voice again. Bombshell dropped, my mother seems to have wandered off.

'What does that mean, exactly? I mean, in practical terms, how does canonisation work?'

He clears his throat. 'Well, Mammy is getting a little ahead of herself. The process is very complex and can take decades, even centuries. It's not assured that your brother will ever be a saint and, if he is, we may none of us be here to see it.'

'I see.'

'I mean, with no offence meant to Ferdia, it took Joan of Arc five hundred years and she had quite the CV.'

I laugh. Though clearly rehearsed, the joke is solid. Satisfied with himself, he goes on.

'So in the next few months the cause will be officially opened and Ferdia will be named a Servant of God. Then, over the coming years, evidence will be gathered and his writings will be assessed to ensure they're in keeping with Church teaching and morality. Witnesses to his life will be asked to give testimony, including ourselves, and eventually a full account of his life, called a *positio*, will be presented to the Congregation for the Causes of Saints in Rome. And after all that, if they conclude that he lived a life of heroic virtue, Ferdia will be declared Venerable. But then . . . well, then, I'm afraid, we'll need a miracle.'

He pauses again for laughter, which this time I don't supply. 'What qualifies as a miracle?'

'It generally means that someone has prayed for the intercession of the candidate in heaven and, without any other explanation, an illness or injury has been healed. With one verified miracle the Venerable Servant of God can be beatified. And after a second they can be canonised, becoming a saint. But, as I say, that possibility is, for now, very remote.'

'So that's what the prayer cards are for?'

'Exactly.'

Another long silence.

'It is a huge honour,' my father says, as though I've missed the point. 'I know it's a lot to think about. But for your brother it's a living legacy.'

'OK,' I say. 'Well anyway, I'm afraid my battery's dying so I'm going to have to go.'

'Just one last thing,' he jumps in. 'We'll be having our usual anniversary mass in March. Nothing formal for now, just a chance to celebrate the news. With a meal in the hotel afterwards.'

'Oh right. That sounds nice.'

'So you'll come?'

I say nothing, wondering if he bought the low battery story, if I could get away with hanging up. It's been ten years at least since I went to one of these masses, so long that my parents don't usually share the arrangements any more.

'I'll have to think about it,' I say eventually. 'I don't know if I'm free that weekend.'

'Three-line whip, I'm afraid.'

I nearly laugh, mildly outraged that he thinks he has any claim on my time. But maybe there's something in the air or in the way that he's asked because – after waiting another thirty seconds to prove I'm making the decision myself – I agree to go.

'Great,' he says. 'OK.'

'OK. Bye.'

'Nice to hear from you, Jacinta. And we'll speak again soon, I hope.'

'Yes. Look after yourselves. Bye.'

'Bye now. God bless.'

I end the call and consider flinging my phone against the wall, like I used to when I was away at university. Back then, it acted as a sort of counterbalance to the flatness of my conversations with my parents, gave physical expression to how broken everything felt. But right now, I don't actually feel the kind of coursing anger that a display like that takes. My bum and legs are numb from sitting on the ground and the chill is spreading upwards like a fog so that my mind feels clumsy and heavy, like a dead hand trying to grip a pencil. Eventually, I force out a laugh, thinking that this surely puts me in the gold league of inadequate second children. But there's no relief in it, no cleansing power, because for that I'd need someone to laugh with.

Can you imagine it? I'd say to them. Can you imagine me there in the front row in Saint Peter's Square? The lesbian sister of a literal saint.

*

Back at home, I sleep for a few hours. Blank, heavy afternoon sleep that leaves me no more rested than when I closed my eyes. The sun is setting now and through my window I watch the white facades of the houses opposite turning a harsh, wintry gold. Already the conversation with my father seems like it happened a long time ago, and it strikes me that although I asked him how my brother would become a saint, it hadn't occurred to me to ask why.

I look at the picture of Ferdia on my wardrobe door, an original, developed from film, which I've Blu-Tacked to each of the nine wardrobes I've had in the last decade. It was taken on a family holiday in Clifden, during a brief intermission in a week of rain. We've seized the moment, gone for a walk on the beach, just the two of us in the howling wind. Ferdia's dark hair is standing almost vertical and his cheeks are blown back into a grin. Our clothes are gritty, damp with sea spray, and as I point the camera I have to brace my small body against the gale. He shouts something to me but the wind and the waves are too loud. I can't hear.

'What was it about you?' I ask aloud, the first time I've spoken to the picture in years.

But my brother doesn't respond.

## Chapter Three

THIS IS WHERE I imagine the story starts. The pope's helicopter appears over the tree line and my mother feels a low swoop of nausea, though she doesn't pay it much heed. The morning is sunny, warm for September, and the huge expanse of the Phoenix Park is close packed with congregants. A million-and-a-quarter souls, the old farmer next to her said earlier, a small battery-operated radio pressed to his ear. He's dressed in a brown suit and, as the crowd around them roars and waves frantically upwards, he stands quiet and still, eyes brimming with tears. The excitement is getting to everyone.

It's not until she faints during the Eucharistic Prayer – slumping softly against the thick crowd in what many interpret as a fit of religious ecstasy – that my mother starts to worry she might actually be unwell. Still the truth doesn't occur to her and, some minutes later in the medical tent, she gasps in outrage at the St John's Ambulance volunteer, a man in his fifties, who asks, very tentatively, if she might be expecting, snatching her hand away from him as he takes her pulse.

'All right, take it easy,' he murmurs, patting her shoulder. 'I just thought . . .' Her eyes follow his to her left hand

and the wedding band seems to clamp around her finger as she realises that after all those years of not ... and of promising that she would never ... now everyone is going to know that she has. She can't bring herself to look at my father, who's keeping himself busy in the corner, examining the construction of the marquee.

They were six months married then. As a child, as far back as she could remember, my mother had wanted to be a nun. Newly eighteen, just a few weeks after her Leaving Cert, she took the train from Carrick-on-Shannon to Dublin, joining the Carmelites in Kilmacud as a postulant. Though my grandparents had wanted to drive her the whole way, she refused, ready to be alone with God at last. But something happened in the months that followed. A weakening she couldn't explain, a failure of the spirit. She left the convent and trained to be a teacher instead. On her first day of work, she met my father, a few years older than her, diligent and very devout, inclined to rattle the rosaries in his pocket as he taught algebra.

Theirs was a slow, old-fashioned courtship and she didn't think it was very serious at first. But when she told her parents and sisters about him, they were so delighted that she decided to make a go of it and ultimately, propelled by the force of their approval, closed the door on religious life for good. It was painful but she put her trust in God, assuming He had marked another path for her. Looking back later, she could see that He had, and that the secret of her divine purpose was never contained by convent walls but hidden in the nestling depths of her own body, in the cluster of cells that announced itself that morning in the Phoenix Park and – in the first rush of realisation – made her scalp burn with shame.

Ireland was already on the turn then, though you wouldn't have known it from the size of the crowd. Something new had started growing, something that, left unchecked, would fundamentally change the body it inhabited, dragging resources and nourishment away from their established purposes and towards itself.

People like my grandparents, good Catholic people, didn't want their daughters to be nuns anymore. They weren't praying for their sons' vocations with the same deep yearning. And after generations of naming children according to their religious devotion, after a continuous decades-long march of Marys and Josephs and Patricks and Bernadettes, after a brief bloom of John Pauls, people began to look elsewhere for their baby names, to the pagan past. Gráinne. Fionnuala. Fiachra. Oisín.

Ferdia.

That was what my mother called her new baby, born in the first beam of the first summer of a new decade, as across Ireland women and children decorated their May altars with daffodils.

Ferdia. Man of God. A child soldier in ancient mythology, friend and foster brother to the great boy warrior Setanta – whom others called Cúchulainn – and forced to face him in single combat on the plain of Muirthemne. For days they fought brutally in the hours of sunlight and then, in the dark of night, cried together and slept together and bound each other's wounds, until eventually, with no other options remaining and surrounded by the greatest army Ireland had ever seen, Setanta dealt Ferdia his death blow and sobbed over his corpse. A war of greed fought with the bodies of children. The nation's founding saga.

\*

I scroll through a folder on my phone, searching for a picture from the day they came home from the hospital, my mother looking slim and sharp in a black pencil skirt and a puff-sleeved blouse, her mouth red, almost vampish. It's a photo of a photo, I took it years ago while flicking through an album at home. And when I find it, I see that the catch of the light on the plastic page protector almost completely obscures the bundle of blankets in her arms. My baby big brother, Ferdia Devane.

Right from the start my mother believes, with an almost-blasphemous zeal, that he's been marked out by God. He sleeps well, feeds like a dream, can be trusted to gurgle and smile in any set of arms.

'There's never been a baby like that in our family before,' says my grandmother, peering into the cot where Ferdia lies, awake but quiet. Wide-eyed. Reflective.

'I know,' my mother says, dropping her face towards his. 'You're my little saint, aren't you? Aren't you my little saint?'

My parents have bought a semi-detached new build in Maynooth, fifteen miles west of Dublin and home to what was once the largest seminary in the world. Every day of her maternity leave, my mother wheels Ferdia through town for mass in the college chapel, to be doted over by elderly ladies and blessed by an endless rotation of priests. By the time he's three, and she still hasn't gone back to work, he's playing ball games on the quad with young seminarians. By the time he starts school he knows the names and stories of all the chapel's frescoed saints – Brigid, Patrick, Bernard and Malachy, Columbanus, Columba, Laurence O'Toole – and begs to arrive early so he can say a small prayer of hello to each of them.

His reputation spreads and, from time to time, the priests ask my mother if Ferdia could give a personal tour of the chapel to some visiting dignitary. He's the perfect advertisement for the Irish Church as he tells them, in a voice high and clear as a chorister's, how Brigid gave her father's jewelled sword to a hungry beggar, how Patrick ate the same food as the pigs in his years as a slave, and how Laurence protected the people of Dublin from foreign invaders. The glory of Christian Ireland is held in the marble and stained glass of the chapel and the child's voice lends it life and hope. Of course, the high-ups in Maynooth can see the challenges ahead. They know, long before their congregations, that the glory days are over. Vocation numbers are falling and drop-out levels rising. In another forty or fifty years parishes will wobble and collapse for want of priests. And, most troubling of all, the faithful are becoming restive. Instructions are less likely to be followed. Confidences are becoming harder to keep. But never mind that, Monsignor Visiting Papal Envoy, look at this brilliant young man explaining the legacy of the early Christian monks in Ireland. Witness before you the hope of the Church.

It's against this backdrop that Ferdia, around the time he turns six, becomes obsessed with making his First Communion; speaking about it constantly, praying for it, waking up in the night crying about it and telling my mother that without the sacred host his body feels weak and empty. Eventually, instead of consulting a psychologist, my father speaks to the parish priest, asking if it might be possible to arrange a special dispensation so that his son can receive the sacrament a year early. Permission is granted and in the professional photo taken on the day, which still hangs over the sofa at home, my seven-year-old brother looks tiny and glowing in his beige suit, swallowed up by the expanse of the frame but radiant with delight.

\*

There's a knock on my bedroom door. I sit up quickly and grab a book.

'Do you fancy joining us for dinner?' asks Sasha, one half of the straight couple I live with.

'Ah no, sorry.' My voice crackles from lack of use. Though there's nowhere else to sit in the room, still I worry that Sasha will think I'm a waster, lying in bed all afternoon. 'I'm going to a gig with some friends.'

It is true, though until this moment, I realise, I'd been planning to bail. Sasha nods and withdraws, looking vaguely relieved. She and her husband own the flat and though they're desperate to be decent landlords – 'we like to think of ourselves as the good guys,' Thomas says, whenever I raise an issue – their faces cloud over when we collide in the kitchen or coming in and out of the shower. It's as though I'm a faint smell of cooking. Not actively unpleasant but not something you'd choose to have in your home, all other things being equal.

And it's probably for the best that I'm forced out of my warm sheets and into the blue air of the January evening. I decide to walk to the venue in Dalston, moving slowly through the quiet of Stoke Newington and Canonbury, looking through tall uncurtained windows where people are stirring pots and preparing packed lunches in expensive kitchens. These streets are so tightly packed that I could walk this route every night of the winter and look in a different set of windows each time. Close to Newington Green, I hear the opening of Pachelbel's Canon and stop to listen, searching for the source of the music. A father and son playing together in a terracotta living room lined with books. The little boy looks tiny, taking up barely a third of the stool they share, but I can hear that he keeps racing ahead with the melody, then slowing down again so his father can catch up.

*

I don't have to search hard for stories of the young Ferdia. They're like smooth stones in our family, passed from hand to hand and weathered by the telling. Like the foot of Christ on some giant crucifix, polished with the touch of a million lips.

Gradually, my mother starts to fade from view, just as the mothers of brilliant boys have done for all of history. Ferdia toddles into centre stage and I lose sight of her. She starts working again when he's five or six, part-time, as a substitute teacher at my father's school. But she resents the work, resents him for encouraging her to do it and the students for sitting there, lethargic and demanding. They don't like her either because children always know when they're resented, and have that deep collective knowledge of how to punish the adults who slight them, with blank-faced silence, whispers and smirks. There are other pregnancies too, I know that, though no one's ever told me when or what went wrong. By the time she's thirty-four, it's like the life force has drained out of her. She dresses in slacks, loose-hanging cotton jumpers and flat, sensible shoes. She wears brown lipstick to mass on Sundays and worries about her prayerful and precocious boy, about how the other children are treating him at school.

And then I'm there, dropped screaming into the middle of it all, a colicky, bad-tempered baby with a great greasy helmet of cradle cap.

'They're like sun and rain,' my grandmother says when she comes to help out. 'Funny how it happens like that.'

My mother's mother is a hard-working woman, not given to nonsense and possessed of a stolid lifelong faith. The kind of granny you'd never ask for a second helping of dinner. The kind of neighbour who, if her neighbour were taken ill, would run their household and feed their children without hesitation. The kind of mother who – had the need arisen – wouldn't have thought twice about packing her daughters off to the Magdalene Laundries.

But she softens in the evenings when she comes to sit next to my brother's bed. His little frame is weighed down by a lasagne of woollen blankets, her grey hair is hazy in the glow of the night light.

'Once upon a time, there were three little shepherd children alone on a mountainside . . .'

'Because even children had to work back then, didn't they, Granny?' says pious little Ferdia.

'They did,' says Granny, seriously. She's been telling this story to various grandchildren for years and he's the first to really appreciate it. 'They'd be out all day watching over the sheep in the scorching sun, with only a bit of bread and cheese to keep them going and a drop of water in a flask. But then, on this special morning, a lady appeared dressed in white and more beautiful than you could possibly imagine, with such a light shining around her that your eyes could barely stand it.'

(I can't speak for Ferdia, but in my mind this mystery woman looked a lot like Princess Diana.)

'And the three children, hardly even knowing what they were doing, dropped to their knees and started to pray and pray and pray, like they'd never prayed before. Until eventually, the lady reached out her hand and beckoned the oldest of the children to her –' Granny mimics the motion, her fingers shiny pink '– and leaned down to whisper a secret. And the oldest girl, Lucia, said to the others "we mustn't tell anyone!" and they agreed. They'd say nothing.'

'But the smallest one couldn't keep the secret, could she?' says Ferdia, his little hands gripping the quilt.

'She couldn't,' Granny agrees. 'She was a very holy little girl but a blabbermouth all the same. And so she told her mother and her mother told a friend and before long the whole town and the whole country and nearly all the world knew: the Blessed Virgin Mary had appeared on a summer's day to three little shepherd children at Fatima.'

As she finished the story, Granny would stroke your forehead, the grit of her palms catching a little at your hairline. And then she'd say a decade of the Rosary so that you'd fall asleep to the steady roll of her voice and the click of the beads.

Ferdia was so moved that he used to kneel for hours at the feet of a resin statue of Our Lady of Fatima that stood on the dresser in my grandparents' good front room, so devoted to it that my grandmother got him a miniature one of his own. It's still on his bedroom shelf, I think, near the window, bleached almost white by the sun.

And then, all of eight, he gets told that he's got a new baby sister, and what does he think she should be called?

'Jacinta,' he says without missing a beat, after the blessed little blabbermouth. Everyone's charmed, as ever, so moved by his devotion that they don't think twice about the name, or if it suits the baby just born. And until I start primary school, I love it too. The miracle of Fatima is my favourite game. I play myself, Jacinta, with a white pillow case wrapped around my head to shield me from the sun. And Ferdia, though he's approaching his teens now, commits fully to his role as my brother, Francisco, clutching his stomach and wailing when I tell him we have to forsake our lunch for the conversion of sinners.

But things change a few years after I get to school, when I start to get hassle for my name from middle-class children who don't associate it with the dry hills of Portugal but with the streets of Dublin's north inner city and the women – born in the decades after the apparition – who sell fruit and vegetables there. Jaaaacinnnntah, do ye have any orrandges? they shout at me. Are dey five for a pow-wind?

It's not just the name that gives me trouble either. I'm an odd child from an odd family, and the biggest problem is that I don't realise it. I haven't grasped that by the mid-nineties, Sunday mass is the beginning and end of a normal family's religious practice. My classmates eat whatever they want on Fridays, they rarely say grace before meals, they've never knelt down in the sitting room to say a decade of the Rosary, which we do every evening – a parent in front of each armchair and two children at the couch. If I'd known all that, if my parents had explained, I would have kept quiet about what our house was like, and held back in classroom discussions about Christ's parables. On the first day back after Christmas I would have lied and said I got a Game Boy from Santa instead of bringing in my new set of expensive-looking blue-glass beads. I might have had more friends.

But then, I loved God too. Our house was different because Ferdia was in it and the intensity of his belief was magnetic. He was like a world-class athlete, streaking out in front but pulling the field with him so that even if you couldn't keep up, even if you were getting lapped, there would be these moments when you could sense him next to you, hear the roar of his breath and the force of his focus, and just for a second you'd pull yourself a little straighter, lengthen your stride. It made me feel powerful to pray with him. He made it feel like the most natural thing in the world.

\*

'JAY!'

The voice lifts over two lanes of stalled traffic. I look up. My friend Clem is waving extravagantly in a full-length orange puffer coat and my heart lifts at the sight of him. He crosses the road and we hug. I hold on a little longer and tighter than normal.

'You OK?' he asks and I shrug. Clem knows me well. He's a born Londoner and when I first moved here, in a dark and sleety February, we worked in the same tiny coffee shop and talked non-stop from eight to five each day. The move had been harder than I expected – the city was big, rent was expensive, I was lonely – and his friendship saw me through.

'I've had a bit of a day,' I say now.

'Want to tell me about it?'

I hesitate. When I left Ireland, I decided two things. First, I would start introducing myself as Jay. I'd been rehearsing the name in my mind for years and it felt clean and unassuming as a freshly shaved head. Second, I wouldn't tell anyone about Ferdia or my family. I'd had enough of being tragic, of the long sideways glances and of people hiding their whispers behind lifted hands. *A priest? He must have been young though? And he never regained consciousness?*

'Nah,' I say. 'I'm fine, just didn't get much sleep. How are you?'

We start walking together and Clem tells me about the family party he went to last night, where not one of his aunties or uncles had asked a single question about his life.

'I was honestly sitting with Uber open on my phone, you know? Refreshing it again and again. It helped to know that if things got really bad it would only take me twenty minutes and twenty-eight pounds to get to Vauxhall.'

'Sounds rough.'

He kicks at an empty chicken box on the street. 'I mean it could be worse, right? None of them are, like, actively bigoted.'

'Right,' I say. 'But we are allowed to expect more than that.'

We walk on, not speaking again until we reach the venue, an old-school pub with a grimy performance space in the back. The doors haven't opened yet so we order pints and sit at a table by the toilets, waiting for the rest of our friends – Ash and Cat and Cat's girlfriend. We all booked the tickets at the same time, after a Wolf Alice show at Ally Pally, when we were drinking wine and passing around a joint in Cat's living room. It was late on Friday night, we were buzzed, the weekend was in front of us. When a song by this queer French band came on the speaker we all went into raptures. They're coming to London in a few months, Cat said, and we took out our phones and bought tickets, there and then, believing we could stretch the vibe out for months, cast it into the dark beginnings of the new year.

But it hasn't worked out that way. Two of that group have already bailed on tonight and everyone else is crabby. I can tell Cat wishes the rest of us weren't here, that it was just her and the girlfriend. Ash is so hungover he's struggling to hold down his soda and lime and Clem, who's told us he has a 6 a.m. spin class tomorrow, keeps glancing at his watch. They still manage to drag a conversation out but I don't participate at all. The whole scene seems unreal to me, my friends' faces unfamiliar in the low light, like I've stumbled into a group of strangers.

The doors open. We buy more drinks and hover near the back of the space. It's freezing. But there's Fleetwood Mac on the sound system and as Clem starts moving gently to the beat, I can sense his energy changing. He loves music, will dance to anything. Cat and her girlfriend are swaying too, pressed close to each other, flirting and kissing. But Ash and I stay static. I put my coat back on and we lean together against a pillar, swiping through our phones. My parents haven't been in touch again since this morning and I wonder if they've even considered the impact the news about Ferdia might have on me. I take a mouthful of my beer but it's not going down right.

'Do you want some of this?' I say to Ash, and he grimaces but takes it. We pass the cup back and forth between us, not speaking. We're the moody ones in the friend group and variations of this scene have played out plenty of times before. But tonight, after a few more minutes, Clem has had enough.

'Is this what you're going to do with it?' he calls over the music. 'Your one wild and precious life?'

We laugh. He takes our hands and drags us upright. As the room fills we get shuffled a bit closer to the stage and other bodies warm the air around us so that I have to take my coat back off again and tie it awkwardly around my waist. When the band comes on they launch straight into a loud, bass-heavy opener. The noise helps with the feeling of disorientation I've had all day, letting me lean into the feeling of unreality.

From there on, the ritual of the gig takes over. The energy builds with each new song, our swaying turns to dancing. We grab each other's hands and shout, the air between us glinting with spit. I'm still exhausted but there's pleasure in it now, in all the effort and sensation of moving a tired body. At the end, the band step back on to the low stage and play their final tune, their one big hit, the one we listened to at Cat's the night we bought the tickets.

We sing along loudly in vague approximations of the French lyrics. Clem and Ash are dancing furiously now, their faces lit up with sweat. Cat is holding her girlfriend's hand but she wraps her other arm around my waist and I stretch mine across her back and the three of us sing on and on – because the band keeps adding choruses – and I'm at home then, for a few minutes at least, in my life, in my body, with my friends.

But later, back in bed, I struggle to sleep. My ears are still buzzing, my heartbeat is jagged, and I'm thinking about the other Jacinta again. My grandmother never told us the end of her story and it was years before I realised that, of the three shepherd children at Fatima, only the eldest, Lucia, survived the Spanish flu. Francisco went first and Jacinta followed less than a year later, a grisly death from purulent pleurisy just a few months shy of her tenth birthday.

The room is cold and I pull the covers over my head, my phone screen misting over as I study their shared Wikipedia page. I've read it before but I've never paid much attention to the section on beatification and canonisation, which details how, in the investigation of her sanctity, they dug Jacinta up twice. Though I should probably know better, I click through to the pictures. In the first, from 1935, her small face pokes out of its shroud like a porcelain doll's. A lone priest looms over the grave, verifying the state of the body, which is immaculate, incorrupt. And maybe that's why a crowd gathers for the next exhumation in 1951: a cardinal, men in white coats, Jacinta's parents. They've all come to witness the miracle but they look perturbed. The state of the relic has changed and they're staring at a decomposing child.

I hear Thomas getting up to use the bathroom and close the tab quickly, feeling complicit and queasy. The boiler in the hallway bursts into life as he runs the taps, then dwindles back to silence. I stay huddled under the covers, trying to breathe heat into the trapped air. I'm getting sleepy but when I close my eyes I'm back at Ferdia's graveside on the rainy day we buried him, smelling the damp off my own good coat. The cemetery is next to the dual carriageway and we have to shout our Hail Marys over the roar of passing trucks. As they lower Ferdia in, the coffin straining against the grubby black straps, I step forward to throw a rose after him. It lands with a thump, and as I stare downwards, mesmerised by the gleam of the wood and the garish red of the bloom, all penned in by endless miles of coarse mud, I feel dizzy. I stumble backwards and in the dream I drop into space, falling for as long as it takes me to jolt awake, heart thumping and drenched in sweat.

In reality, when I stumbled in the cemetery, the gravedigger caught me by the forearm before I fell.

'You're all right, a ghrá,' he said, not letting go until he was sure I was steady. His hand left a smear of clay on my sleeve. I felt embarrassed. No one else had moved. In that moment, I think my father and mother forgot that they had another child, were lost to everything beyond the gape of the ground in front of them.

# Chapter Four

IT'S WEDNESDAY NIGHT, nearly nine, and I'm fidgeting in the cold, waiting for the Holborn traffic lights to change. An hour ago I was at home in my pyjamas, wondering if I could be bothered getting a bowl of cereal. Then Lindsay texted:

*Long shot, but would you like to come for a curry?*

I'd showered quickly, spraying perfume on my damp skin before pulling on clothes that I could get away with wearing to work tomorrow, humming a little tune on my way to the Underground. When I reach the restaurant, I stop outside and look over the top of the frosted glass. Lindsay is already there, at a table by the wall eating poppadoms. She's wearing a grey fisherman's jumper, the sleeves pushed up to her elbows, and her jaw-length shag – not a Shane haircut, she insists – is rumpled and a little greasy. I push open the door and when she looks up and smiles, I feel a rush of something warm and stupid.

We met on a rainy Friday evening last November, at after-work drinks with my office. Lindsay was due to have dinner with Hannah, her friend and my colleague. The pub was humid, the wood panelling slightly oily and the carpet fragrant with run-off from people's coats. I had already drunk nearly two pints and was thinking about going home when Lindsay arrived, pulling off her fluorescent bike jacket, her eyes scanning the group, stopping at me. I smiled. She bent over the back of Hannah's chair, gave her a quick hug, then pointed to me and asked if I needed another drink. I fell for her, urgently and desperately, was turned on even by the large wet patches where the jacket met her jeans. After we'd been speaking for an hour or more – mostly about her post-doc research in feminist politics – I asked when she had to leave for dinner. She cocked her head at me with a little smile and I realised, looking around, that Hannah had already left.

'Oh right,' I said, beaming despite my best efforts to play it cool. 'But still, you must need to eat?'

'I hate eating in town on Friday nights.'

I took a long drink.

'Well, I don't live too far away . . . if you like scrambled eggs on toast?'

'Sounds perfect,' Lindsay said and I grinned again.

She wanted to leave her bike somewhere safer, so we took a detour on the way to the station. Though the rain had eased off, the dark streets were quieter than normal and the air felt fresh as we walked, Lindsay wheeling the bike between us, my skin singing in the chill. I was nervous. I don't usually invite people back to mine, but Sasha and Thomas were away that weekend and Lindsay was Lindsay.

When we stopped in the shadow of Senate House, out of sight of the main road, I perched on one of the bike racks while she looked for her keys, trying to keep talking though I wanted her so badly by now that even the sight of her hands working the lock was agony. She straightened up, pushed her hair out of her face.

'OK. Glad that's finally out of the way.'

I laughed, stayed leaning on the other rack with my feet stretched out. Lindsay stepped towards me and I reached for her hand. She held it loosely, moved slowly closer until her legs were spread on either side of mine. Though I'm taller than she is, she was looking down at me and she lifted her palm to my cheek, tilted my chin upward with her thumb.

'All right, mate?'

'All right.' My voice came out steady, though my breath felt shallow and thin. When we kissed I surged forwards, wrapping my arms around her waist. She pushed back, holding behind my head to stop me from tipping over, kissing me harder, biting my lip.

'Fucking hell, Jay,' she murmured after a few minutes, resting her forehead against mine.

'Yeah, I know,' I whispered, and we laughed, made a break for home, where she surprised me by actually demanding eggs on toast before coming to bed, then again by staying all of the next day. We fucked drowsily as soon as we woke, then chatted over coffee, watched a film on the sofa, had sex there, went to a pub around the corner and ate pies and mash under a patio heater in the beer garden. By evening, twenty-four hours after we'd met, I felt so close to her that it seemed we were old lovers rekindling an affair. I walked her to Finsbury Park station and we said goodbye with three lingering cheek kisses, the done thing in the Netherlands, apparently, where Lindsay isn't from.

Tonight though, she's quiet. She stands up when I reach the table and kisses my cheek but then sits back down and starts toying with her napkin, saying nothing. I catch the waiter's eye and gesture that I'd like a mango lassi, same as hers.

'You OK?' I ask.

'Yeah.'

'You sure?'

Lindsay sighs. 'Well actually, I found out today, from Facebook, that my ex is pregnant.'

'Oh,' I say. Children aren't something we've talked about. 'With a woman?'

Lindsay looks up at me.

'No, with a baby,' she says and we both laugh, so loud that the only other person in the restaurant turns to stare. Lindsay slides her hand across the white tablecloth and plays with my fingers.

'Obviously it doesn't really matter,' she says. 'It's not something I particularly want, anyway. But I don't know how she managed it so fast. They tell you it'll take years, right?'

'Yeah, sure,' I say, not really knowing what she wants from me. I'm looking down at my plate but then Lindsay lifts my hand from the tabletop and my head follows, like a puppet's, until our eyes meet.

'Am I being too much?' she asks. 'Are you the wrong person to talk to about this?'

'No, not at all. I'm just a bit tired.'

'Everything OK?'

'Yeah, fine.' I draw my hand back. I haven't told her about Ferdia's cause for canonisation. I still haven't told anyone. 'Was that why you broke up? The kids thing?'

'No,' Lindsay says quickly. 'Though actually, it wasn't not why we broke up either. We were at the point when everything is so interwoven that any problem can travel fast through the network, you know? Infect the whole?'

I hum thoughtfully and wait for her to continue. I find it incredibly attractive that Lindsay speaks this way, in chains of jumbled metaphors, with underlying notes of scouse. But a lot of the time I don't quite understand what she's saying.

'The biggest problem was that we couldn't get on with each other's families. Every weekend visit home – total war. And that does then affect the way you think about kids, doesn't it? You don't want them to have a fucked-up family.'

'Do you mean you didn't want them to have those specific grandparents?'

She laughs. 'Yeah, you could say that.'

Our food arrives. Because Lindsay got here first, I told her to order for the two of us, and I smile now as the waiter puts down potatoes, rice and peshwari naan.

'This is an impressive range of carbs.'

Lindsay shrugs. 'Irish Catholic family, what do you expect?'

'What?' It comes out sharply. 'You're Catholic?'

She looks up. 'I'm from Liverpool and my name's McLoughlin. What religion did you think I was?'

She's laughing but I feel caught out. Not only had I assumed she was Protestant, but I'd also believed that some of her most annoying habits – insisting the dishes get done before bed, not allowing shoes in the flat – were the proof of it.

'It has really changed the way I think about relationships though,' she goes on, spooning neon paneer masala on to her plate. 'I don't see any reason to risk a good thing by involving loads of superfluous people.'

'Are we talking about your ex again?' I say, feeling irritated now.

'No, I just mean in general. Why is it so important to fold someone into the family? Especially if you're queer and the odds of disaster are so much higher.'

'But you are close to your own family?' I say, thinking of how she'd disappeared to Liverpool for nearly two weeks over Christmas while I'd been in London.

Lindsay chews for a few seconds before answering, sensing something has shifted.

'Yeah. My mum and I talk every day,' she says, as though that's completely normal. 'But then I know that I like my own family, don't I? Whereas yours . . .' She blushes. This is the first time she's let herself slip out of the abstract, the first time she's mentioned me.

'You wouldn't like them,' I cut in, trying to sound chilly and sardonic. But still I see pity flash across Lindsay's face and look down at my food, poking dal through the rice.

'You don't see them much?'

I shake my head.

'It must be hard.'

'It's hardly unusual, is it?'

'Yeah, but with your brother and everything . . .'

I look up. On that first morning in my flat, Lindsay had noticed the picture of Ferdia in my room. I'd explained, as briefly as I could – it was sudden, an accident playing football, I was young, so was he – and then I'd gone to get a glass of water, assuming she'd know not to bring it up again.

'Listen, are you into family or aren't you?'

Lindsay is reaching for more naan but stops mid-movement. 'Sorry?'

'Well, if you're not interested in being involved with people's families then I suggest you don't go digging for gossip about them either.'

She raises her eyebrows. 'That's clearly not what I meant.'

'I'm sure it wasn't.' I check my watch. 'Anyway, I have to be up early in the morning so I might head off soon.'

She stares at me, her jaw working. We've never argued before.

'I'm sorry, Jay,' she says eventually. 'I should have been more sensitive.'

The apology is genuine. But there are tears backing up behind my eyes now, walled in by a hard, almost painful frustration. I'm furious with Lindsay, can barely stand the sight of her. We walk apart when we leave the restaurant, our hands jammed in our coat pockets and our shoulders hunched against the wind. Back at the Holborn intersection she asks if I'm getting the tube. I shake my head, nod at the Sainsbury's.

'I have to pick something up.'

'All right.' She steps closer, kisses my cheek. 'I've got that conference this weekend, but see you next week maybe?'

I nod, knowing that I should apologise for overreacting and that, if I do, Lindsay will invite me back to hers. But I cling on to my anger instead and, after hovering a few seconds more, she walks away.

It's after ten now and the night air has dipped below freezing. My skin feels raw and exposed but still I decide to walk the hour home, to let my feeling of injury harden and chill. I convince myself that I'm embarrassed for Lindsay, speaking to her mother every day like a child. But then, even when I was a child, I didn't demand that kind of attention. My mother would stay asleep until long after I'd woken up and I see myself sitting in bed on my own, reading picture books and waiting, trying to guess the right moment to stick my head into the dim, morning-breath reek of her room, to ask if it's nearly time to leave for Montessori. There's a dullness in her eyes as she looks back at me, her stare so flat that I worry she's died right in the moment of turning her head. But then we hear a sound from across the hall, heavy boy's footfalls, and a spark runs through her, there's life in the old bones now and a shimmer of light in her eyes as they catch a glimpse of Ferdia on his way to the bathroom.

Of course, this isn't what we tell people. As far as anyone else is concerned – my grandparents, aunts, uncles, even my father – Mammy gets up and makes us breakfast every day. Cereal and toast in summer, porridge in winter, keeping Ferdia's warm in the pan until right before she and I set off, when he finally tumbles out of bed and appears, tousle-haired, at the kitchen door.

'The Lord Himself couldn't convince that boy to get up a minute earlier than he has to,' she laughs sometimes, when people ask if her son is really as perfect as he seems.

The car is freezing when I get in, the windows so thick with frost that I feel hidden in my own blue kingdom for a few minutes until, through a little act of magic, the ice on the windscreen melts away to reveal my mother, focused and capable in a cloud of steam, the big kettle in one hand. We listen to classical music on the short journey and I feel like a child in a Christmas film, wrapped in a woollen coat and red beret, peering out the window at a frozen world.

'I hope your brother's on time for school,' she's saying, and I laugh along, though I can tell that Ferdia doesn't like these jokes. When we tease him about sleeping late his jaw tightens and his shoulders tense. But I laugh all the same, liking the idea that she and I are in a gang together, that we drive to school every day, listening to a Schubert tape in the car and making fond little jokes about my older brother. I don't think it matters that, by the time I start primary school, I get myself out of bed more days than not, dress myself in a uniform that's not as clean as it could be, pour myself a bowl of cereal in a cold kitchen. I don't feel the need to tell anyone that Ferdia, though he really does love a lie-in, always notices when the house is quiet and gets up much earlier than he needs to, early enough to walk me to my school and then turn around and walk back to his, a forty-five minute round trip.

'What are you doing?' my mother says to him one night when she comes into the kitchen and finds him carefully buttering bread for our sandwiches the next day. I'm sitting on the edge of the kitchen table, my legs dangling. I've been chatting to Ferdia while he works, summarising the plot of one of my favourite books, speaking quietly so I can't be heard from the sitting room, where she's sprawled in front of a stream of quiz shows. 'I make your lunch.'

Ferdia stares at her. 'I was just trying to give you a hand.'

'Give me that.' She grabs the butter knife from him. 'That's not enough spread.'

She's not wrong. Ferdia always scrapes the butter thin, chooses a slice of either ham or cheese. But now my mother piles both onto the bread, wraps the sandwiches neatly in tin foil and puts two small bars of chocolate in each of our lunchboxes.

'I'll leave these in the fridge for you,' she says. Her voice is soft now and she kisses his cheek. 'Don't forget in the morning.'

'Thanks very much,' he says. 'I won't.'

The next day I want to ask Ferdia how he felt about it, what he thinks is going on. But he and I don't discuss my mother, not even on our morning walks. We never acknowledge that something is out of place, that her moods are so variable and the darkness of her lows is frightening. And though I don't like being the first child to arrive at school, shivering by the front gates, my coat and beret helpless against the cold, I do like my walks with Ferdia. There's something about being with him that makes the time feel special, luminous, so that even though we live in an estate and the route takes us along main roads crawling with traffic, when I remember it I see us – a gangly boy and a tiny girl – crunching through frosted fields, kicking rusty leaves, strolling down country lanes in the sunshine with gorse blooming in the ditches. We don't speak much. We don't need to. My brother is at home in silence like no one else I've ever met and I get to know him in the quiet. We become friends.

# Chapter Five

'Jay!' BART, MY MANAGER, shouts at me from across the office while I'm still unwinding my scarf. 'I've given the guy from the composting company your number. He's going to call this morning. Will you deal with it?'

I give him a thumbs up. My colleagues are still shaking off sleep, wrapped around their coffees or nestled inside over-ear headphones. It's the morning after my argument with Lindsay and I'm tired. I haven't worked on the brief that Bart is talking about and, beyond my suspicion that the company is a green-washing operation secretly owned by some large plastics manufacturer, I know nothing about it. I go to the kitchen, make myself a coffee and a toasted bagel, then message Hannah when I'm back at my desk, asking her to share the initial brief and the notes from the previous meetings. I can see instantly that the creative plan we've offered them is semi-ironic trash. A family of sentient coffee cups dance their way to the commercial composting plant, thrilled that they're going to be mulched together, rather than floating the ocean alone. And Bart has gotten bored, it's clear as day. He's stopped responding to the company's emails, or feeding back on our team's work. He wants the project done and the money paid without ever having to think about it again. I brace myself for a strained conversation with the client, probably some junior marketing executive who's stuck his neck out to get funding for a proper agency campaign and is worried it's all falling apart.

My phone rings.

'Good morning, Jay speaking,' I say brightly, wanting to reassure him. But there's a short silence on the other end of the line.

'Am I speaking to Jacinta Devane?'

I stand up quickly and make for one of the meeting hubs, confident that this isn't the composting guy. The voice is Irish, the tone formal.

'My name is Father Matthew Richter,' it says and I shut the door behind me, though these tiny glass boxes are barely soundproof anyway. 'As I'm sure you're aware, Jacinta, I've been appointed vice-postulator for your late brother's cause for canonisation.'

My throat tightens. 'This isn't a very good time. I'm at work. I'm expecting another call.'

'Yes, I do apologise for contacting you out of the blue,' the priest says, his words deep and smooth, the rural notes of his accent overlaid with an international clarity. An emigrant's voice. 'But I'm unexpectedly in London for today and tomorrow and I hoped we might meet.'

I don't speak. I'm angry that he's imposing himself like this, I want to tell him to fuck off. But my colleagues are a few feet away. They can see me. They might hear through the glass.

'I have plans tonight.' The lie comes out high-pitched. 'I'm sorry.'

'Don't you apologise,' he laughs. 'I'm the stranger contacting you and asking you to meet me with no notice. It's just that I know that this stage of the process can be quite overwhelming for family members like yourself. So since I was here I wanted to make myself available to speak to you.'

He waits for me to answer. I know he's trying to trick me – the play is subtle as a brick – but still I'm tempted. In all my thinking about Ferdia and the cause, the Church has been a shadowy enemy, too vast and intangible to take on. It might be satisfying to put my anger to a real person. It could help.

'Could you do tomorrow evening?' I ask eventually and he inhales loudly.

'I'm afraid I fly out at five. But I could meet you for lunch? For breakfast?'

Across the office, Bart stands up to fill his water bottle, walking the long way to the sink so he can pass right in front of me. He looks through the glass and mouths, 'All good?' I nod but still he lingers, waiting for me to speak.

'Well, it definitely sounds like there might be merit in meeting in person,' I say loudly. Bart nods and moves on, I drop my voice again. 'But I don't want to do it during the work day. I have somewhere to be at seven this evening, but would half-five suit?'

'Absolutely perfectly,' says Father Richter. 'Do you know Garret's Bar? It's got plenty of space so we should be able to speak freely.'

Garret's is a hotel bar less than five minutes' walk from my office. It seems a strange coincidence and I hesitate, wishing I had a moment to think. But Bart is still wandering the office, looking over people's shoulders at their screens, chatting and laughing. It's only a matter of time before he circles back to me.

'OK,' I say. 'I'll see you there at five thirty.'

'That's great. I'll look forward to it, Jacinta.'

I hang up, already half regretting what I've done. I wish I could clear the rest of the day, spend it planning exactly what I want to say to Matthew Richter. But then, of course, the composting guy does call and I have to arrange a real meeting in person to cover for the fake one, and prepare for it, and travel to their office in Stratford. All I eat is an M&S samosa on the train, holding it in one hand and making notes on my phone with the other, about sainthood and advertising strategy.

\*

I leave the office around five twenty-five. On my way, though I know it'll make me late, I walk seven times around the perimeter fence of Bedford Square Gardens, breathing the cold air slowly, trying to make room for Ferdia in my thoughts. I want to act as his advocate in all this but lately I hear nothing when I search for his voice. And instead of seeing him in my head, I see his picture from the wardrobe door. This happens sometimes, I tell myself. It doesn't mean he's gone forever.

All day I've been avoiding the thought that my father, though he must have given my number to Matthew Richter, hasn't bothered to warn me that the call might come. I can't understand why. As always, it's hard to pin my father down, to place him in the story of the family. After being made a school principal in his thirties, he wasn't there much when I was little. He would leave for work before I woke up and come back moments before I went to bed. And he's an outsider, still, in my mother's big family, never in on the joke or part of the fun, always taking care of some job or other, speaking with the hotel manager or checking the bill. His own parents – quiet, habitual people with a semi-detached house in Blessington – died when I was a child. He had a brother too, Ambrose, who died here in London a couple of years before I was born. No one's ever told me what happened to my uncle; I assume suicide, or some kind of traumatic accident, or maybe even AIDS. Though we never met, I imagine him in my life sometimes. There's an Irish pub near my house where I think we'd meet on occasional Sunday evenings, swapping notes on the music we both like. We have things in common, Ambrose and me. He's a runaway too.

In the summers, though most of my father's colleagues were off for three months, he never took more than two weeks' holiday. The four of us would go on a short trip, to Connemara or West Cork or to Wales on the ferry. Then he'd drive us home and leave again for his annual three-day retreat at Lough Derg. I find it difficult to imagine him there, his pale bare feet circling the stations for hours, his body tense against the rain as he lowers himself into the mud to pray. Even after he arrived home, the rules of the pilgrimage required him to continue his fast until midnight. In solidarity, the rest of us would join him in missing dinner, which was fine by me because to compensate my mother would send Ferdia to get our lunch from the chip shop, pressing a twenty-pound note into his hand. You'd smell him coming back before you'd see him, a rich waft of grease and vinegar, the oil from the food soaking through the brown paper bag as he unpacked it. Burger and chips for me, chicken and chips for my mother, battered sausage and chips for Ferdia. Onion rings to share, curry sauce, and three cold cans of fizzy orange.

My mother would leave the radio on while we ate, turning it up any time there was mention of a car accident, afraid my father had fallen asleep behind the wheel and been killed. The only thing she was more worried about was his being shot on the way through Northern Ireland – 'they know by the look of you that you've come from Lough Derg' – so she insisted that he skirt the long way around the border, adding hours to the journey.

'Poor hungry Daddy,' she'd say every few minutes and Ferdia and I would falter briefly, looking down sorrowfully at the gleaming mountains of food. 'Poor exhausted Daddy.'

The evening would be getting shadowy by the time we'd hear his car in the driveway and his key in the lock. Though tired and pale, you could see his shoulders had loosened and there was a lightness in his smile. It was the only time I felt I could run down the hall and have him sweep me into a hug. His clothes smell stale with a hint of incense.

I jump down and wait for him to open a plastic carrier bag full of gifts: bottles of holy water, prayer books, sweets he'd bought in a garage shop on the road home.

'Was it as good as you remembered?' asks Ferdia from the end of the hall and my father nods. Ferdia, I know, is counting down the minutes until he's fifteen and allowed to go to the lake himself. He's got a longing for more intensive penance, for deeper and more challenging prayer. At one point he goes through a phase of kneeling for hours on the floor of the back kitchen. It's freezing in winter and roasting in summer and one day while I'm doing my homework I hear the clatter of a basin falling and find him in a dead faint on the lino. Then my father brings him to talk to the parish priest, who insists that Ferdia has to consider his health, banning him from self-mortification of any kind. He's cold with our parents for a week or two after that.

When Ferdia died, my father held things together, that's what everyone said. *Thank God for Brendan. I don't know where he finds the strength.*

But here's what I remember. The day after the funeral I heard him moving around the house early. Though it was cold and my body felt heavy as a bag of rocks, I went downstairs to check that he was OK and found him standing at the counter in his usual suit and tie, eating a piece of toast.

'You're going to work?' I said and he jumped, staring at me like I'd risen from the dead.

'Just a half day. There's one meeting I need to get to.'

My mother stayed in bed all morning and I drifted around the house in two jumpers, working my way through a tray of egg sandwiches our neighbours had left in the fridge, half listening for the flushing of my parents' en suite toilet, the only sign that my mother was at home and alive. Late in the afternoon, I fell asleep on the sofa and when I woke the house was dark. My nose and throat felt congested, my head cloudy, so I went for a walk to the local shop and bought a can of orange. When I got home, my father's car was in the drive and there was a crack of light under the kitchen door, a sound of something frying. I slammed the front door behind me and stamped up the stairs, threw myself down on my bed, eking as much noise as I could out of each action. He would come when he'd finished his rasher sandwich, I thought, or after the news? But half past nine came and went and he didn't come to see me. I spoke to no one that entire day, had no respite from the roar in my brain, so relentless that it broke through the walls of my mind and coursed horribly down my arms and legs.

By eleven o'clock my father still hadn't moved from his place in front of the TV. I tipped the flat, syrupy end of the drink down my throat and changed into a fresh pair of pyjamas. Lying back in bed, I put on my MP3 player, tired of listening for the sound of his footsteps.

\*

Matthew Richter is young for a priest, fifty-five or fifty-six, with broad stooped shoulders. He's sitting in the far corner of the bar, tapping at an iPad with his two index fingers.

'Father Richter?'

He looks up and smiles, his mouth thin, his reddish-grey hair faded on the sides and slicked on the top, like a Premier League footballer or a French intellectual. Under his black jacket he's wearing a green knitted jumper, the white collar just visible at the neck. When we shake hands, his palm feels dry.

'Can I get you a coffee?' he asks, gesturing at his own empty espresso cup. I ask for a tea and he walks to the bar, banging loudly at the bell to summon the young woman who's clearing tables nearby. I sit and look around. The place is sterile: poured concrete walls, fake monstera, colourful mismatched seats.

'What's brought you over?' I ask when he's back and sitting opposite.

'Conference,' he says, taking a sip of espresso and grimacing at the taste. 'In Westminster Cathedral. I won't bore you with the details.'

I nod and begin to pour my tea. It's almost translucent and I stop when the cup is a third full. I'm certain he's lying, that he's come to London specifically to meet me.

'A bit of an awkward trip, I'd have thought. From here to Westminster?'

'Not ideal,' he agrees smoothly. 'But the prices near there were prohibitive. So close to Big Ben, I suppose.'

'And the palace,' I say.

'Of course.' He smiles. 'And I'm told Westminster Abbey is popular.'

The joke catches me off guard and I laugh, genuinely. Looking pleased, Father Richter lifts his tablet and slides it into his satchel then sits back and watches me. I try not to break eye contact.

'Well,' he says. 'The first thing I want to say is that I'm so sorry about your brother.'

This startles me and I laugh again. 'That's OK. It was a long time ago.'

He smiles sadly. 'Still. I've spoken to a great many people who knew Ferdia and his extraordinary qualities just shine through. I can't imagine what it must have been like losing him the way you did, so suddenly.'

I fill my cup the rest of the way and pick it up carefully. My grip is a little shaky. There's something so grim and meaningless about the way Ferdia died, a freak accident playing five-a-side soccer. It might have felt more coherent if he'd been martyred somehow, defending oppressed Christians or pulling a child from the path of a train. But there was no greater narrative to what actually happened, no way to find sense in it beyond the chaotic and random workings of the universe.

'You never met him yourself?' I manage to keep my tone light. Father Richter shakes his head.

'Sadly not. I was at the Irish College for a time but I arrived shortly after Ferdia's passing. Your mother and I have often said what a shame it was.'

'That he died?' I say, my temper flaring. I hate euphemisms for death. 'Or that he didn't have the pleasure of meeting you first?'

Father Richter raises his eyebrows slightly then holds up his hands.

'OK, Jacinta, I think we need to talk about the elephant in the room. My strong impression is that you're not a fan of what's happening here. Is that fair?'

'It's understating it a bit, but yes.'

'OK. Well, I'm sorry to hear that and I would like to hear more about your concerns. But to begin, I want to reassure you that the goal here is not to whitewash or to force a prescribed narrative about your brother.' He sits forward in his chair. 'Do you know that the term devil's advocate originates with the Congregation for the Causes of Saints? It described a canon lawyer who would be appointed specifically to make the most vigorous case possible against a candidate's sanctity, in the interests of a thorough and robust process.'

'Yes,' I say, irritated by his tone, patronising and priestly. 'I do know that actually.'

'Well then you know that we're not in the business of silencing critical voices. And your voice is critical to what we're trying to achieve.'

'Which is what, exactly?'

'Which is, at this stage, to establish as clear and meaningful an account of Ferdia's life as we can for the purposes of the positio.'

I roll my eyes. This answer is disingenuous, focusing on the details of the process rather than the big picture of why it's all happening. I want to splinter Father Richter's smug calm, to find my way under his skin.

'And what if I were to provide some information you haven't heard before?' I ask.

'Such as?'

I shrug. 'What if I told you that Ferdia used to torture baby birds, or attend Protestant mass wearing our mother's underwear. Would that change things?'

The priest smiles. 'There will be a very thorough investigation and, in the fullness of time, we will submit the *relevant* information to the Vatican. Our colleagues there will then examine it in a great degree of detail. If that process reveals compelling evidence that undermines the candidate's claim to holiness, then the cause would be unlikely to progress.'

I hum in acknowledgement but say nothing. Father Richter watches me a moment, then speaks again.

'Though you do raise an important point, Jacinta. You may well learn things about Ferdia that you didn't know before. We have a duty to investigate the candidate's flaws and failings as well as their virtues and that can be challenging. But at the end of it we want the fullest possible picture. And you can offer a perspective on Ferdia, on his kindness and care as a brother, that no one else can.'

'Jay,' I say. I don't like what the man is getting at, am slightly sickened by the thought of him digging around in Ferdia's private life. There are lingering questions I have about my brother, but this isn't how I want to find the answers.

'I'm sorry?'

'You keep calling me Jacinta but I prefer to go by Jay.'

'Oh, I apologise.' He squints at me briefly, as though trying to figure something out. For the first time, I feel I have the upper hand. 'No one told me that.'

I nod, wondering what my parents did tell him about me. Father Richter coughs.

'Listen, Jay. That coffee was borderline undrinkable and your tea looks insipid. What would you say to an aperitivo?'

I look at my watch. It's just past six. I can't remember what time I said I'd have to leave for my imaginary dinner.

'I could have a quick one, I suppose.'

He smiles and turns to look for the bartender, who's now sitting on her phone a few tables away.

'Could I get an Aperol spritz, please?' he calls. 'And for my friend . . .'

I ask for a pint and he frowns a little, but quickly composes himself. 'You'll bring us some olives and nuts too, will you?'

'I can if you'd like,' the woman says, and looks at me. Our eyes meet and she holds the glance fractionally longer than she needs to. She's hot in a sulky sort of way. I smile.

'Do you like olives?' Father Richter asks.

'Yes,' I say, struggling not to laugh.

'A lot of Irish people don't.'

He says it so condescendingly that I feel a protective rush towards my old enemies, the boiled-vegetable-eaters of Ireland.

'And where's home for you?' I ask.

He tells me he grew up in Cavan and I can hear it, very faintly, in the way he names the county. 'But I've been mostly based in Rome for more than twenty years.'

'And Richter is a common name in Cavan, is it?'

He smiles. 'My father was from Köln.'

'So you speak German?'

'German, Italian, Latin, French, Irish, Greek. Probably in that order.'

I fight an unexpected flash of sympathy. There's something of the lonely schoolboy in his arrogance, his need to show me how clever he is.

'Did you not want to be a parish priest?' I ask. 'You must feel a bit removed from it all in Rome.'

He frowns. 'Well, we don't actually get to choose, as I'm sure you know. I was in a parish for a few years but ultimately I was moved back to the Holy See. And, of course, I do perform some pastoral work around the city.' He sounds defensive and, though I have on my best politely interested face, gets flushed as he continues. 'I believe that this work matters a great deal, Jay. The saints are one of the most powerful channels between ordinary Catholics and the divine. They give people a vision of holiness that they can relate to, that they can emulate themselves. To invest in that is to invest in our spiritual future.'

The bartender arrives with our drinks. He grabs his spritz directly from the tray and takes a sip.

'I'm sorry,' he says, 'but I can barely taste the Aperol in this.'

'Excuse me?' says the woman.

'I had the same problem last night. There isn't enough Aperol in here.'

'It's a standard measure.'

'Well, it's not right. Your colleague added extra for me last night and I'd like you to do the same, please.'

She takes back the glass and walks away. I'm mortified but Father Richter, as though nothing out of the ordinary has happened, rearranges his trouser legs and changes the subject.

'So, you'll know that in his lifetime your brother built a reputation for holiness. That was reflected at the time he died, I believe, in obituaries, attendance at the funeral et cetera.'

I nod, not wanting to think about the funeral, about all the people who pressed into our space, lost and needy. The Aperol spritz reappears, more vivid now, and Father Richter takes a long happy pull on his paper straw before continuing.

'In the years since, the archbishop has observed an unusual degree of continued interest in Ferdia's life. People offer masses and visit his grave to pray. We have a mailing list, I'm sure you know, with well over ten thousand members. And there have already been reports of miraculous interventions.' I look up sharply and he clarifies. 'Nothing that would meet the Congregation's standards just yet, but we've heard of people's mental health problems easing, skin conditions responding well to treatment . . .'

I take a drink to avoid eye contact, embarrassed by his conviction that Ferdia is sitting up there in heaven, interceding with God over people's psoriasis flare-ups. My beer is an IPA, not quite fresh, with the thick organic taste of a compost bin.

'Of course, your parents have also been powerful advocates for Ferdia. Even before I was involved they kept meticulous records of everything that was going on, preserved his writings and belongings. And they maintained contact with many of his friends and admirers both in the archdiocese and in Rome, which meant that when the question of the cause officially crossed the archbishop's desk, he had many encouraging voices in his ear . . .'

'So it's all about who you know?'

I try to sound innocent but Father Richter frowns and runs a finger around the rim of his glass. His nails are craggy.

'I'd ask you not to misinterpret me. This is a deeply reverent process first and foremost. But, of course, there is also a degree of marketing involved. And we must be ready to identify occasions when the interests of Ferdia's cause overlap with the interests of decision-makers.'

I nod, satisfied that he's taking me seriously, that I'm getting some real answers out of him. 'OK, so tell me this then: what's in it for the archbishop?'

Father Richter pauses, and I think that he's deciding how honest he should be. Then he shakes his head slightly and smiles. 'Well, he's very conscious that, although Ireland has an extraordinarily rich legacy of saints, in the main they come from very long ago. They didn't live in the world that young Irish Catholics are living in today.' He takes another drink, looks at me. 'And it's hardly betraying any confidences to say that we're aware the Church in Ireland has a problem with relatability, with trust.' He swallows. 'But the archbishop has observed that what few young priests we have don't seem to be implicated in the same way. Some have built very large followings on social media and young people come to them, on those forums, for support. So that's how we've pitched a lot of this, as modern and innovative. We're trying to build a cause that, on our side at least, will be digital-first and appeal to the community of Catholics online.'

'So you're trying to make him, like, a patron of the internet?' I notice that my tone has changed, realise that I'm actually interested.

'Don't start,' Father Richter says, picking it up too. 'I've heard them all. "A saint for Snapchat". "An influencer for God".'

I laugh. 'They're truly dreadful straplines.' He grimaces dramatically. 'And it doesn't make sense to name a specific platform either . . . Snapchat will get overtaken by something else eventually, long before the cause is complete.'

'Of course,' says Father Richter. 'But we are dealing, in the main, with men of a very different generation. I've had to take a "there are no bad ideas" approach.'

I think about the most difficult clients I've ever had and imagine how much worse the bishops must be.

'So why now?' I ask. 'My parents have been trying to make the cause happen for years, right? What's changed the boss's mind?'

'Well—' Father Richter shuffles forward in his chair. He seems excited by the turn the conversation has taken, the chance to explain his strategy. 'Of course, I can't speak to His Grace's thought processes and I'm sure he spent lots of time in prayer and contemplation, but it certainly didn't hurt our chances when the Holy Father announced that he's coming to Ireland this summer. If we could just manage to catch his ear, or convince him to mention it at some point, or even to visit some site associated with Ferdia's life . . .'

I watch him as he speaks, his hands flying, his eyes lit up with the possibilities. To me, it seems absurd that the pope would take a specific interest in Ferdia, would elevate our boring suburban family to his tier of historical significance.

'Do you really think that could happen?' I ask.

Father Richter shrugs. 'We've spoken with the Irish cardinals, with our contacts in Rome. But this pope is very much his own man, of course.'

He picks up his glass and drinks the last of the spritz, hoovering noisily at the ice.

'Will you have another?' he asks, my lie about other plans now forgotten.

I nod, though having hardly eaten all day, I'm already feeling the effects of the first one. 'But I can get it.'

'No, not at all,' he says and looks around for the server, who ignores him, forcing him to walk to the bar. I watch him go, trying to re-establish some distance, to tap back into the dislike I felt for him at first. But there's a sadness about Matthew Richter, like there is about so many priests, a sense of something unmoored. He sits back down heavily, with a glass of red wine so large that it threatens to slop over the sides.

'It's good to speak to you,' he says, raising it gingerly towards me. 'I've heard so much.'

I take a drink. 'All bad, I'm sure.'

'What?' Father Richter shakes his head, looking theatrically confused. 'Your mother and father only ever speak highly of you.'

I don't believe him. My parents have been embarrassed by me my whole life. Too loud, too argumentative, too queer. I can't tell if Father Richter is naive or if he's lying to get his way.

'They do want you to be involved,' he goes on. 'But only because of the contribution you can make.'

'And what would that look like?' I ask, making air quotes. 'Being involved?'

Father Richter straightens up, seeming relieved to be back on his own territory, on the technical detail.

'Well, the cause has been opened under the category of heroic virtues, rather than martyrdom, say, or giving one's life for others.' He takes a mouthful of wine, swirls it noisily around his mouth. 'So through the positio we need to demonstrate Ferdia's holiness, as manifested by his exceptional or heroic example of the three supernatural virtues and the four cardinal moral virtues. In Ferdia's case, that will be judged based on an in-depth assessment of any of his writings, be they essays, papers, diaries, emails, blogs. And the testimony of any living witnesses to his life. Including, I hope, your good self.'

'What are the virtues?' I ask and Father Richter smiles.

'You're testing me now.' He closes his eyes. 'Faith, hope and charity are the supernatural three, of course. And then prudence, justice, fortitude and temperance.' He opens them again. 'You'd be asked to speak to your experience of Ferdia in relation to each one.'

'To be honest, I barely know what those words mean.'

He nods, patronising again, as though I've expressed a genuine worry about the reach of my vocabulary. 'It is complicated, but we'll help you prepare for the hearing.'

'You mean vet my answers?'

There's a quick shift in his face, a flash of irritation.

'No,' he says, controlling it. 'It's just that people often find the hearings quite challenging. It can feel as though your loved one is on trial which, in a sense, they are. We find that it helps to have planned your answers in advance.'

He takes an olive and chews it, looking at the wall over my head. It's hard to believe, here in a bar in central London, that the process he's describing is real, that these hearings actually happen all the time. I can envision a large room, a gathering of priests at a mahogany table, stacks of papers, portraits of scarlet-robed cardinals on the walls. But I can't add myself to the scene. It's impossible, my body fights back and all at once, though I've been perversely enjoying myself up until now, I've had enough.

'It's probably time for me to go,' I say. Father Richter spits the olive stone out, catching it in his hand.

'Do you have another ten minutes? There are a couple more points I wanted to mention.'

I narrow my eyes. So much for his claim that this meeting was for me. But I shrug agreement and he coughs, takes a swallow of wine before speaking again. 'Well, I know this is personal, Jay. But the panel at the hearing will ask you about your own faith, about your standing in relation to the Church?'

I run my tongue along my top teeth. 'All right. And?'

'And,' he says slowly. 'I was wondering how you might answer that?'

I look at him. 'Well, I'm a lesbian.'

Father Richter deals with the word better than most. A slight double-take but a quick recovery.

'Is that to say you no longer go to mass?'

I sigh and he raises his hands defensively. 'Many gays and lesbians do, you know. And Pope Francis—'

I shake my head, not wanting to hear whatever 'who am I to judge?' nonsense the man is about to come out with.

'Listen, Matthew.' I take a long drink of my beer. 'I am in extremely regular commission of mortal sin and I haven't been to confession in over a decade. My soul is, if you'll forgive the phrase, absolutely filthy.'

I smile as I say this, expecting him to laugh along. But his face has closed over, his mouth is tight. Whatever positive feeling briefly existed between us gone.

'OK—' he begins, but I cut him off. The beers have done their work and I feel combative.

'More importantly, I've found so much more virtue, more hope and charity and justice in the queer community than I ever did in your institution. So the key question, really, isn't about my standing with the Church, it's about the Church's standing with me.'

There's a long pause. I feel breathless, triumphant. When the priest speaks again, his voice is clipped and even, but cold with anger.

'Well, I suppose all I would point out is that your brother built his life in *our institution*. And now he's being considered for its greatest honour, which will ensure that his memory lasts long after all of us are gone, long after today's fads and political hot topics –' his lip twitches, drifting towards a sneer '– have disappeared. Whatever your own views, I thought you would appreciate that.'

He pauses and I shake my head, smiling incredulously. I'm surprised at how this late stage of the conversation has unfolded. I hadn't expected either the intensity of my own challenge or of his response. I take out my phone, trying to gather myself, and as I check when the next bus is due, I can hear him taking long deep breaths.

'I'm sorry, Jay,' he says eventually. 'This wasn't how I wanted this chat to go.'

I glance up from my screen. He looks like a child after a tantrum, pink-faced and confused, and I can see that a man with such limited patience must have struggled with life in a parish.

'That's OK,' I say, glad of the opportunity to be gracious. 'But I think we've probably reached the limits of what we're going to achieve, don't you?'

He nods and I stand up to go, pulling my coat around me. I reach out my hand and he takes it, his palm a little claggy now.

'I'm only in this for Ferdia,' he says, not letting go. 'That's the only reason any of it is happening, because we believe in him. I'd just ask you to think about that, about your brother rather than any of the failings of the Church.'

'OK,' I say, desperate to leave now. I can see the woman behind the bar watching us. 'Thanks for the drinks.'

'Don't you think it's what he'd want?'

I pull my hand from Father Richter's. 'I honestly don't know.'

'Well, maybe you could think about it some more?'

'Yes, fine,' I say. 'But now I have to go.'

'God bless you,' he says quietly.

I turn and walk away.

# Chapter Six

That friday night, I go for after-work drinks with Bart and the accounts guy and a couple of the graphic designers, gulping down G&Ts in the sweaty glare of a patio heater, imitating the wavering voice of one of our clients, a kind woman who works for a luxury umbrella company.

'It's still a bit rough,' I begin in her high-pitched Australian accent. 'But could we do something with Noah's Ark? You know, each set of animals carrying a different umbrella? I mentioned it to my husband in bed last night and he thought it was fantastic.'

My colleagues roar with laughter and Bart claps me hard on the shoulder. I grin at him, empty my glass. It's been a long week, everyone's said so, and most of the team have made their excuses and gone home. But Bart gave me this job when I had no experience and part of our unwritten agreement is that I'll come out after work, get my rounds in, participate in the relentless mockery of the people who pay our salaries. And I have nothing to go home to anyway, besides all the claggy, complicated feelings that the week has brought up.

Lindsay and I have made peace after our argument, texting each other memes and articles through the last few days, but she's away at a conference for the weekend. Clem is working. Ash is visiting his parents and Cat's moving her stuff into her girlfriend's flat. There's no one I can make small, near-spontaneous plans with. And I'm frightened by gaps like this, disturbed by dark spaces in the calendar. Even one weekend spent at home alone makes me feel that the life I've built, and of which I'm so proud, is insubstantial, patchy, like thinning hair.

So when Bart invites me on to his friend's house party, I agree. We stumble to a corner shop for bags of cans and crisps, then take a cab to a corporate-looking high rise in the East End, where everyone is already very drunk and bored, beyond the help of new arrivals or better music or coke. I find myself propped against a large oak-topped kitchen island, talking to three women about an art exhibition on freezing your eggs. I think it's art anyway, though it could be a reality TV show, or one of their actual lives. There's a gutted wheel of Camembert on a plate between us and I keep tearing off small strips of skin and eating them, nodding vaguely at the other women and wiping my fingers on my black work trousers until, eventually, Bart comes in and throws an arm around my neck.

'I'm so glad you came,' he says.

'Thanks for inviting me.'

'Are you having fun?'

In the office he always smells so fresh, of power showers and dry cleaning and expensive, understated aftershave. But now he has a slightly stewed scent.

'You're not going to leave, are you?' he says, leaning in. The women smirk and I want to tell them that actually there's nothing happening between Bart and me, that his physical over-familiarity is quite typical of a straight man interacting with his one lesbian friend-slash-employee. But in the end, I don't care enough to explain and push my way out to the balcony instead, where a couple are trying to conceal the drunken argument they're having from the rest of the party.

'Could I steal a cigarette?' I ask, sidling over. The man holds out his packet. I take one, turn away then quickly back. 'And a light?'

The woman sighs angrily. Shortly after that they go back inside and I'm left alone, pretending to smoke. It's nice out here, clear and numbingly cold. I can see the dark line of the river winding through the lights and I trace its progress west, craning dangerously over the balcony when I run out of view.

\*

I wake early the next morning, tectonically hungover and crawling with suppressed anxiety about Ferdia, my family, the cause. For hours, I lie very still in bed, texting Lindsay and watching comedy reruns on my laptop, reading about the lives of the saints on my phone. We learned dozens of their stories as children and I still know, almost instinctively, who I'm meant to pray to for what: Saint Anthony if I've lost something, Gerard Majella for pregnant friends,

Christopher ahead of a long journey. But in my conversation with Father Richter, I felt at a disadvantage, lost and ill-informed, with no real understanding of where the saints sit in Church teaching.

I start with the basics: Peter upside down on the cross, Francis talking to the animals, Augustine the fuckboy sleeping his way around Carthage. I look at paintings of Saint Agatha's severed breasts, sitting pert like two supermarket cheesecakes on a plate, and stare a long time at Bernini's *Ecstasy of Saint Teresa*, at the saint's open mouth and the curl of the angel's fingers as they grip the arrow. In the early Church, I learn, most saints were local heroes, declared by the simple acclaim of their communities, their legends flexing to accommodate the beliefs and superstitions of the congregation. This means that the further back you go, the better the miracles get. The early saints fight snakes and dragons, seize land from feudal overlords with expanding cloaks, camp on the backs of whales and turn bathwater to beer. If they're decapitated, which they often are, they may continue to walk through the streets, carrying their own fallen heads with the bloody lips still preaching. These holy people acted as bridges between the old beliefs and the new order. They brought God closer to home, made Him accessible, gave Him the sorts of characteristics and gifts that ordinary people expected of their deities. But as the Church's power grew, the whiff of paganism became too strong for the papacy and over time it seized control of the means of saintly production, creating hoops for the blessed in heaven to jump through. Power shifted from the periphery to the core, from the faithful to the curia.

And still, they kept the most disturbing parts of the process intact. Late that morning I come across a photograph of a relatively young Pope John Paul II, kneeling, his head bowed and his hand pressed to a glass box with the wax-cased body of a young girl inside.

This is Maria Goretti, one of the most popular saints of the twentieth century. She was eleven when Alessandro Serenelli, her twenty-year-old neighbour, tried to rape her and then, when she resisted, stabbed her fourteen times with a farm tool. She was dead within twenty-four hours and yet (the hagiographies claim) she found it in her heart to declare forgiveness for her attacker, an act of Christian virtue that – although secondary to her admirable commitment to her own chastity – set her on the road to beatification. In 1950, she was canonised as a virgin martyr of the Church in front of a crowd of nearly half a million people.

Serenelli was still alive then, out of prison and very contrite, a lay brother in a religious order. He was invited to the mass in Saint Peter's Square, given a front-row seat for the rite of canonisation, with a clear view of the blessed girl's portrait, which would have hung from the front of the basilica. He was deeply moved, we can only assume, because for the rest of his life he remained very devoted to Maria Goretti, calling her – the child he murdered – 'my little saint'.

The nausea gets the better of me after reading that and I have to run to the bathroom to throw up. Afterwards,

I crouch on the lino floor, my pounding head propped on the side of the bath. Whenever I try to stand up I heave again, though there's nothing left inside me but a thin, lemon-tinted froth that strains and burns my throat. Thomas and Sasha are out cycling today and I'm thankful that I don't have to worry about running into them when eventually I stagger to the kitchen and force down two ibuprofen with a mouthful of Diet Coke, straight from the two-litre bottle in the fridge. Without them here, I can air out my worries, laying them on the floor in rows before I wrap them up again for the week ahead.

*

Time operates strangely in the lives of the saints. They mature too rapidly and then die too young. Ferdia was still a child the first time he sat all night at someone's deathbed. He was fourteen. Bernadette was ninety. They knew each other from weekday morning mass, which my brother attended every day during the school holidays, arriving early to join in with the Rosary and staying afterwards to speak to the old ladies about their illnesses and bereavements, and about which of their legion of granddaughters it would be best for him to marry.

For years, Bernadette had insisted that she was prepared, ready to go back to God, to see her husband in heaven. He had died fifty years before, very suddenly, in the early hours of a Thursday morning, leaving her with four children and no income. In all those years, the children have never seen their mother cry or complain. But now, as her breath begins to stutter and fail, Bernadette panics. She doesn't know, suddenly, if there's anywhere for her to go, senses a terrible emptiness on the other side. She keeps mumbling about Mary and grasping for her beads, shouting weakly at the children when they try to take her hands or stroke her brow, too weak even to clear the spit that gathers at the corners of her mouth.

Ferdia arrives mid-morning, straight from the church, where Bernadette's friends had gathered in a tight, sad cluster after mass. He brings a smile and a prayer card – Saint Joseph, patron of the dying – and he intends to stay just a few minutes. But every time he gets up to leave, Bernadette writhes in bed, gasping as though she's been stricken with a terrible pain. So he stays all day, praying with her until she drifts into unconsciousness. The family crowd in to say their goodbyes then and Ferdia retreats to the corner, forgotten, praying on and on into the night as the old woman's breath rattles and falters and eventually stops. The room is filled with grey light by the time the parish priest arrives to say a blessing, and to offer the staunch, shivering boy in the corner a lift home.

When I wake up later that morning no one tells me exactly what's happened, only that Ferdia's in bed and I can watch TV but with the volume very low. My mother makes a big pot of chicken soup and my brother, when he comes down from his room in the early afternoon, eats bowl after bowl.

'Good man,' my father murmurs, watching him from the end of the table. 'That'll set you right.'

I wonder now about the burden that all of this put on Ferdia, about how suffocating it must have been to live as a saint in a teenager's body. But back then, he was an icon to me. His word was gospel, his approval was a blessing, to let him down was the worst thing in the world.

I'm crazed with excitement the first time my parents leave the two of us at home alone, with a couple of rented DVDs and money for a pizza. I spend the first hour running steeplechase loops of the sitting room furniture, ignoring Ferdia when he asks me to sit down, to be careful. I only stop when the food arrives and we sit in front of the TV together, watching an action film that I'm marginally too young for. When the last crusts are gone, I inch closer to Ferdia on the sofa, covering it up as restlessness, until eventually we're shoulder to shoulder. He smiles down, puts his arm around me and I nestle into his body. Though I know that my parents would see this kind of closeness as gratuitous, I feel safe, calm, cared for. But then there are doughnuts for dessert and the sugar goes straight to my head. I resume my household assault course, rocketing around the sitting room for a few minutes more before moving upstairs, shrieking laughing and jumping on my parents' double bed, which I never do when they're at home. I'm having the time of my life and, though Ferdia keeps telling me to settle down, it doesn't occur to me that I'm actually being too much for him. I run from my parents' room to his, climb on to his bed and begin to bounce.

'I'm serious, Jacinta,' he says from the door and his voice is crackly. It's taking a long time to break. 'This isn't funny anymore.'

I grab the duvet and wrap it around myself like a cloak, though it smells strange and musty, like Ferdia himself does sometimes.

'This isn't funny anymore,' I mimic, straining my voice to growl and squeak like his. I'm still laughing at my joke as he crosses the room in two huge steps, his face suddenly snarled with fury.

'For fuck's sake,' he shouts and lunges at me. I topple backwards off the bed, my head cracking against the lip of the windowsill as I fall, the pain so sharp and shocking that I barely understand what's happened, and can't believe that my brother might have pushed me. My view of the room is disorienting; my head by the skirting board and my legs and feet still tangled in the duvet. When he vaults over the mattress I expect Ferdia to lift me up but instead he towers over me, still shouting.

'Why did you do that?'

He's so angry that he barely looks like himself. I've never seen him lose his temper with anyone but now he bends and grabs me roughly by the shoulders.

'Is it bleeding?'

His fist thumps the wall somewhere over my head and he crashes out of the room. It isn't bleeding. Later a bump will form, hard and hot, but it will be under my hair where my parents will never see it. And, though for days my fingertips will be drawn constantly to the tenderness, I won't say anything and neither will Ferdia. Beyond an initial gruff sorry, called through my door half an hour later when he's calmed down and I'm lying in bed – dry-eyed and stunned – we never speak about it again. If we had, if he had properly apologised, I'm not sure I'd even remember what happened, let alone feel the strange burn of humiliation that comes back to me now. He was a teenage boy who lost his temper. These things happen. But it's the secret that creates the shame and, like an old potato in a drawer, gives it a cool, dark place to sprout.

\*

In the afternoon, Lindsay is presenting at her conference and she stops replying to my texts. Though the worst of the hangover has passed, still I feel needy and emotional. I open her Twitter feed, scroll through her posts from the day, which are measured and professional, showing none of the acid or impatience she speaks with in real life. I imagine her drafting them on her phone, biting her top lip, focused. Her current contract ends in the summer and she's being careful about what she says, worried about having to leave King's, leave London, leave academia altogether. I'd go with you, I was tempted to say when she explained it to me, wherever you go I'll go with you. But four months in, we're still pretending that we're in the early days. That a weekend apart isn't a big deal and a possible separation is an irrelevance. I never admit that most lunchtimes I leave the office and go for a long slow walk, circling the library where I know she works, hoping I'll run into her. When it happens, I pretend it's a coincidence and so does she.

I realise I'm hungry and drag myself out of bed, pulling on jeans and an old gardening fleece of my mother's, planning to walk to the bagel shop around the corner, already imagining the warm bite of the bread, the salt of the pickles, the fatty chew of the meat. I glance at my phone before putting it in my coat pocket. Lindsay hasn't responded but I send another message anyway.

*I hope your presentation went well. Bet you nailed it.*
*I miss you.*

Outside, the air is cold and misty but everywhere you can feel the building energy of a Saturday evening. My phone buzzes.

*Thanks, babe. Lots going on here but speak to you later x*

I'm envious of Lindsay's work, of her commitment to it, her belief that it matters. I never chose my own job, I took it because Bart offered it to me when I worked in a café where he often held meetings, and he decided that he liked my vibe. I've been there five years now. The people are mostly friendly. The money is fine. But if, on my deathbed, I'm asked to account for my life, I know I'll struggle to defend the time I've already spent this way, drafting and distributing marketing emails, not really helping anyone.

Ferdia always knew he was going to be a priest. When I was a toddler he would set me down on the sitting room floor and preach the gospels from the step in front of the fireplace. In our local parish he did every lay job going: altar server, faith friend, lector, columnist in the church newsletter, weeder of the peace garden, hander-out of baskets for collections at mass, stretcher-carrier on the annual pilgrimage to Lourdes. He spent all of his mid-teens in correspondence with various priests and orders, contacting colleges across America and Europe. At first he planned to be a Carmelite, drawn to the simplicity of the call, but in the course of these conversations he's encouraged to become a diocesan priest instead.

'Just like what they said to the pope,' my mother tells people. 'They think he's destined for greater things.'

She's behind him all the way; having lost her own vocation, she's always believed in his. But my father's not so sure. He wants Ferdia to take a year out to think about it and for a while our lives are full of their quiet arguments.

'A bit of experience of the world of work never hurt anyone.'

We're in the car, driving to see my grandparents in Roscommon. It's dark. My father is speaking to Ferdia in the front seat and I'm pretending to sleep in the back. My mother must have travelled ahead.

'The priesthood is work, Daddy. And it's my work. You know that I have a vocation.'

'And if so, then what harm will waiting do? Another year won't make much difference to the Lord.'

My father is trying to keep the mood light but Ferdia doesn't laugh.

'Why would I expose myself to temptation?' he says, and my father coughs, glances around quickly to check that my eyes are closed.

'There is something to be said for the temptations,' he nearly whispers. 'Do you appreciate that? It's a big sacrifice for a man. You'd want to know for sure.'

A shiver runs through me in the back seat. Though I don't quite know what my father is talking about, I can sense that a boundary is being breached. Ferdia doesn't reply for a long time and when he does his voice is cold, almost condescending.

'I already know for sure.'

He never gets angry during these talks. He's calm and immovable, has answers prepared for everything. In the end, he wears my father down and, just turned eighteen, prepares to leave for Rome, where he'll spend six years studying at the Irish College. And at this, my mother is suddenly devastated. She's always assumed he'll be a seminarian at Maynooth, twenty minutes from home, and he hasn't corrected her.

'There's no sense in that,' she sobs, the night he admits the truth. 'There's no sense in that at all.'

I'm sad about him leaving too, though no one ever really talks to me about it. I'm nervous about being left alone with my parents. But then there's also a part of me that's looking forward to Ferdia's absence, the way the rest of the solar system must secretly hope for the burning out of the sun.

When I order my bagel, the man in the shop smiles and makes a joke. He's the only person I've spoken to all day and it's nice to laugh. I miss that about my years as a barista, the chats, the certainty that you could make someone's day a little better just by being friendly. I go back to the flat. Sasha and Thomas are still out so I sit alone at the table and eat.

\*

The evening before Ferdia left, while my mother roasted a leg of lamb, my father took out a bottle of whiskey. It was his best one, an expensive single malt, gifted by a wealthy parent whose delinquent son he had shielded from expulsion.

'You'll have a drink with me?' he says, gruff and embarrassed. Ferdia nods, appreciating the solemnity of the moment even as he struggles not to flinch with each tiny sip. I work quickly through my glass of Coke, confident I have the better deal.

'Do you like it?' asks my father.

'I do,' says Ferdia, sipping again and wrestling his grimace into a smile. 'You can tell it's good stuff.'

My father bows his head and raises his glass. 'Your grandfather gave me a glass of poitín the night before I went to university in Dublin. So you've gotten off lightly.'

They both laugh briefly then drop into silence, cradling the thick bases of the good crystal tumblers in their hands. The TV is off but I turn and stare at the blank screen, desperate for relief from the intensity of the moment, the dense, unspoken male emotion.

I'm nine and it was only a few hours ago, on seeing him zip his suitcase shut, that the reality of my brother's decision became suddenly clear to me, all the different fibres of it fusing in my mind. Nine is old enough to scent the thin perfume of loneliness that surrounds the priests I've met, the air of bewilderment as they shuffle around the altar, the thickening cloud of shame and scandal that I can't reconcile with my shiny-eyed brother. What's more, one of my classmates' sisters has recently had a baby and I was nearly sick with jealousy when I heard, had to fight off an image of Ferdia with a child in his arms. I know I'd be a great auntie, much better than the girl from school, buying the baby presents and bringing it to the playground. When it got older we'd go to the cinema together and it wouldn't have to bring a bag of popcorn from the shop because I'd buy some at the theatre, buttery and hot. I feel completely at ease with this future self, in a way I never do when I think of having a husband or baby of my own.

'Though I am actually thinking of giving it up,' Ferdia says, breaking the quiet. 'The drink, I mean. I'm thinking of becoming a pioneer.'

My father glances at him but then turns and stares out the window for a long time, his throat working. Even I can see how thoughtless Ferdia has been, spoiling his little father-son ceremony that way.

At dinner no one says much at first. It all feels so final, as though Ferdia is going into a closed order, or to the missions, and we might never see him again. It doesn't help that we're in the dining room, eating off the good Christmas plates and surrounded by the lingering smell of hoovering and polish.

'You'll say grace, Ferdia?' my father asks as my mother puts down the last plates of soup.

Ferdia nods, solemnly reaches out his hands and clears his throat. I'm prepared for a bit of Latin, or at least some reflections on the plight of those in poverty around the world. But instead –

'Bless us, oh God, who sit together, bless the food we eat today, bless the hands that made the food, bless us, oh God, amen.'

It's the children's grace, the same one we say at school, our thirty high voices racing through it so we can get our lunch boxes open a fraction of a second quicker. It sounds absurd in Ferdia's low mumble and I decide that he's panicked and forgotten the words to all the others, which doesn't bode well for his chances of memorising the whole of mass.

The meal is lavish by our standards: French onion soup to start, with chunks of warm baguette for dunking. Then the lamb, brought out on a large platter, studded with garlic and rosemary, shimmering with lemony oil and served with smooth mash, whole-roasted carrots and a china dish of mint sauce. It's not the sort of food my mother has made before – even at Christmas our vegetables are boiled mushy – but in the last few weeks I've noticed her slipping cooking magazines into the shopping trolley. Tonight she's wearing a silk blouse I've never seen before, whether because it's old or new, and I think she looks beautiful.

'This is delicious, Mammy,' I say after two bites of lamb.

'It really is,' says Ferdia. 'Thanks for making so much of an effort.'

She smiles at us mistily from across the table. We always sit in the same configuration at dinner in the kitchen: Ferdia and I on one side, wedged against the wall, my mother opposite Ferdia, my father at the head. In the dining room we maintain the same pattern and I find it strange to think that tomorrow I'll move up into Ferdia's seat. I've always been jealous of it, resentful that he gets to be at the centre of the conversation while I get an empty chair for company.

'Though we'll be eating it for weeks,' my father says. 'I'm sure we could have made do with a slightly smaller bit of lamb.'

My mother drops her eyes to her plate then. 'I can make some sandwiches out of it,' she says plaintively. 'For Ferdia to bring with him.'

Ferdia laughs. 'I do think they'll feed us, Mammy.'

He's joking but tears are rising to her eyes and I'm suddenly furious with all of them for first making such an effort and then ruining it. I want to cry myself or lift up my plate and then slam it back down on the table, but instead I take a deep breath and turn to my brother.

'What do you think your room will be like?'

When I think of Ferdia off at college, I picture him sitting up late in a white washed attic room like I've seen in books about the early Irish monks, crouched at a slanted desk in a small pool of light. He smiles.

'Not very glamorous. A single bed and plain walls with a desk in the corner and a small wardrobe. But it's not like I'll have many clothes to put in it anyway. Black shirt, black shirt, black trousers, black jacket, another black shirt.'

I grin. 'Do you have to share with someone?'

'No,' he says, 'thank God.'

'Wouldn't do you any harm,' my father says loudly. He poured himself a second whiskey before dinner and seems to be feeling it. 'I slept with forty other boys at boarding school.'

'And I shared with Breda in digs, right up to the day I was married,' my mother says, seeming to have forgotten her time in the convent.

'Exactly,' says my father. 'You young ones don't know how good you have it.'

They're both speaking directly to me, my mother confiding, my father teasing and jovial. They're being brave, I can see now, trying to shield Ferdia from the scale of their grief at his going. But I'm flustered by the attention; the forced cheerfulness making me uncomfortable in a way I can't quite understand. My parents' lives, even when they joke about them, are beginning to sound sad and confined to me, with so little breathing room that Ferdia's life in the seminary will seem free by comparison.

As the meal wears on the dining room warms up and blurs around us; the table lit by tall tapering candles. I feel something in myself softening and swelling. Ferdia seems to sense it too; he keeps looking up from his plate and gazing around at each of us in turn, at the room, and then down at his own hands.

When my mother moves to take the plates he jumps up himself. 'Let me do it.'

She pauses, half-lifted out of her chair, and stares at him, as though he never clears his own plate. 'Can Jacinta help you?' she asks, and I pull my chair back in readiness. But Ferdia puts his hand on my shoulder.

'Would you please just sit down?'

After he's cleared the dishes we hear him clatter out of the kitchen and up the stairs, hear the bang of the bathroom door just overhead and the thrum of his pee hitting the water, so loud and protracted that I nearly giggle. Then he goes into his room.

'Is he gone to bed?' my father wonders after a few minutes, only half joking. We're beginning to feel awkward, the three of us alone, afraid that the moment of goodbye has passed and we've missed it. But then Ferdia thunders back down the stairs and appears in the door, like a Valentine, with a bottle of brandy in one hand and a box of Roses in the other.

'I wanted to . . .' His voice comes out high and unsteady and he pauses to clear his throat, resetting to an unnaturally deep pitch. 'I wanted to get you all something, just something small, to signify how grateful I am –' there's a crack in his throat but he keeps on '– for all you've done for me.'

My mother gasps, then coughs out three noisy sobs. My father has to look down at the table, rapping it gently with his knuckles. Ferdia stays standing at the far end, clutching the gifts in his hands, uncertain of what to do next. So I stand up and take them off him, set them on the table then turn and give him a hug, my arms tight around his torso, my ear pressed to the rapid beat of his heart. He hugs me back and kisses the top of my head.

'Well, we'll have to have a drop,' says my father eventually. 'You'll partake, Margaret?'

'Yes, lovely.' She blinks through a mess of mascara.

'And what about you, Ferdia?' he asks, uncertain after the episode with the whiskey.

'Why not? I won't be a priest for another few years.'

'Good man,' says my father. 'Lord make me chaste, but not yet!'

They all laugh loudly at that. My mother leans over the table to loosely cover my ears and I shake my head forcefully, as though to throw her off, though really I'm thrilled with this gentle moment of contact. The brandy is poured and another Coke for me, which I gulp before realising that everyone else has paused.

'Well,' says my father portentously, standing and raising his glass towards Ferdia, who shifts in his seat. 'Your mother and I certainly can't deny that we're deeply saddened at this parting. The Lord God has blessed us with two children and, though we may not say so often, we trust you know how much we cherish you both. And though Jacinta, thanks be to God, will be with us a few years yet, the time has come for us to let Ferdia spread his wings and fly. We've done our best for you, we hope you've found it worthy, and now all that remains is to wish you well on your road. Wherever it may lead, know that our thoughts and prayers go with you, and that no matter what happens you'll always have a home here.'

He pauses then and his lower lip juts out like a child's as he struggles not to cry. His left hand is pressed to the tabletop and Ferdia reaches out and rests his palm on top of it. My father looks at him, surprised by this small tenderness from another man, even such a young one, even his own son.

'God bless,' he says quietly and again my mother's high breath fills the silence that follows. We all sit a moment as though frozen, before my father begins slowly clinking his glass against each of ours, and the rest of us follow.

'Cheers, big ears,' I sing out as I meet Ferdia's eye and he grins at me, teeth white and eyes shining in the dim, looking like a boy from an old black-and-white photograph, about to go off to America, or to war.

# Chapter Seven

THE NEXT MORNING, with all the renewed vigour and purpose of the no-longer-hungover, I go for a swim in the local pool. It's Sunday morning, peak chaos, children skidding around the pool edge, ignoring the lifeguards, screaming and dive bombing and pretending to drown one another. But under the water it's calm and I swim slow lengths for nearly an hour. When I leave the changing rooms and walk through the park, the morning is sunny and blue, the air so cold that it turns my damp hair frosty.

Before he left for Rome, Ferdia helped me to set up a hotmail account so we could email each other. I haven't logged back into it for years but now, in a quiet café close to home, I do. No one else ever emailed me back then and Ferdia only had time to write once or twice a week. But still I used to check the account every day, on the family computer in the dining room, getting up early to avoid blocking the phone line and dropping in again at night. His life in Italy was almost unimaginable to me then, so distant and exotic that I struggled to picture the world outside the photos he sent me of Piazza Navona or Saint Peter's Square. He sent pictures of himself too, smiling with the other seminarians, and I would stare at them endlessly. Though Ferdia still mostly wore his ordinary clothes, it was strangely thrilling to see him in the black cassock and priest's collar he was allowed to wear for special occasions, the skirt somehow making him more handsome. But then he sent one of himself serving mass and the addition of a white lacy surplice ruined the effect entirely, left him looking girlish and infantile.

Despite Ferdia's encouragement, neither of my parents were willing to get their own email accounts and so these pictures, which he carefully scanned in an internet café, came only to me. I'd hoard them for a day or two before showing them to my mother, enjoying the power I had over her as a channel to Ferdia. But when it came to replying to his emails, to sharing stories of my own life, I was embarrassed at how grey and sad it all seemed.

*Dear Ferdia,*

*How are you? Is the weather nice in Rome? It's been a very wet September here, unfortunately.*

*I wanted to write to ask something about Saint Patrick. In school at the moment we're learning the ancient Irish myths and legends and he keeps turning up! For example, when Oisín comes back from Tír na nÓg and falls off his horse and becomes an old man, Saint Patrick comes to baptise him before he dies. The same thing with the Children of Lir when they're turned from swans back into people. And it doesn't make any sense to me because Saint Patrick was a real person but the myths are made up. Why do you think they have done that?*

*Lots of love,*

*Jacinta*

Reading back over the email now, I smile, remembering that I worked on it for hours, drafting and redrafting, obsessively checking my punctuation. I wanted Ferdia to know that I'd changed in his absence, matured. I was trying to show him that I was someone special too.

*Hi J,*

*Thanks for your email, it's always brilliant to hear from you. We've had a lovely few weeks of weather in Rome, until last week it was still warm enough to sit outside and eat. But this week it's definitely turned and you can feel winter coming in. It's going to get a lot colder here than it does in Ireland – I might need a new coat!*

*Thanks as well for your really good question about Saint Patrick. First of all, I agree that it's not true that Patrick baptised Oisín, and it's a bit clumsy of whoever wrote the book to mix up the stories like that. But as Catholics, we believe that God has always been at work in the world, even before He sent Christ to save us, and we believe He was at work in Ireland even before He sent Patrick to convert us. And by superimposing the saints into the old stories, I think what the writers are trying to do is to show the presence of God even in ancient Ireland. Does that make sense?*

*You've actually hit on a big question for religious thinkers. When we tell the stories of the saints, or even of Christ Himself, should we stick as close to the facts as we can? Or is it more important that the stories capture the spirit of God's Word even if we can't exactly prove every detail? I think it's probably the second one – but I'd love to hear what you think.*

*I've attached a photo from when I went to the Vatican last week. If you look closely you can see Pope John Paul II in the window in the middle – he's not small, he's far away. Could you show it to Mammy for me? I think she'll like it.*

*I miss you, little sister. God bless.*
*F*

These emails are the highlight of my week but they're always too short and I log off feeling flat. In these lonely years after Ferdia leaves, I need more from him than he can give. Coming to the end of primary school, I still have no friends and spend break times reading on a quiet step in the corner of the yard. I had liked playing football, even if the boys always picked me last, but then one day the teacher held me back after class and said that maybe I was getting a bit old to be playing, that I should spend more time with the girls instead. I know it's unfair but there was something in the way she looked at me, some strange mix of pity, discomfort and dislike. I couldn't bring myself to argue.

At home, no one really talks to me either. My father is always at work and, following Ferdia's departure, my mother has dropped like a stone into one of her depressions. Though I try to fill the gap my brother's left – bringing her tea and toast in the mornings, tidying away her dirty cups and sweet wrappers before my father gets home – still she seems surprised and irritated when I'm around. It's as though, if she can't have Ferdia, she'd sooner have the house to herself.

I get my period one Tuesday morning but I say nothing until Thursday night, when the toilet paper I've been stuffing into my underwear finally fails. I go to my mother's room and knock. She doesn't reply but still I crack the door open and step in. The floor is messy and cluttered, the air thick with the smell of unwashed clothes. Though neither of them ever acknowledges it, I know that my father spends a lot of his nights in the spare room, which is fresh and austere.

'Mammy?' I say.

She's lying on her back on the unmade bed. I go and stand by her and she swivels her eyes to look at me, but doesn't move.

'I have a mark on my uniform,' I say. 'I'll need to wear my tracksuit tomorrow. Can you write me a note?'

'It's only one day,' she says, already frustrated with me. 'Can you not just wear it and we'll clean it at the weekend?'

I shake my head and the tears come on so suddenly that I can do nothing about them. My face crumples and when I speak again my voice is shrill and wobbly like a child's.

'It's blood,' I say.

My mother closes her eyes and sighs. I'm imposing on her. 'Fine,' she says. 'Bring me your diary.'

When I come back with it, there's a pile of five sanitary towels on the bedside table.

'You can have those,' she says, clicking her pen to write the note. I take them away. I put my stained skirt in the laundry hamper and by Monday morning it's washed and ironed and back in my wardrobe. But my mother doesn't speak to me about it again. A few days later, I come into the kitchen as my father is unpacking the weekly shop.

'I got those there for you,' he says, nodding at a cube of pads on the kitchen table. 'And there's some Häagen-Dazs in the freezer.'

I pick them up and leave the room quickly, my cheeks burning. For years afterwards, without my asking, he buys me a new pack every time he shops, so that by the time I go to university I have a backlog of dozens.

I realise then, approaching my teens, that while Ferdia might answer my questions about religion, when it comes to everything else, I'm on my own. I can tell that there's something about me that pushes other women away, that shuts me out of the tight gossipy clusters of girls at school and the kinds of intimate mother-daughter chats that you see on TV. I start buying teen magazines, reading the advice columns and the make-up tips and the how-to guides to puberty and body hair and flirting with boys. I read them on my step in the school yard, hoping that eventually one of the other girls will stop, ask for a lend, or sit down next to me so that she can read it too.

\*

When Ferdia comes back to visit, he brings home the first proper best friend either of us has ever had. Brian Fallon is from Donegal, gangly, with a soft voice and a habit of keeping his eyes lowered when he speaks to you. His bus journey north from Dublin is far longer than the flight from Rome so he always spends one night with us to break up the trip. My mother loves him, spends days planning what we'll eat on the days they arrive. Brian is like another son, she says, and the only thing better than one priest in the family is two.

This is the first time an outsider has ever infiltrated our house and I find it strange. But I like Brian. I like his smile and the way his clothes sit on his skinny frame. When he arrives at the house he always says hello to me and shakes my hand. But I'm shy of him too; there's something in his eyes, when he flashes them upwards, that makes me feel I'm about to be caught out.

While my mother cooks, the three of us go to play football on the small green opposite the house. I play in goal, shouting instructions while they charge around like little boys, wrestling each other off the ball and pumping their fists when they score, which is seldom since they both prefer to let me save. I feel at ease, part of the gang, often laughing so hard that I can't see the ball to catch it. But back in the house, when my mother offers each of them a single can of not-quite-cold beer, I have to sit and listen as they tell my parents about everything they've studied and heard in the preceding months, about every new priest or bishop they've met. My mother hangs on their words so closely that she barely touches her dinner. After a few minutes, she'll run to get a copybook and make a note of a theological concept they've mentioned.

'That sounds very interesting. I'll have to read some more about that.'

Though I try to hide it, I'm bored by the theology. I prefer when they tell stories about the day-to-day life of the seminary: about pasta-making disasters, vestments dyed pink in the wash, missing sacks of communion wafers and doddery priests lost in the corridors. The college building is haunted, Brian insists to me one afternoon, and if you dare to walk the halls at night you can hear the echo of ghostly choirs.

'Though, of course, we don't believe in ghosts,' Ferdia interrupts. 'Being, you know, Catholics.'

Brian shrugs. 'You say what you like, Ferdia. But I won't be taking any chances.'

My brother grins, shakes his head. Up until now, he's spent his whole life being taken too seriously by the adults around him and he lives up to it a lot of the time, delivering his opinions slowly, every word weighty and momentous. But Brian laughs at him when he talks like that.

'Has Ferdia told you about the mouse in the guest accommodation?' he says to me on another visit. 'We had a very eminent bishop staying a few weeks ago and – to the embarrassment and distress of the entire community – our wee friend crept out while he was brushing his teeth.'

I giggle. 'What did he do?'

'Well, at the time, His Grace went down to the front desk and asked to be changed to another room—'

'Which he was,' says Ferdia, picking up the story. Brian looks at him and smiles. 'But the next day over breakfast he asked what was being done to deal with the rodent problem. And one of the monsignors tells him that they've tried everything they can think of but nothing has worked. Then, quick as a flash, our friend Brian here pipes up. And what does he say?'

Sitting opposite me, Brian grins. 'Would you consider confirming the mouse, Your Grace? That always works to get rid of people.'

Silence. Brian's bright face falls and I want to laugh to make him feel better. But both my parents have picked up their knives and forks and are applying themselves studiously to their roast beef.

'I'm sorry,' he says. 'Maybe that wasn't appropriate . . .'

'Don't be stupid,' says Ferdia. 'You're fine.'

My father clears his throat and Ferdia rolls his eyes. 'Ah, come on, Daddy. Let's all remember Saint Thomas More: Lord allow me the grace to be able to take a joke and share it with others.'

My mother perks up then. 'I haven't heard that one before.' She takes hold of her copybook. 'Is it a real prayer?'

'It is,' says Ferdia, pointedly. 'I recently heard that one of the new cardinals – a guy called Bergoglio – prays it every day and says it helps him in his duties.'

That's enough for my mother and she laughs abruptly at nothing. Ferdia laughs with her though my father holds his frown. Brian winks at me across the table.

\*

Walking back from the café, as the afternoon turns navy and damp, I search my phone for a particular photo of Brian and Ferdia. It's from the day they were called to candidacy for the priesthood and they have their arms slung around each other like a pair of underage footballers or a newlywed couple, so full of energy – the best of their cohort, everyone said – that it was impossible to think of them ever becoming old men, lifting the Eucharist with exhausted arms.

'Do you ever run into Father Brian?' my mother used to ask when I first moved to the UK. We had last seen him at Ferdia's funeral, which he was asked to serve, skinny and pale next to the presiding archbishop, his hands shaking as he held the book. Though he was ordained the next year, he didn't last long in the priesthood before he dropped out and moved to London.

'It's a big city,' I'd tell her. 'And I doubt he'd thank me for stopping him in the street.'

But the truth is I know exactly where Brian Fallon is and what he does. After years in the wilderness – no new Google results, no social profiles – he reemerged in 2016 as a fully-trained psychotherapist, practising in Dalston. Late that evening, after I've spoken to Lindsay on the phone, packed my bag for Monday morning and made a pot of soup for the week, I look him up again. His website is white and minimal. On the About Me page there's a picture of him on a mountainside somewhere, the sky swirling grey and the ground mossy, his face creased as he smiles at someone to the left of the camera.

*I'm a fully qualified psychodynamic therapist, working from my own private rooms. I have extensive experience working with anxiety, depression, childhood trauma, family breakdown, addiction and sexuality. I aim to create a peaceful and reflective atmosphere that gives clients the freedom to dig deep into their feelings and experiences. I believe that laughter and joy have an important place in the therapy room, alongside more difficult emotions, so I invite you to bring your full self to sessions.*

I smile, immediately hearing the words in Brian's voice, though I haven't spoken to him in more than a decade. Underneath there's a contact form and I fill in my name, my phone number, scroll through a drop-down menu and select 'Other' as the reason for my query. But then I get stuck, staring for a long time at the large empty box at the bottom of the page.

I've emailed Brian once before. After Ferdia's funeral, when the meal was over and people were beginning to drift away, I disappeared to a corner of the hotel gardens where I hoped no one would find me, needing a break from having my shoulders sympathetically squeezed. Brian had had the same idea and I found him sitting on a drippy wrought-iron bench with his long legs stretched in front of him. He was staring into the shrubbery and I stood and watched him for a moment before I coughed softly. He jumped up.

'Oh God, Jacinta, sorry. I'm just getting ready to leave.'
'OK,' I said.

We hovered a moment, then Brian reached into his inside jacket pocket and held out a business card. I'd never seen anyone do this outside a film and almost laughed. But then I noticed how badly he was trembling and sobered up again.

'If you ever need to get in touch ...' His voice was thick and uncertain, his words slurred. 'I mean, if there's ever anything I can help with ...'

'Thanks, Brian,' I said, appreciating the gesture but thinking, even then, that of the two of us I wasn't the one who needed help.

'I mean it,' he said, and looked at me, swaying, a few seconds more. I wanted to give him a hug, to tell him that Ferdia would be proud of him and we were going to be OK, maybe even stronger somehow. But instead I just looked back and we stood there, a few feet apart, both too exhausted, too wrung out to cry, until eventually he nodded and walked unsteadily away.

All that day, I'd been looking over my shoulder for Aisling, the girl I'd kissed at the party less than a week before. Though it felt like a betrayal of Ferdia, I couldn't stop thinking about her. Even then, drifting around the hotel gardens mere hours after we'd put him in the ground, I imagined her appearing from the direction of the train station, breaking into a run when she saw me and crushing my body against hers. I didn't see her for months afterwards but I pictured myself with her every night, many mornings, most afternoons. I could bring myself to the brink with just the thought of her slightly chapped hands brushing my cheek, or holding my waist. And it was a relief to let thoughts of Ferdia recede, to briefly have all that cold emptiness filled before the reality flooded back and I lay awake for hours with my grief and my guilt and my confusion about what it all meant.

Eventually, I took Brian's card out of the copy of *The Glass Bead Game* that Ferdia had bought me the previous Christmas.

*Dear Brian,*

*I hope you don't mind me getting in touch but I've got a question I'm not sure who else to ask. Before I go on, let me assure you that this question is entirely hypothetical. Say a woman was to find herself interested in a romantic relationship with another woman, and this woman is a Catholic. What exactly is the Church's teaching on what she should do next?*

*I hope things are good with you.*

*Best wishes,*

*Jacinta Devane*

Reading this email again is painful. I can see myself at the PC in the dining room, typing as fast as I'm able, terrified of my parents walking in. I know I could never have this conversation face-to-face, but the Brian on the other side of my screen isn't entirely real to me, is separate from the man I met a few months ago and might one day meet again. This shields me from the full significance of what I'm doing, so much so that I don't really believe he'll reply, or even read it. When my parents go for a walk the next evening, I don't rush to the computer. I finish what I'm watching on TV. I go to the fridge and eat a scoop of last night's mince, drink a mouthful of Coke from the bottle. Only then do I go to check my email, only then does the taste of scavenged food turn sickly in my mouth when I see that Brian has already responded.

*Dear Jacinta,*

*Thank you for getting in touch. It's lovely to hear from you and I hope you and all the family are managing as well as you can in this difficult time.*

*First off, I'd like to thank you for trusting me with this question. Although it is entirely hypothetical, I'm sure it wasn't easy to ask. And recognising the trust you've placed in me, I think the most respectful thing I can do is give you an entirely honest answer.*

*The Church's teaching on sexuality is quite clear. Sex is acceptable in only two interconnected contexts. First, for purposes of procreation within marriage. And second, to increase the closeness and intimacy of married couples. Neither of these purposes can apply to couples of the same gender, and as such all sex between such couples is considered a sin.*

*But it is important to note that the Church doesn't consider being same-sex attracted as a sin in itself. Gay people were created by God and so their existence in and of itself cannot be sinful. The problem starts when you act on those feelings. So in practice what that means is that gay or lesbian people are called either to live chastely, like priests and nuns do, or to redirect their feelings and marry a person of the opposite sex. If that seems difficult, the advice is to seek Church-provided counselling and learn to manage your feelings of attraction.*

*I know this probably isn't what you were hoping to hear and I'm sorry about that. But if you have any questions or would like to talk more about anything, I'll always be very happy to hear from you.*

*Take care,*

*Brian*

The email winds me and I shut off the computer. My parents arrive home from their walk and for the first time in weeks they're in a good mood – the light on the canal was lovely, they say – but I shout at them over nothing and storm off to my room, hiding under the duvet and crying for hours, livid with shame. I'm angry with Brian and with myself for contacting him in the first place. I never want to think about it again.

But still, the secret has been spoken and, after months of stasis, without my even noticing it, my thinking begins to shift. A few days after receiving the email, I agree to go to my friend Fionnuala's birthday party, though since Ferdia died I've been refusing to see my friends outside school, not able to face the stares and whispers.

The party is a barbeque on Shankill Beach and I notice Aisling as soon as she arrives, in denim shorts and a men's dress shirt, laughing with a guy I don't know. I wait for her to see me and then, the moment she does, her face freezing, I turn away and look far out to sea. For what feels like hours, we avoid each other. To shield myself from my friends' awkward chat, I've volunteered to take care of the foil barbeques and am kept busy handing out paper plates of blackened meat, which people stuff in hotdog rolls and cover with tomato sauce. But eventually, dizzy from the smoke, I stand up to look for another beer and find her behind me.

'Hey,' she says and smiles.

I nod. 'Are you looking for a burger?'

'I'm vegetarian actually.'

'Oh, right.'

I shift my feet a little, trying to place myself more squarely in the path of the wind, worried I smell of meat grease.

'I was actually wondering if you needed a break? I'm thinking of stretching my legs a bit. Taking a walk along the beach?'

She speaks quickly, the last few words of every sentence lurching upwards into a half question. But to me everything seems very slow, my heartbeat getting harder and louder.

'Sure.'

Though it's past eight now, the midsummer evening is long and clear. I know nothing will happen between us, that nothing can when there's nowhere for us to hide away. And still I feel unsteady as we walk slowly from the crowd. The water is quiet at this time, in the shelter of the bay, and all I can hear is the roll of stones under our feet.

'So how have you been?' I say eventually.

'Yeah, fine,' says Aisling. 'What about you?'

We've fallen into step and I count thirteen footfalls in the silence after this question.

'I'm sorry,' she says.

'It's OK.'

'I meant about your brother.'

'Oh, yeah. Thanks.'

'I was so upset when I heard,' she says. 'I wanted to come to the funeral but my mam and dad wouldn't let me take the day off school.'

'I guess we don't know each other very well.'

'Yeah. And I didn't actually know if you'd want me to be there?' Her voice is tentative. 'Or if maybe it would have embarrassed you in front of your friends?'

I suddenly feel so much older than Aisling. I picture my parents, sitting in the living room sharing a chicken curry from the local Chinese and watching a film they've seen before. *Rocky*, maybe, or *Indiana Jones*. They've done the same thing every Saturday since Ferdia died and although it's felt like a prison to me for all that time, right now I want to be back there with them, safe in our shared pain.

'To be honest, that wasn't the sort of thing that was on my mind,' I say flatly and Aisling apologises again, even more quietly this time. We keep walking but when I next look at her I realise I've made her cry. I stop and touch her arm but she waves me away.

'No, please just ignore me.' Her voice is wavering, threatening to break into a wail. 'I can't believe *I'm* the one crying.'

I laugh then, grab her arm and pull her into a hug. She sinks her head into my neck and we hold one another, easy and close, for such a long time that I forget who's comforting who. She rubs my back gently and I hear the rhythm of my breath change, and then hers does too, and though I know everyone at the other end of the beach can still see us, I pull her tighter against me.

# Chapter Eight

IN A QUIET PUB off Newington Green, Brian Fallon's thick-rimmed glasses fog up as he steps in the door. Briefly blinded, he has just the same baffled aspect he once had on the altar. But then he blends back into the Islington aesthetic, in tan trousers, a thin grey jumper and a navy wool coat.

'My goodness,' he says, approaching the high table where I'm sitting. Something in his gaze still makes me shy and I stumble as I stand up and reach out my hand. Brian squeezes it, then leans forward to kiss me, fleetingly, on the cheek. 'You've changed.'

'You haven't at all,' I say and it seems true because he's still so lean and moves languidly to the bar to order a drink. But when he sits down opposite me I can see the fade in his face, the lattice of wrinkles like spun sugar. We look at one another a moment, both half smiling in the low light.

'Well, sláinte,' I say.

'To old friends,' he replies, his Donegal accent still so mossy and gentle that my nerves about this meeting melt away. Already it feels completely natural to be here with him, to have him tell me, without preamble, that he doesn't drink anymore, raising his bottle of non-alcoholic beer as proof.

'My first few years in London were . . . well, they were intense.'

'Not in a good way?'

He smiles. 'No. I believed that I had all this life experience, this wisdom that other people my age didn't. But actually, the priesthood kind of races you along to a certain level of maturity and then stops, sets you in aspic for the rest of your life. When I left . . . well, I realised I had a lot of unused stupidity to burn through.'

'Know the feeling,' I say. 'Kind of.'

'I'm sure you do.' Our eyes meet and he smiles, wry and warm.

'There's something I want to tell you,' I say, deciding to get the revelation over with, though I don't really want to talk about it, would much rather chat on with Brian about nothing in particular.

'OK.' He moves a little on his stool, bracing his feet against the legs.

'They're looking to make Ferdia a saint.'

The words seem to echo around the near-empty pub. Brian blinks, raises his eyebrows slightly. 'I mean, you probably knew they were thinking about it. But they're officially starting the process now.'

He toys with the bottle in his hands, staring at it.

'I thought the vice-postulator might try and contact you, so I wanted to let you know first.'

'Thank you. I really appreciate that, Jacinta.'

'Jay.'

'Sorry?'

'I go by Jay now.'

Brian pauses to absorb this, then smiles. 'Nice. Well thanks, Jay.'

'I only found out myself a few weeks ago. I don't really see my mother and father that much and I think they probably preferred not to tell me until it was certain. I mean, they probably knew I wouldn't be happy about it.'

Brian nods but otherwise doesn't react.

'You don't seem surprised?' I pause, he doesn't reply. 'You already knew?'

He nods again and I flush, embarrassed by my big reveal.

'Matthew Richter has already been in touch with me,' he says.

'You could have just said.'

'I know, it's a bad habit of mine.'

'Lying?'

I mean it as a joke, but he flinches.

'Not telling people things they won't like hearing.'

We don't speak for a minute. People are filtering into the pub now, bringing blasts of cold air with them, and I watch as two middle-aged men hug, already laughing, delighted with the sight of each other.

Then I say, 'I have kind of found that it's bringing it all up. Trying to remember these things about Ferdia. It's dragged me back.'

'I can imagine,' Brian says quietly. 'But you know, they can't oblige you to give your testimony if you don't want to. They're not the police.'

The way he says it reminds me of the old Brian, whom Ferdia always referred to as 'the best religious thinker in the college'. Though alone, my brother would happily lecture the family on theology, philosophy, Latin or Greek, he always deferred when Brian was there, would nod along as his friend embarked on long, enthusiastic, perfectly reasoned journeys into the world of the spirit. It's comforting to find that, so long out of the priesthood, Brian still speaks about the Church with the same supreme assurance, though now every word is chilled and reserved.

'Even so,' I say, 'it's hard not to get sucked into it. I mean, I told Father Richter exactly what I thought of the whole thing. But you can imagine how excited my mother is . . .'

He nods. I'm leaning right across the table now, my hands reaching towards him. The tealight between us is in a red jar, like a votive candle, and I briefly rest my fingertips against the hot glass. Then I draw back.

'What did you tell him?' I ask.

'Richter?' Brian grins. 'Well, I admit I was tempted to meet him for a theological debate. But instead I told him he could fuck right off.' I laugh, imagining the priest's face, and Brian laughs with me, for a moment, before his smile fades. 'But seriously, I decided it wasn't a good idea, for exactly the reasons you've described. You know, all that happened that night . . . with Ferdia. I don't think I can risk going back there.'

His head jolts very slightly, as though to loosen the memory, stop it taking root.

'It must have been awful,' I say and he flashes me a look of such genuine gratitude that I wonder if anyone has ever acknowledged it before, how shocking it must have been, how lonely and painful. Then he shakes his head again.

'I know it's nothing compared to what you all went through.'

He takes a drink. I want to tell him that grief isn't finite, and that no one's pain is worth more than anyone else's. But it seems silly to say so to a trained therapist.

'You know, Jay,' he resumes. 'Maybe the worst thing about leaving the priesthood was that I felt that Ferdia would be disappointed in me, that I was letting him down somehow.'

I nod. For me, that thought is like a dark pool, rippling below all my anxiety about work, about wasting my life.

'How did you deal with it?' I ask and Brian shrugs.

'Well, initially I didn't. But over time, I realised that it was actually a kind of magical thinking. That I was hanging on to the idea that Ferdia was out there somewhere, capable of being disappointed in me.'

'And you don't believe that he is?'

'No, not anymore.' Brian pauses. 'Do you?'

'No,' I say quickly, though there's still something nerve-racking about admitting it, a feeling I might get in trouble.

Brian nods.

'That makes this process extremely complicated for you. I mean, obviously the world is full of people with different religious beliefs, but most of the time – if we leave the moral and political aspects of faith aside – that doesn't surface in any really impactful way. You can rub along pretty happily with religious friends or colleagues without coming up against the fact that their understanding of how the universe is constituted is fundamentally different to yours.'

'Yeah, of course,' I say.

'But this situation is entirely different, right? In that people who believe in the process of canonisation believe that the candidate is an active participant. It's basically the only remaining time when we try to verify the interaction between heaven and earth. And if you don't believe in that, then of course your relationship to the cause is going to be entirely different. Your parents, presumably, believe that Ferdia is in the next life, that he still exists, he's still their son, and they still have an obligation to him. Whereas you . . .'

'Have to make do with a gaping void?'

I'm trying to make a joke but it doesn't come out that way. Brian blinks, suddenly worried, reaches across the table and rests his hand on mine.

'Sorry,' he says. 'We don't have to talk about it if you'd rather not.'

'No, it's OK.' I turn my wrist awkwardly and squeeze his hand. 'I would like to. But only if you don't mind?'

'Not at all.'

There's a silence then, but not an uncomfortable one. It's a strange feeling, being with someone who's known me since I was a child but who I haven't seen in so long. It's like my two lives are drawing together and suddenly,

I can imagine Ferdia here too, so easily that I glance at the empty stool next to me.

Then Brian speaks again:

'What I was trying to say, but expressed extremely badly, is that it's reasonable for you to put your own needs first. That's what makes sense with your belief system.'

I smile. There's something very endearing about Brian's confidence that he can reason his way through any problem.

'But it's not that simple,' I say. 'I mean, atheists are still concerned with the wishes of their dead friends, right? They still try to protect their memories.'

'Sure,' says Brian.

'OK. So, with that in mind, do you think Ferdia would have wanted to be a saint?'

Father Richter has planted this seed in my mind, complicating my relationship with the process. I can condemn the Church happily, any day of the week. But Ferdia's preferences, whatever they might have been, are harder to brush aside. Brian sighs.

'I honestly don't know. I mean, he would have had his doubts about the expense and fanfare, I'm sure of that. But he was *obviously* very committed to being virtuous.'

There's something in his tone that makes me smile.

'You sound a little resentful?' I say and Brian grins.

'You know as well as I do that the saints are a nightmare to live with.'

We both laugh. Then Brian drifts back into his thoughts and I glance around, waiting for him to go on. The pub has filled up now, traffic is flowing to and from the bar.

I think the people at the table nearest us are on a first date and I turn to ask Brian if he agrees. But his head is bowed and there are tears on the tabletop.

'Oh God, Brian . . .'

He waves my concern away.

'It's fine. I just . . . I know this probably isn't what you wanted to hear from me. But if we were to accept that saints exist, Catholic or otherwise, there would be no doubt in my mind that your brother was one.' His voice breaks again and he tilts his head backwards, fanning his face with his hands. 'I don't think I'd realised that before now.'

Watching him, I feel a sudden clarity, understanding that I came here without knowing the question I really wanted answered.

'Brian?' I say tentatively. 'There's something I want to ask you, but if you'd rather not speak about it, you can just tell me so.'

He takes a handkerchief from his pocket, blows his nose loudly and then smiles at me, the old knowing smile. 'Ask away.'

'Were you in love with him?'

Brian exhales loudly, puffing out his cheeks. 'Well firstly, I have to say I'm impressed. I never thought a Devane would ask a question like that straight out.'

'You don't have to answer,' I say again.

'Truthfully, I'm not sure I *have* an answer.' He looks out the window, on to the square. Figures in dark coats shuffle by, stiff in the cold. 'But if it's any comfort, my husband wonders the same thing.'

My mouth falls open and he laughs, holds up his left hand. 'Last May.'

Old anger slices at me, sudden and unexpected. Why didn't he tell me he was gay when I was a teenager, when I sent him that email? But then Brian's smile falters and quickly my better self burns through.

'Congratulations,' I say and he flushes, relieved. 'It's obviously going well?'

'It is. Thank you.' He beams, looking shy and proud, and I am happy for him now, completely. 'There was a long time when I couldn't even imagine being with anyone. In my head I was still a priest. And then, well I didn't believe I deserved to be happy after all that happened.' He shakes his head. 'Even after all that had settled, I thought I had too much baggage for any self-respecting gay man to take me on.' He laughs awkwardly. 'But Tristram – yes, that's his actual name and yes, he is a Protestant – he hardly blinked at the priesthood or the addiction stuff. But the one thing he did want answers about was Ferdia.'

I don't reply right away. It's a strange feeling, not only voicing these questions about my brother, but having them validated. It's not just me, other people are trying to figure him out too. This man, Tristram, a total stranger.

'Why do you think that was?' I ask eventually and Brian shrugs.

'It was still live, I suppose. Live pain. I'd spent so many years doing everything to avoid it . . .'

He trails off. I wonder how bad things got in those years, imagine a blank-eyed and emaciated Brian stumbling in and out of clubs, wandering in the grey hours from Soho to the Embankment to gaze at the beige swirl of the river. But I don't pity him. No, I envy him the crash-and-burn of it, the redemptive journey out the other side. Blessed are those who hunger and thirst. I imagine my parents at home right now. My mother watching *Mastermind* in the sitting room, my father reading a book at the kitchen table, their lives flattened out and faded.

'I mean, yes, obviously I was in love with him on some level.' I look at Brian again, taking a moment to absorb what he's said. 'But it's hard to know what that even means when there was never any question of it being acted upon.'

'So you don't think Ferdia was . . .?'

Brian cocks an eyebrow.

'Of the parish?' he says archly and I laugh.

'I just wonder if you ever talked about it.'

'No.'

There's no give in this answer, no room for doubt. I feel a rush of tears, slowly sip my drink as I try to hold them back.

'He wouldn't have appreciated it,' Brian says eventually, more softly. 'And I didn't want to risk it.'

'Your friendship?'

He nods. 'There are very few religious, priests or nuns, who can really inhabit the vow of chastity. Even those of us who officially manage it tend to fail implicitly. And I suspect that a growing number don't really believe in the vow in the first place, don't think it's necessary or healthy.'

'But Ferdia did?'

'He was very committed to it. The same way most of us would work to really understand and enact the vow of poverty, Ferdia was like that with celibacy.' He hesitates. 'But that meant the scandals hit him even harder than the rest of us, I think. I mean, it was terrible for everyone. But in some respects, they affected him more.'

'Really? I don't remember that,' I say. 'Though I suppose he might not have wanted to talk to his little sister about it . . .'

A flash of pain. I take a drink and Brian, sensing something has happened, waits a minute before he goes on.

'None of us liked to admit when we were having doubts, anyway. You knew people would either be disappointed in you or they'd feel vindicated, as though they were right all along that the priesthood was the wrong choice.' I nod, thinking of my father's doubts. 'So though I didn't entirely agree with him about celibacy, I had to respect what he was trying to do. The other seminarians are the only people who really know what you're going through, and obviously he would have felt that about me more than anyone. So if I'd questioned him, if I'd thrown doubt on our friendship . . . I think it would have been shattering.'

Brian looks down at his hands. Across the bar a table of three men explodes into laughter.

'Sorry,' he says in a rough whisper. 'You think it's getting better and then . . . it's still so fresh, isn't it? You remember how young we were –' he looks up, his eyes shining '– and how stupid.'

I nod, remembering the day a few years ago when I realised that I had grown older than Ferdia ever would. In an instant, the tenor of my memories had changed, as though I had stepped out of his shadow and seen, in the full glare of daylight, how young he actually was, how naive, how badly in need of protection.

'Was that why you left?' I ask Brian. 'Over celibacy?'

He shakes his head. 'It was actually obedience that did for me in the end. I couldn't get my conscience in line with what they were asking of me. That, and I was just so unhappy.' He drains his bottle. 'Can I get you another?'

'We don't have to,' I say, though there's nothing I'd like more than to stay here with Brian, to keep talking into the night. With him, I feel closer to Ferdia than I have in years, like together we can steal him back from the bishops, the saint-makers, the miracle-seekers, can hold on to him as he was.

'I'd like to,' says Brian. 'And you're not going to turn me back to the drink if that's what you're worried about.'

I laugh. 'Go on so. It's the pale ale.'

I take out my phone while he's at the bar. I have a text from Lindsay, a photo of her reading the secondhand copy of *Gilead* I'd bought her for Christmas. She's done it ironically – her eyes staring over the top of the cover and straight into the lens – but hasn't managed to disguise how sweet she's being. When she first unwrapped it, she seemed disappointed and I was hurt, though I'd tried to disguise it. It was the first gift I'd ever given her.

Now I stare at the photo for a long time, my eyes running over her hair, her shoulders, her fingertips where they grip the book. She looks so beautiful to me and I want to express it to her right then, how deeply I feel. But Brian is coming back from the bar so I quickly type, *gorgeous x,* and put away my phone.

We talk about Tristram then, Brian's husband, an orthopaedic surgeon whose salary allows Brian to split his time between private clients and voluntary counselling work with young offenders.

'Do you enjoy it?'

'I do,' he says. 'It might seem strange but my favourite part of the old job was hearing confession. If you got it right, you could see the lightness in people as they walked away. And I feel that way now, that I can give people space they might not get anywhere else.'

I say I never felt that way about confession and he frowns.

'I mean, obviously I know how terrible the power dynamic is and I know that many priests, well maybe most priests, are awful about it. But the –' he waves his long hands looking for a phrase '– the raw operational concept of it, of giving people a calm space where they can speak their guilt and shame. There's a lot in that.'

I ask if he misses it. He smiles but shakes his head.

'I sometimes miss the person I was when I believed in it.'

'But you don't regret leaving?'

'I'm not sure I had any option.' He pauses. 'It can be harder, I think, for lay people to walk away from religion. There's no ritual about it, no one to guide you.'

I make a small humming sound.

'So, what about you?'

'I'm not sure there's much to miss. Even when I believed I never thought I was good enough. I still felt on the outside.'

'Of the Church?'

'And the family. Mammy and Ferdia, whatever they had.'

Brian nods, as though he understands exactly what I mean.

'You don't see much of them these days?'

'Not really. Every few Christmases, the odd visit in between.' I pause. I never know how to explain to people how, without any open conflict, our family ties had disintegrated after Ferdia died. 'We just have nothing left in common.'

'Are you angry with them?'

'No, not usually. I don't see the point. But since they told me about Ferdia's cause.' I make my hands into loose fists. 'Honestly, I haven't felt this way in a long time. I'd burn down Saint Peter's if I could.'

Almost imperceptibly, Brian winces.

'Are you not?' I ask him. 'Angry, I mean.'

He doesn't answer for a moment then says evenly. 'I try not to expend too much emotion of any kind on the Church.' He laughs quietly. 'It won't love you back and it won't hate you back either.'

'And?' I prompt, not sure what he's getting at.

'And to be honest, I think you need to consider conserving your energy too, not letting this canonisation thing eat you up. Because whether you're for it or against it isn't going to make a bit of difference to the Vatican.

So if you let yourself get swept up in it, it might stop you ever getting closure.' He pauses. 'These campaigns are circuses, Jay. They need huge amounts of money, political will, support from the faithful. And still it might take decades. Or it might never happen at all.'

I think of my mother's voice as she told me the news. For her, I can tell, the intensity is the appeal. Ferdia was always her purpose and now that mission is renewed, intensified. Being dead, he's more helpless than ever, like a newborn, dependent on her for everything.

'Do you think he'll make it?'

Brian shrugs. 'The Vatican is very eager to create saints at the moment. But no matter who you are, the odds are low.'

He looks at the wall over my head and I can see his mind working over something. I finish my drink, my hand tight around the glass. The pub is full now and getting noisy. Brian looks back at me and leans right across the table, so that he can speak quietly and still be heard.

'Listen, Jay,' he says. 'I don't want to intrude, but have you had any help with what happened? Have you ever spoken to anyone about it?'

I laugh. 'Do my parents seem like big believers in talk therapy?'

'What about since you left home? Have you ever considered it?'

I shrug. 'Can't really afford it, to be honest. I asked the GP once and they said I could put my name down but that it would take at least two years.'

'Well, if there comes a time when you can afford it . . .'
'Yeah, I know.'
'These things have a long tail. It's OK if you're still struggling.'
'Thank you,' I say, trying to tamp down my defensiveness. 'But I am actually fine. It was bad for a long time, but I'm OK now.'

Brian nods and lets me close the book on that one. Our drinks are done again and this time I know it's time to go. The streets outside are shiny and we step out of the warmth of the pub into a thin soaking mist.

'Well!' says Brian, turning to face me.

'Love a casual catch-up,' I reply and we laugh, then step forwards into a hug. It's slightly awkward at first but instead of pulling away quickly, Brian tightens his grip around my shoulders.

'Thank you so much for suggesting this,' he says. 'It was great to see you.'

'You too,' I whisper. My face is pressed to his shoulder. I don't want to let go.

'And tell your mother and father I was asking for—' He stops and backs away, lifting his collar against the mist. 'Actually no, maybe don't say anything.'

# Chapter Nine

A FEW WEEKS INTO the first term of my fourth year of secondary school, I come out of the main building and find Ferdia leaning against a lamp post. He's wearing black jeans and a black puffer jacket, the white of his clerical collar peeking over the zip. I stop short, hardly believing it's him, then look over my shoulder to check that none of my friends are around. Because I have friends now. Halfway through the last year of primary school, my parents announced that instead of going to the local secondary, where all the kids I knew would go and where my father was principal, they'd be sending me to a well-heeled convent in the city centre. I saw my chance for transformation and, in the six months that followed, focused with singular twelve-year-old intensity on becoming the kind of person I felt I needed to be – studying my teen magazines, changing my hair, my walk, my clothes. I ate less. I practised being silent even when I had something to say. I learned to be cruel to other girls to shield myself. And most importantly, when the first week of First Year came, I acted like my parents didn't exist. I lied about Ferdia, telling everyone he was in Galway training to be an Irish teacher. And in all my three years at the school, I'd never talked about God.

'What are you doing here?' I ask him.

'I'm back for a retreat. Did you not get my email?'

I shake my head and he laughs, though it must hurt his feelings that I've drifted out of contact, taking longer to respond to his messages, telling him less about my life. I don't want him to know about the weekends I spend in the city centre parks, swigging from naggins or cans provided by boorish private schoolboys, too many of whom I kiss in back alleys, hating the feel of their doughy hands on my body.

Still I feel a weight lift when I see Ferdia and, when we hug, a knot unties in my chest.

'Sorry. I just didn't realise it was this week you were coming.'

'That's OK,' he says, ruffling my big back-combed hair as I draw away. 'It's good to see you.'

He buys me a takeaway mocha and we go for a walk in the Iveagh Gardens. The season is just on the turn, the light low, warm through the frail green of the trees. Though we haven't seen each other in months, Ferdia is quiet and the whole city seems to hush around him. After a while we stop and sit on a bench, watching two children play chasing with their dad, their shrieks shocking and alive in the dusk.

'Are you nervous to be a priest?' I ask.

He looks over at me. 'I am. Very.'

'But everyone says you'll be brilliant.'

I can hear the note of resentment in my voice and Ferdia picks it up too. But just then, the bigger of the two children accidentally body slams the smaller, knocking them over. A wail breaks across the green and we both laugh.

'See?' I say. 'Being a second child is tough.'

Ferdia elbows me softly. 'I'm nervous because I know my limits. I know I'm going to spend the next, what, sixty or seventy years ministering to a disappearing congregation. And I have this vision of myself as a seventy-year-old man with nine parishes to look after. And for what? For a church that's . . .'

He trails off, stares upwards at the fading blue of the sky, looking young and moody in his black clothes. It was only a few months ago, at the end of his fifth year in seminary, that Ferdia was admitted to candidacy for ordination, earning the right to dress as a priest in his daily life. This is the first time I've seen him since.

'So why are you doing it?'

He shrugs. 'I don't have a choice. I was born with my vocation, that's what I believe at least. But that doesn't mean it's easy.'

There's a loneliness in his voice that's almost too heavy for me to bear. And still, I feel proud. Because something has clearly shifted in the months since we saw each other last. Ferdia is speaking to me like another adult, like a friend. He needs someone to talk to and he's chosen me.

'Is there anything I can do?' I ask seriously.

He clears his throat. 'Just promise me you'll stick around?'

'What do you mean? Like, in Ireland?'

'No.' He laughs awkwardly. 'I just mean, you know, there's going to come a time when Mammy and Daddy aren't around anymore. And you might have children and a husband, or a partner –' his voice falters a little '– but I'll only have you. So I'd just like to be in your life, wherever you are.'

'Of course you will be.'

'Thank you.' He's quiet for a minute. 'I don't think I've been here for you. Not enough.'

I don't say anything. Ferdia reaches out and puts his hand on my back, just below my shoulders.

'Are you OK?'

I shrug roughly and he moves it away. 'Yeah, I'm fine.'

'Because if there's anything you want to talk to me about . . . to tell me. I know I haven't been great, but I am here to listen. I'm always here.'

I think about this moment all the time; the evening chill starting to brush my cheeks and the noise of rush-hour traffic building outside the garden walls. When I dream about my brother now – and I still do, a few times a year – I dream that he's dying again, slowly sometimes, but unavoidably, and there are things I need to tell him, or ask him, things that need to be spoken about. But I can't speak: I develop a stutter, or laryngitis, or see him far away in the distance and can't shout loud enough for him to hear.

'I'm fine,' I say.

'You don't sound entirely sure.'

He's looking directly at me now and I feel a cold surge of fear, like I'm about to be exposed somehow.

'Well, is there something you want to tell me?' My voice is cool and angry.

Ferdia jerks back a little. 'What do you mean?'

I shrug. I've been practising this technique at school. Whenever someone seems about to learn something about me, or laugh at me, I throw something back to destabilise them. But though it's effective with my classmates, I didn't imagine it would work with an adult. Ferdia looks genuinely nervous and I almost laugh. But then I see a change in his face and his shoulders relax. I'm a teenager again and he's not.

'I'm always here,' he says again and I nod, thinking I might cry if I speak now. A few minutes later the attendant comes by.

'Locking up shortly, folks.'

We get up and walk back through the manicured beds. It's hard to see our way now in the gloom.

'Are you heading back out?' I ask, thinking we might get the train together. But he shakes his head.

'Brian is around town today too, meeting some friends. I said I'd go for a drink.'

\*

In the weeks leading up to his anniversary, I always try to think about Ferdia a bit more, to remember moments like these, when it was just the two of us. But this year, I'm preoccupied with my visit to Ireland, with deciding what to wear and preparing answers to the questions my aunts and uncles will inevitably ask. *And you're still a . . . what was it? A marketing executive, yes. And what's that when it's at home, hah?*

The week before I'm due to travel, I go to see my hairdresser, a stylish Czech lesbian I call the Child of Prague. I booked the cut right after I agreed to go, close enough to the trip for my hair to look sharp but far enough away that it won't seem newly done. I don't want to look shiny and coiffed, like my aunts, who'll all be rolling into their salons over the next few days, or like my mother, who'll have asked hers to open early on the morning of the mass. I can picture them already, lined up in the chapel in their navy dresses and pastel cardigans. I've already washed and packed my black work trousers and a fitted black polo neck. Nothing that stands out. Nothing they can comment on.

But then, as the hairdresser fastens the gown around my neck and asks if I want the same as last time, a tidy up of the indeterminate bob I've stagnated into, I say no, that I'd like her to add an undercut and to make it look as gay as possible.

She laughs, asks if I have a date. I say no, a family occasion, and she rests a hand on my right shoulder, tugs gently at the locks on the left side of my face.

'So I guess they're not supportive? Your family?'

'Not really. Yours?'

'They're fine.' She shrugs. 'Normal. Kind of uncomfortable if I'm too extra but otherwise OK. Have you shampooed your hair today or yesterday? Will we just spritz it?'

I nod. I've been seeing her for nearly a year now. It's the first time I've ever had a regular stylist because normally

I don't like the power they have over you. But Nat is different. The first time I came to the barbershop, I brought John McGahern's memoir with me and instead of asking the usual questions about my weekend plans and styling products, she asked about his work and we spent the entire time talking about the different ways censorship operated under communism and Catholicism. She lived in Cork for a year when she first left home and you can still hear it in the slight stretch in her accent. I have a benign crush on her, which she takes kindly in her stride.

'I came out to them after I arrived in Ireland,' she goes on, spraying water on my hair. 'Over a shit Skype connection. I thought that even if it went badly I'd be far away at least. But it was OK.' She laughs. 'I owe *a lot* to Martina Navratilova.'

I laugh too. She leans forward and pulls the damp ends of my hair taut against either side of my face. I shift slightly in my seat.

'Are they Catholic?'

She scrunches her face a little. 'I guess, technically. We've all been ... what's it called with the water?'

'Baptised.'

'Yeah, we've been baptised. But we don't go to church or anything. The Czech Republic is one of the most atheist countries in Europe.' She unzips her case and takes out the clippers. 'Only behind France, I think.'

'That's interesting.'

'Yeah, not like Ireland at all, right?' I shake my head. 'So your parents, they weren't happy when you came out?'

I shudder suddenly, just as the clippers touch my scalp. She steps back and I smile apologetically.

'Actually, we've never really talked about it.'

'Oh.' Her eyebrows lift in the mirror. 'That's interesting.'

'I mean, I have come out to them,' I clarify. 'When Ireland was voting on marriage equality I sent them a long email explaining everything. It was a big thing back then, you know, asking your older relatives to vote yes, laying out your heart for them to trample.'

Nat hums, drawing a clean line around my right ear. 'Do you know how they voted?'

'No, I don't,' I reply slowly. 'They just kind of ignored it.'

'You mean they didn't respond?'

'My father sent an email thanking me for getting in touch, said I'd given them lots of food for thought.'

She releases my hair from the clips, the fresh shave disappearing under the other layers.

'And?'

'And we've never spoken about it again.'

It sounds pathetic and though I try to flash a quirky smile, my reflection slumps a little.

'Hey, where are you going?' Nat places the tips of her two forefingers under my chin and lifts my face upwards, smiling at me in the glass. 'Life is fucking hard, man. We need to pick our battles.'

I smile back, swallowing hard.

'Don't worry,' she says. 'People cry in here all the time.'

\*

That evening, Lindsay and I meet at the back entrance to the British Museum. She's there first and my face breaks into a smile at the sight of her, wearing an enormous grey overcoat she recently bought in a charity shop. Her lips are moving, her eyes closed. She's jiving softly to whatever's on her headphones and I slow down before stepping out of the shadow on the other side of the street, wanting to enjoy the moment a fraction longer before she realises I'm here.

'You look amazing!' she calls when I do move into the lamplight. 'I love your hair.'

I smile, lean in to kiss her. We're going to a book event, a conversation about Russia, socialism and financial crime that I'll struggle to entirely follow. When she texted me this morning, Lindsay said that she appreciated it might be too obscure, and that several people had already refused to go with her. I agreed immediately. And I like the bookshop where it's being held. I enjoy the performance of being there: nodding seriously every few minutes, carefully sipping my free red wine. The people are so well-dressed and intentioned, deferential to the speakers, yearning for answers. It's like mass.

Afterwards we go for a pint in a pub opposite the museum. It's decent, despite a slight ambiance of gravy, and Lindsay is teasing and gentle, running her hand across the shaved part of my head, paying me compliments. I laugh, I loosen up, feeling that I've shaken off my wobble in the hairdresser's. But then, when she goes to the bathroom and I pull out my phone, my mother has sent a link to a long profile of Ferdia in the *Irish Catholic*, with extensive quotes from her. I scan it quickly.

> Margaret Devane is cheerful and matter-of-fact when discussing her son's life. He was a devout Liverpool fan, she says, and sometimes as interested in playing PlayStation as he was in the sacred mysteries. Did he give her any trouble? 'Well, he could be exasperating at times but sure that's true of all teenagers.' She laughs often as we speak. But as soon as I mention Ferdia's sudden death thirteen years ago, aged just twenty-four, she becomes quiet and withdrawn. 'Nothing can prepare you for a moment like that. When the phone call comes . . .' She struggles a moment to compose herself, then goes on quietly. 'Well, you change forever. It's very difficult to trust again, to believe that life can go on.' Did her own faith help her through? 'Oh yes, absolutely. I pray to Ferdia every day, for his intercession. . . .'

When I read that, a sudden pressure gathers in my right temple. I scroll away, back to the picture at the top of the page, the same one of Ferdia in his vestments that we propped on top of his coffin during the funeral. Afterwards, I carried it out of the church, clutched desperately in front of my chest like he was a missing dissident.

'Jay?' Lindsay, back at the table now, reaches out to stroke my hand. 'Is everything all right?'

'Yeah, fine,' I say. 'Why?'

'You seem pretty far away.'

'No. Not at all.'

She smiles. 'OK. Because I asked you about forty seconds ago if you'd like another drink and I'm still waiting on an answer.'

'Ah.' I squeeze her hand. 'Sorry.'

'Don't apologise. I quite like it when you brood.' She winks badly, her whole face heaving around the closed eye. I tell her that I'd love another drink but then, when she brings them back, I struggle to concentrate, can't keep up with what she's saying about the clampdown on free expression under Putin.

'I'm sorry,' I say, the third time she asks me what I think and I have to admit that I haven't been listening. 'It's nothing to do with you, I'm just having a strange day, I don't know why.'

She nods. 'Is it the pollution? It's been so bad this week. I feel like I can't breathe.'

'Maybe.'

'Seriously.' She rubs her fingertips across her forehead and holds them out to me. 'Black as soot. I need country air or my growth will be stunted by the smog.'

She's beautiful when she's in a mood like this, her face bright and flickering, her hands flashing in wide arcs. I want to vault over the table and tell her that I love her, but at the same time, I can't get the image of my mother praying to Ferdia out of my head.

'That sounds nice,' I say.

'Well, let's go then. Let's get out of London on Saturday.'

'And go where?'

'I don't know. Folkestone? The Chilterns?'

I feel panic rising. Too many things are happening at once. 'Wouldn't that be a bit smug and middle-class coupley for you?'

'Well, yes,' she says seriously. 'But I won't let my class consciousness get in the way of your respiratory health.'

I laugh. Lindsay hooks her index finger around mine. 'Come on. We'll go for a big walk then find some nice pub in the middle of nowhere, drink five pints and scandalise the locals. It'll be nice.'

I smile back at her and say again that it does sound lovely. 'But I've got to go to Ireland the following weekend. There's stuff I need to get ready.'

'Oh right,' she says. 'Why didn't you say?'

I shrug. 'Didn't seem like the sort of thing you'd be interested in.'

'I'm not sure that's fair,' she says, hurt but trying to smile through it.

I sigh. 'You say you're not into families?'

'Seeing them, no. But I do want you to talk to me.'

'Well anyway, I'm sorry about the trip.'

Lindsay shrugs and the conversation moves on. But when we finish that round of drinks, she says she's tired and that it's time to head home. I ask if I can come too but she shakes her head.

'I have to be out the door really early. Probably best not.'

My heart sinks. Though Lindsay has turned me down kindly, and though she goes on chatting as we walk together to Russell Square, something has shifted and I'm suddenly sure that this is the beginning of the decline, that I'm about to lose hold of her. This news about the canonisation process, this dive back into the oily well of grief, has come at the worst possible moment, just when things were starting to go right. The soiled air of the station catches in my throat and I feel myself gulp a little for breath.

When we reach the point where our tunnels split, Lindsay stops.

'Seriously, is everything all right?' She dips her head slightly to catch and hold my eye. I know she's really asking and am so grateful to her for noticing.

'Yeah, of course, I'm fine,' I say, and she nods, leans in to kiss me three times, her cheeks soft but decisive against mine.

As I walk down the tunnel, I scroll to the article about Ferdia again and stare at the picture, trying to remember the exact way his face cracked into that smile, the sound of his laugh, the grip of his arm around my shoulders. I realise, as the first tears spill over, that some version of this happens every year, that no matter how hard I try to convince myself that Ferdia is no more dead on his anniversary than he is at any other time, the pain of it still intensifies as the days start to stretch out and blossom appears on the trees.

\*

Time seems to change after that afternoon in the Iveagh Gardens; it blurs in my memory so that I can't tell if things are moving very quickly or very slowly, if I'm looking at them from too close up or too far away. That visit is his last to Ireland and on the Saturday before he leaves, the two of us drive to Roscommon to see our grandparents. We don't talk about anything much in the car, a little shy with each other after being so earnest the week before. But Ferdia's in a good mood, excited about getting back to Rome. He turns the radio up loud and we sing along.

My mother's family has always been a large presence in our lives but somehow insubstantial too; I'd struggle if you asked me to tell you what any of them was like. Numerically, too, we're less dense than you'd expect. My uncles John and Damian are bachelor sons who've never left home, who still sleep in the same twin bedroom they've shared their whole lives. They're both alcoholics: Damian practising, John recovering. And my aunt Breda, the youngest of the family, has never married either. My mother and her two older sisters, Maura and Kathleen, were left to do all the breeding. Allow for one untimely death and we're left with five grandchildren from six children, which is a poor innings no matter how you look at it.

Besides Breda, who lives in Dublin, they all drop in and out of the big farmhouse that afternoon, wanting to catch a rare glimpse of Ferdia before he goes. Though we only intend to stay a couple of hours, by six o'clock we're still there, eating our second meal of tea, bread and fruitcake.

As the rest of us are finishing up, my grandmother disappears into the cavernous cupboard under the stairs.

Over lunch, Ferdia mentioned that the zip on his suitcase has split and she's decided to give him a battered old leather one belonging to my grandfather, their shared initials stamped on it in faded gold. After several minutes of noisy excavation, she finally wrenches it out on a current of paint brushes, golf balls, school textbooks and tins of shoe polish. A flood of expired life. As she straightens, she skids a little and I jump up to stabilise her.

'Thanks, a stór,' she says, kicking away the small round thing that's rolled under her feet. A baby's head, one of its eyelids drooping.

She's frailer than the last time I was here, just the other side of the summer. More forgetful. Though she mostly hides it well, several times today she's dozed off next to the fire while everyone else is talking and once, on waking with a jump, she barked out a few sentences of angry nonsense. We all ignored it, more from shame, I think, than kindness. But she's vigorous enough as she beats the dust off the suitcase and brings it to Ferdia.

'Granddad got this for our honeymoon,' she says. 'And it cost a lot of money at the time, though it might not look like much now.'

'It's perfect,' says Ferdia. 'But are you sure you can spare it?'

'Sure we've no big trips left in us now. Do we?' She directs this to my grandfather, who ignores her.

'Where did you go?' I ask, having returned to my perch on one of the hard chairs in the corner, out of her line of sight. She turns to look at me, surprised and uncertain.

'On your honeymoon,' I prompt, as gently as I can. 'Where did you go?'

'We went to the Holy Land,' she snaps, as though it's obvious.

'Can you imagine that?' my uncle John chimes in. 'On your honeymoon.'

He winks at me in a way that makes me feel pinned to my chair. Though I don't think John is actually a creep, he drinks too much to notice when he's acting like one. No one else says anything and eventually I stand up and start gathering the plates.

'Are you in a hurry to leave?' my grandmother asks sharply. I look to Ferdia for help.

'I asked Jacinta not to let me spend the whole evening chatting,' he says and nudges the suitcase with the tip of his black shoe. 'This thing won't pack itself.'

'Of course,' says my grandfather. 'You need to get on the road while there's a bit of light left. We won't keep you.'

He speaks gruffly, reaching for the remote control, but there's a shimmer in his eyes. He's frightened, I think, by the change in my grandmother.

'Well, at least make sure you wrap up a few pieces of that for the journey,' Granny says, gesturing at the plate of brack in my hand. I nod. As I deposit the plates on the sideboard, she's lowering herself on to her knees, clinging heavily to Ferdia's forearm for support. When I come back for the cups, he and my grandfather are kneeling too and untangling their beads. As they begin murmuring their Hail Marys, I wind cling film around the pieces of cake. John's disappeared for this bit of the proceedings and no one seems to expect me to join in either. When I finish what I'm doing, I turn to watch them, their backs turned to the centre of the room, their voices low and earnest.

'Well, please God we'll see you again,' my grandfather says when he's back standing, taking Ferdia's two hands in his.

'Of course you will,' says Ferdia softly. 'And I'll be sure to ring.'

'Don't worry about that,' my grandmother says briskly. He leans down to kiss her cheek. 'We know you're busy. Just say a prayer for us every now and then, that's all we ask.'

'Well, I can promise that.'

'Send my regards to himself,' bellows the returned John, lifting his hands and shaking them to show that he means the pope. 'And watch out for those Italian women. You don't want to fall at the last hurdle.'

Ferdia picks up the suitcase and I take the brack, a little irritated now by all this fuss. Rome is only a Ryanair flight away and he comes to visit all the time. But later, I wonder if they sensed something that I didn't. The brightest flames burn fastest, people tell me again and again after my brother's gone, as though things were destined to turn out the way they did. I hated their resignation the same way I hate the people who pray to him now, the miracle-seekers, preparing their cancers and thyroid problems to be laid at Ferdia's heavenly feet.

Late at night, I've been watching beatification and canonisation masses on YouTube, mesmerised by the hordes of priests, the holy blood and organs carried along the nave, the haloed portraits and garish bursts of song. It makes me queasy to think of my mother and father, ten or twenty years from now, elderly, in new suits, shuffling along with Ferdia's heart in a box.

It's carnage in the comments section, too:

> *Pray for us Blessed Oscar, from the Philippines.*
> *Please heal my husband's cancer of the tongue.*
> *Keep my daughter in your prayers, Saint Anna. She has been sexually assaulted and denied justice.*

When I lost something when I was little, my grandmother would tell me to give a penny to Saint Anthony. But she never said where Saint Anthony was, or how you could reach him, so I used to open the back bedroom window and hurl the coin as far as I could into the garden, assuming he was out there somewhere, near the rhododendron. And that's how these people seem to me now, flinging their need into the void and hoping it will get forwarded somewhere. They're no different to the Catholics of a hundred or a thousand years ago. Given the chance, they'd tear loose scraps of the holy flesh, snap away fragments of bone, shear off brittle dead hair and suck the blessed blood with straws. Because that's what you get, isn't it, when you build a church in the darkest pits of people's despair.

> *Hi Fr John. Well done on nearly being a saint. Please pray for my big brother who is very sick in hospital. Lots of love, Caoimhe, age nine.*

When we step outside my grandparents' house, the evening is getting dark, enough that my grandfather flicks on the lights on his way across the room. I kiss them both goodbye. We get in the car. And when I look back from a long way down the narrow road, just before we turn the bend and the house disappears, I can see the two of them silhouetted in the door, still waving.

\*

By the time I reach the platform, there's a hollowness in my chest. I feel too tired to last the three minutes until the train comes, until I can sit down and have my pain confirmed by the face in the dark window. The line is almost deserted and I press my fists into my eye sockets, let three sobs shudder through me. Then there's a hand on my back, just below the shoulders.

'Come on,' says Lindsay, slightly out of breath, wrapping me into a hug. 'Come home with me.'

I cry all the way, my face buried in her shoulder, a dark damp patch spreading through the grey coat. She kisses my head. She doesn't ask what's wrong. Back at hers she brings me tea and biscuits and we watch a couple of episodes of a nineties English sitcom that I've never heard of. When the credits roll, I turn to kiss her, tugging and grasping at her body, ready to block out my feelings and go back to normal. But she slows me down, drops kisses along my jaw and neck, matching my hard hands with her soft ones as she sweeps her palms along my face, my sides, my hips. The sofa is narrow and she has to stand up to pull off my skinny jeans. We laugh. When she touches me, I take a deep breath, unspoken feelings still tremoring just below the skin.

'Are you sure this is OK?' Lindsay asks and I nod, pulling her head down so I can kiss her. She moves gently, builds slowly, keeping her eyes fixed on my face and smiling at me now and then, a sweet private smile, as though we're standing on opposite sides of a crowded room. I'm still wearing my jumper and socks and there's no expectation of anything, no pressure to come. After a while, I move her hand away and she lowers herself down on top of me. I wrap my arms around her ribs, breathing in time with her breath.

'Thank you,' I whisper after a little while. She tilts her head, kisses the top of my jawbone, just by the ear. I gasp, still sensitive, and she laughs quietly.

'Anytime.'

# Chapter Ten

I STAY THE REST of the week at Lindsay's. Each morning, she brings me coffee and oats in bed then sits opposite me while I eat, cross-legged, bemused that I'm still there. I borrow clothes for work and, if I'm leaving town first in the evenings, we meet outside her building so she can hand over her keys. The week has been bitterly cold for March, leaving trails of lost crocuses in the parks and squares, so I make us a pot of black bean soup big enough to last for days. We have sex immediately after dinner each night, both because we want to and because it maintains the pretence that that's what I'm there for and there's nothing more going on. I'd stay forever, if I could, but by the third evening, Saturday, I can feel Lindsay getting restless. We're lying at opposite ends of her small sofa, sharing a blanket. She's reading Judith Butler and I'm flicking through an old copy of the *New Yorker* that I found under the bed. After a while she looks up at me.

'So, my mum is coming for lunch tomorrow.'

'Oh yeah?'

'She comes down every year to see the orchid show at Kew with two of her mates.'

'That's nice.'

'Yeah, it is. She saves up all year, a tenner a week. They stay in a nice hotel, go to a musical and buy real champagne in the interval. Then she spares a few hours for me at the end of it all, when she's shattered and hungover.'

'Are you looking forward to it anyway?'

'Jay.'

I squeeze her foot. 'I'll leave before then. I promise.'

'Thanks,' she says, not smiling. I'm afraid she's annoyed with me and I climb to her end of the couch and lie next to her, sliding my hand down the front of her leggings.

'I have to finish reading this,' she says, but her voice crackles.

'Really? You *have* to?' I trace my fingers softly along the outside of her underwear. She feels humid; we've been sitting under the blanket for hours. 'Please?'

She closes her eyes, both turned on and frustrated, then throws Butler across the room and winds a hand through my hair.

'Fine.' She tugs my head backwards and I moan quietly. 'Let's go,' she says and walks behind me to the bedroom, pushing me forwards when I stop to look at her. And whether it's because of the days of closeness, or the knowledge that this little holiday from life is about to end, the sex we have then is a world away from anything we've done before. She holds my arms down and grinds against me, burning hot, and I ask her to kneel over my face, whimper into the taste of her, desperate for the feeling of her hand inside me, so aligned with the movement of my muscles that I can hardly tell which is which. When it happens, my thighs are wet and my face is wet and I'm loud, too loud when the walls are so thin, so she kisses me, hard and long, cutting off my breath until I think I might faint but then, when she feels me about to come and gives me my voice again, instead of screaming, I make a strange muffled sound: 'Oh, oh, oh.'

Afterwards, I lie on her shoulder, her arm draped behind my neck and across my chest, our legs heavy and wrapped together.

'You're so hot,' I say dreamily.

'Thank you,' she says. We laugh. She kisses my shoulder, resting her face in the small hollow beneath it.

'Lindsay?'

'Mmmm.'

'Can I speak to you about something?' I can feel the weight of her, sleepy. 'It's about my family.'

She exhales heavily, reorients herself in the sheets. 'Not going to lie, I was hoping you were about to announce a fetish.'

I laugh. 'Sorry.'

I haven't planned to speak to her about Ferdia. I'm used to having a double life, a neat guillotine slice separating childhood from adulthood, family from friends, Maynooth from London. But since the news of Ferdia's cause, I've felt like the two halves have folded, pressing messily on top of each other.

'Well?'

'Right, yeah, sorry.' Another long pause. She shifts away from me to get a clearer look at my face. 'It's my brother.'

My throat is dry now and I look around for a glass of water. Lindsay takes one from her side of the bed and passes it to me.

'I suppose I haven't told you much about him, have I?'

She shakes her head and I clam up slightly, not knowing where to begin. 'Was he older or younger than you?' she asks, trying to help me along.

'Older,' I say, slightly irritated that she doesn't even know that much, though I'm the one who's refused to talk about him, who started a stupid fight the one time she tried to learn more. 'He was twenty-four when he died, I was sixteen.'

She smiles, resting her hand on my ribcage. 'So which of you was the accident?'

'No such thing as accidents in a Catholic family,' I hit back. But we're both too tense to laugh. 'The age gap meant that I hardly saw him for the last few years. I was still at home, obviously, and he was living in Rome.'

Her eyebrows lift at that, interested. She asks what he did there and I can see that she's imagining a job in fashion, art, maybe food.

'He was training to be a priest.' Her hand disappears from my side. 'And actually that's kind of what I wanted to talk to you about.'

Lindsay rolls away, reaching over the side of the bed for her clothes .

'You OK?' I ask.

'Sorry, just cold,' she says, bridging her hips to pull her underwear on. 'Keep talking.'

'Well, a couple of months ago I got a call from my dad and he told me that – there's no way to couch this really so I'm just going to have to say it – he told me that they're launching a campaign to try and have my brother declared a saint.'

Lindsay says nothing, sits up in bed, far away from me.

'I didn't know that was something they still did.'

'It is,' I say. 'Actually, the last three popes have created more saints between them than all the others combined.'

'Oh right,' she says flatly. 'Interesting.'

I cough, feeling very exposed now that she's partially dressed and I'm not. 'It's really been on my mind the last few weeks, you know. It's brought a lot of things up.'

'I bet,' she says, a hint of sympathy back in her voice now. 'So are you going to try and stop it?'

I shrug. 'I don't know how much I can do at this point.'

'Oh come on, there's always something you can do.' Her voice is light but there's something in the tone of the conversation that's putting me on edge. I reach for my own clothes.

'You want to help me tackle a cardinal off the altar right at the moment of beatification?' We both smile. Then I say: 'I'm sure it's hard to understand if you're not Catholic.'

Lindsay's smile disappears. 'I've told you I am Catholic.'

'Yeah,' I say. 'But you were never practising, were you?'

Her mouth twitches and I wonder why this is a competition I'm so desperate to win.

'I went to a Catholic school, if that's what you mean, made my communion and confirmation.'

'Did you go to mass?'

She looks at me for a long time. 'No, Jay, we didn't.'

'Well then, it's different.'

'How's it different?'

'It clearly didn't define your life, did it?'

My voice rises. I'm frustrated with Lindsay for quibbling over the details. I already wish I hadn't said anything. She shakes her head and looks away from me. When she speaks again it's through a clenched jaw.

'My mother went to a school where the nuns kicked the shit out of them, if you must know. It all went a bit sour for her after that.'

A heaviness settles over me, a dull resentment. 'And she still sent you to a Catholic school?'

I'm not looking at Lindsay but I can feel the change in her muscles.

'Excuse me?'

'It's just strange,' I say. 'To send your kids into the same system where you had such a terrible experience.'

'Fucking hell, Jay. Listen to yourself.'

'Or maybe *you* could listen to yourself. Maybe reflect on the fact that I shared something very personal and painful about my dead brother and you immediately made it about you.'

'Well, I'm sorry,' she says. 'But your brother was one of them.'

'One of who, exactly?' I ask, my voice breaking with shock. 'What are you implying?'

'I'm saying that I used to get woken up by my mum screaming with night terrors in the next room.'

I've never seen Lindsay like this before. She's quivering with fury. I take a deep breath.

'I am really sorry about that, Lindsay. But I'd like to clarify that my brother had nothing to do with—'

'He was complicit.' She cuts me off. 'None of their hands are clean.'

I shake my head. 'There's something wrong with you.'

Lindsay shrugs and I get off the bed, start gathering my things from around the room.

'Where are you going?' she says.

'Where do you think? I'm going home.'

'It's after midnight. The tubes won't be running.'

'Then I'll get the bus.'

'Don't be stupid,' she says coldly. 'Just stay.'

I turn to look at her. 'You know you're the first person I've told about this. The first person I've opened up to about –' my voice catches and I swallow '– about the worst thing that's ever happened to me. And instead of listening to me you basically called my brother . . .?'

She rolls her eyes. 'You're exaggerating.'

'Fucking barely.'

I almost shout this and Lindsay winces. Then she dips her head, runs her hands through her hair and sighs.

'OK fine, you're right,' she says. 'I probably could have reacted better.'

She crosses the room towards me but I back away. There's a screaming in my ears, like a pipe has burst somewhere and boiling liquid is flowing through my body. I sit down in the corner of the room and start to cry. Lindsay crouches down to look me in the eye.

'Come on, mate,' she says. 'You can't go out alone like this. Please stay.'

I let her lead me back to bed, let her lie behind me and hold me as I cry. But each time she kisses my shoulder or strokes my hair I break into fresh sobs, coughing them out for what feels like hours.

\*

It's an afternoon in June. Ferdia has just finished his Leaving Cert and is relaxing into his last summer at home before he goes to seminary. He collects me from school and says we're going for coffee, which means that he's going to have a coffee and I'm going to order an immense mess of cream and sugar that the local café calls a strawberry frappuccino. But he has an errand to run on the way, he says, a forty-six-year-old woman in the late stages of bowel cancer.

When we arrive at the house, not far from ours but smaller, a teenage boy answers the door. He has a shaved head, broad rolled-in shoulders and cratered skin. He's dressed in the navy uniform of the local secondary school and I'm so shy I can barely look at him. He offers Ferdia a cup of tea then gestures him up the stairs. I hover next to a loaded coat rack, dangling my schoolbag from one hand. Ferdia looks back from three steps up.

'Can my sister wait in the sitting room, Paul?'

'Yeah.'

The one syllable is compacted in his mouth. I don't want to be here (the house smells sick) but I cross into the beige and pink front room, perch on the corner edge of the drooping sofa and open a home decor magazine for want of something to do with my hands. I can hear the shifting gravel of my brother's voice in the room above me, a few fragments of small talk before it settles into the regular hum of prayer. I can't hear the woman's voice but I picture pale yellow lips, thin clasped hands, a too-heavy head turned towards Ferdia like a tired houseplant to a window. He's radiant next to her, shimmering with health, and downstairs I look at my own hands, pudgy and smooth, and know that they'll shrivel too one day. This has never occurred to me before and I'm deep in a thicket of contemplation when the double doors from the dining room open and Paul with the shaved head is there again. I drop the magazine back on the coffee table, heart hammering.

'D'ye want a cannacoke?' he asks, holding one up. I reach out to take it, both of us gripping the tin with our fingertips for a moment, the thought of our skin touching a shared horror.

'Thanks very much.'

'I'm just doing my homework in the kitchen.' He picks up the remote from the arm of the chair next to him and tosses it onto the sofa. 'Tell me if you want anything else.'

I take this to mean my brother will be a while and so, after putting my drink down very carefully on the coaster – chiding myself for feeling jealous that in this house full of death they have cans of Coke in the fridge – I open my school bag and take out my book. Though I'd chosen it from the 8–12 section of the library, soon after starting

I'd realised it wasn't like anything I'd ever read before. The main characters are heroin addicts living in a squat near Tallaght and, in the section I read on the dying woman's sofa, they want to sleep together but maybe because of the drugs it doesn't seem to work. The woman is dry as a bone, it says, so instead of having sex with her the man takes a bus into the city centre and, with another man, disappears into an automated public toilet on the corner of Grattan Bridge. I'm gripped by the story, which I suspect I'm only getting to read because I'm clever and religious, so the teachers don't feel they need to watch me too closely. I pause at the end of each chapter, tune back in to the sounds overhead and after three chapters I sense a change in the rhythm of my brother's voice. He's not praying anymore, he's saying his goodbyes. Suddenly I'm dying for the toilet so I scurry out and slip through the door under the stairs. The ceramics in here are done in a very tasteful peach but they haven't been cleaned in a long time and I move slowly, trying to hover above the seat. My brother's feet thunder down the steps over my head, I flush, and with four strides he's in the kitchen.

'That's her asleep,' he says as I pull up my knickers and tights, wash my hands under a tiny trickle from the greening tap and dry them on my skirt rather than touch the dank hand towel. Then I apply myself to the little brass lock, sidling it very gently out of its hold, whispering the handle down until it catches noiselessly. I don't want my brother and Paul to know that I've used the toilet, today or ever, I want them to find me back on my sofa corner, engrossed in my book. But still, as I step out of the bathroom, I glance towards the half-open kitchen door.

Paul is sitting at the table, his books spread out in front of him, shoulders rolled tight, hands tucked into his body. And my brother is standing behind the kitchen chair, wrapped around him like a coat of moss, chin to head, chest to back. Ferdia's eyes are closed, he's breathing slowly and deeply, and the moment is so intimate that I startle away from it and pad swiftly down the hall, desperate to reach the sitting room before they look up. I get away with it but in my hurry I miss some details of the picture, don't gather enough information to understand what's actually going on.

We're close to the turn of the millennium and on the news almost every night I hear disturbing things about priests and children, see my parents sigh and turn away, looking pained. No one ever talks to me about these things or explains, so I have no way of telling one thing from another, of distinguishing a moment of care and vulnerability from an instance of something else. Because when even what's healthy and joyful is hidden, you never learn to tell the good and bad apart.

After a few minutes Ferdia comes into the living room to get me and I hand Paul the empty Coke can.

'Thanks, it was really nice,' I say and for the first time he smiles. He has braces and the sight of them floods me with feeling again, with sadness, specifically, that his mother will never get to see his finished teeth. My brother reaches out to Paul, their hands grab tight.

'Mind yourself,' he says. 'And call if you need.'

We step out into the damp and overgrown garden. The picture fades. I've never seen Paul again.

\*

When I wake up the next morning Lindsay's hand is pressed flat against my back, as though she fell asleep still comforting me. I slide gently away and start getting dressed in my own clothes, the ones I was wearing on Wednesday when we went to the book talk. I pause before I pick up my bag and look at Lindsay, who shifts in the blankets and smiles through closed eyes, either not remembering last night or believing that we've come through it.

'I'm going to go,' I say.

She opens her eyes, watches me for a moment as I pull on my boots. 'I'd much rather you didn't.'

'Your mum's coming.'

'Oh shit, yeah.'

She rubs her face, boyish and handsome as she struggles her way out of sleep. Part of me wants to get back into bed with her, just for five minutes, to feel the warmth of her skin and the day's energy building in her limbs, to be part of her easy world, where the rules are clear and everyone's alive and happy and coming around for Sunday lunch. I've spent my whole adult life staring across these kinds of distances, cut off from people my age who can't understand what I've been through and who want to push it away, not realising that loss will come for them too, and sooner than they think. I know it's normal, I know it's not really their fault. But still I'm angry with Lindsay. I wanted her to do better.

'I'm going to go,' I say again and, after a second's hesitation, she nods and closes her eyes.

# Chapter Eleven

I CAN NEVER REMEMBER how much my father told me on the phone that morning when I was sixteen. I don't know how I learned all this, or how much of it is true. But thirteen years ago, more or less to the day, Ferdia arranged a kickabout between the Irish College football team and some Swiss Guards. Every time I imagine it, I picture the guards playing in their red, yellow and blue pantaloons and have to correct the image so that they're dressed in normal sports gear, shorts over black tights.

The night is cool and Ferdia, in goal, is doing squat jumps to try and keep warm, banging a hand off the crossbar with each one. But at least his defenders provide him with plenty to do. They're getting flattened.

'It's no wonder God called you to the priesthood,' he shouts at Brian Fallon, the worst of the bunch, after his man runs a loop around him and blasts a shot just wide of the post.

By a couple of minutes before half time, the seminarians are three–nil down and no one wants to see a fourth before the break. They start to scramble, throwing in big clattering tackles, hurling their big Irish heads into the way of the ball. And still it's not enough: a guard curls a low hard ball from the wing, so fast that Ferdia gets caught off his line and darts back, diving for the bottom right corner. At the same moment, Brian lunges boot first from the other direction and his studs connect clean and hard with the side of my brother's head. Brian screams. Ferdia sort of grunts and at first no one else realises what's happened. The goal has gone in and the other side are cheering and high-fiving one another. Brian scrambles to Ferdia's side and lays a hand on his chest. Ferdia smiles hazily.

'Don't worry,' he says and Brian exhales.

'I thought I'd killed you.'

He laughs. He waits for Ferdia to laugh too, but instead my brother's eyes are sliding out of focus. There's a trail of blood on his jaw and neck.

Brian doesn't call my parents until they get to the hospital and the doctors have confirmed a significant brain injury. It's nine o'clock in Ireland, too late for them to fly, so they pass a sickening night at home, booking flights, packing their bags, praying and trying to get hold of me.

When we finally spoke, I slid to the floor of Síofra's big spare room, my left hand gripping the phone, my right drawing large flat circles on the plush carpet. I asked my father a litany of pointless questions, desperate to keep him on the line.

'Which hospital is he in?'

'Is someone with him?'

'Did they call an ambulance or did someone drive him?'

'Do the doctors speak English?'

'I'm sorry, Jacinta,' he says eventually. 'But we need to get a taxi to the hospital now. Your auntie Breda will be waiting for you at home. And we'll keep you updated.'

I start to cry then, terrified lonely tears, like a child lost in a crowd. 'OK. Tell Ferdia I say hello and I'll see him soon.'

A long, buzzing pause on the other end of the line. 'OK, I will.'

'And . . . tell him I love him, OK? Please.'

I gather my things quickly after that, hoping to leave without seeing anyone. But Síofra is already up and searching through the fridge.

'And where were you for all of last night?' she asks, laughing.

'I have to go,' I say.

'Erm, OK.'

'Sorry. My mam and dad, they're just . . . they found out about the party and they're really annoyed.'

'Oh shit, OK.' She gives me a hug. 'Godspeed.'

I hang on to my friend tightly, fighting tears, then turn and leave the house. Between the DART and the train and the long cold waits for each, the journey home takes me more than two hours. I pray the whole way, desperate begging prayers, believing I can save him, counting Hail Marys off on my fingers.

But after that brief moment of reassuring Brian on the football pitch, Ferdia never regains consciousness. My parents are shown into ICU as soon as they arrive and are shocked by the sight of him, intubated, a dark crusted suture like an ivy tendril poking out from the bandages around his head. They had operated. In an older person they probably wouldn't have bothered, they said, but he was so young. After an hour at his bedside, my mother and father are summoned away to speak to the consultant. Someone has to translate, of course, and so Brian is called on again. He doesn't capture the spirit of the man's fast-flowing Italian but he stumbles through the key message: there's no hope of recovery of any kind and – his voice rises, bulges and breaks – the firm opinion of the doctors is that life support should be switched off.

My father, who's been standing, slumps heavily against a wall. The surgeon goes to him and rests a dark-haired hand on his back.

'I am sorry,' he says in careful English. 'I pray for you all.'

For years, I've been imagining this scene again and again, trying to fill in as much detail as I can, to convince myself it's true. But at this point, one corner of the image goes dark, as though my vision is closing in. It clouds out any glimpse of my mother at the moment she hears that her only son, her blessed boy, her little saint ...

He hangs on for a few hours more, long enough for a cardinal to come and deliver the final sacrament. Back in Maynooth, Breda and I stare at *Friends* repeats all afternoon and she plies me with cup after cup of sugary tea until eventually I fall asleep on the sofa, curled awkwardly under a blanket. I wake up to her hand pressing softly on my ankle.

'He's gone, a ghrá,' she says, though she's never used any kind of endearment to me before. 'Ferdia's dead.'

# Part Two

# Chapter Twelve

On a sunny May morning in 1981, a few days before my brother's first birthday, a spoiled Trappist monk got on a flight from Dublin to London. He was called Larry Downey, an Australian of Irish descent who had been kicked out of his monastery, it was said later, for punching his superior in the nose. The plane he boarded was called the Saint Ita, after the woman known as the foster mother of the Irish saints, who was christened Deirdre but renamed later – from íota, meaning thirst – in recognition of her unquenchable longing for holiness.

Larry was thirsty too. He ordered a brandy when the drinks trolley came around, studied some notes from his briefcase, smoked a cigar. To the mother and daughter next to him, he looked like a prosperous businessman and they found him very polite. But that impression wavered on the approach to Heathrow when Larry disappeared to the toilets, doused himself in petrol and rushed the cockpit, demanding first to be taken to Tehran to deliver some documents to the new Ayatollah and then, when the pilot explained that they hadn't enough fuel to get there, changing tack and insisting that, by way of ransom, the Vatican should reveal the third secret of Fatima.

Because time operates strangely in the stories of the saints. When I was little and Ferdia and I played Marian apparitions, the miracle at Fatima seemed like ancient history. Jacinta and Francisco, with their big eyes and tragic deaths, were children from another world. They had been made Venerable by then and already existed to us as religious icons, outside time and space. But it had only been eighty years. With slightly better luck, they might still have still been alive, like their cousin Lucia, the third of the little shepherds. She had watched her cousins die painful and protracted deaths, two tiny bodies among the five hundred million lost to the 1918 pandemic. But she survived, became the one living witness to the apparition. And though many doubted and smeared her, though religious and secular authorities tried to undermine her, she stuck to her story, recalling word-for-word the three secrets she'd been told by a lady more brilliant than the sun: the visions of her cousins' deaths, of blackened bodies floating in oceans of fire, of demons and shrieking souls, of angels with burning swords and ruined cities and a bishop dressed in white gunned down, and of the spilled blood being gathered up and sprinkled on the souls of the dead.

When Pope John Paul II was shot on Saint Peter's Square, he saw it as the fulfilment of Lucia's vision and believed that he had only survived through the intercession of Our Lady of Fatima. He was so convinced and so thankful that he kept one of the bloody bullets they cut from his body, brought it to Portugal and placed it in her crown.

'My last words are for the children,' he said in 2000, when he beatified Jacinta and Francisco. I was watching it on TV with my mother, who poked me in the ribs. 'Our Lady needs you all to console Jesus who is sad because of the bad things done to Him; He needs your prayers and your sacrifices for sinners.'

The camera panned to a group of children in the crowd, all dressed up as little shepherds, smiling and waving.

'Did you hear that?' my mother said but I didn't reply right away. The whole ceremony seemed overblown to me, formal and pompous, a million miles from the simple story our grandmother had told.

'Why can't they make people saints when they're still alive?' I asked, feeling sorry for Lucia, who looked so old and confused in her thick glasses. Why was she being left out, I wanted to know. My mother replied, as though it should be obvious even to a child, that it was because saints had to be with God in heaven. Which Lucia was too, before long. She died in February 2005. Though she'd been born five years before the sinking of the *Titanic*, Ferdia only outlived her by a month.

\*

When I arrive into Dublin airport – on an Aer Lingus plane named the *Saint Dymphna*, for a young virgin martyr who rejected her own father's sexual advances and was beheaded for it – the duty-free stands are ready for the Patrick's Day influx, piled high with green top hats and rosettes, tiny tricolours, fluffy black-and-white slippers. But it's quiet. Things haven't kicked off yet. A group of English men in off-the-shoulder peach dresses are thumbing their phones as they wait for their bags to arrive and, next to them, a squad of returning peacekeepers look stubbled and shadowy under blue berets.

One of them, a lean man of at least fifty, leans over to the groom-to-be (in full wedding dress and veil) and congratulates him.

'Cheers, mate, I appreciate that,' the younger man says, deepening his voice to compensate for his clothes. 'And, um, thank you for your service.'

The other soldiers turn away politely and so do I, laughing to myself as I pass though the arrivals gates, taking in the good-looking young military families, wives glowing with bronzer and children clutching signs and balloons. A bored RTÉ crew hovers nearby, dispatched to gather some schmaltz for that evening's news.

'Jacinta!'

My mother is craning over the barrier. She looks small, fragile against the crowd, but there's a smile as bright as new blood spread wide across her face. The laugh dies on my lips and I lift my hand in an awkward wave. I deliberately didn't tell her what flight I was on. I planned to take the bus.

I veer right, away from the camera crew, and on the other side of the barrier, my mother follows. I reach out one arm for our usual, perfunctory hug but instead she dives at me, clinging so tightly to my ribcage that I'm caught off balance, have to shift my weight so as not to collapse on top of her. Her body feels spindly next to mine, her hair insubstantial against my face, like worn electrical filament.

'It's good to have you home,' she murmurs.

I pull away, rearrange my bags 'Where's Dad?'

'In the car, driving laps.' She rolls her eyes. 'I only wish he was as passionate about me as he is about dodging parking fees.'

We both laugh, a bit too loudly, and I can see a small red line across the bottom of her incisors. She's been biting her lip.

'Will we head out to him then?'

Her face slackens a little but she catches it, paints the smile back on. 'Well, I just thought we might . . .?'

I don't know what she's talking about and shake my head. 'Might what?' The first of the peacekeepers has just appeared and a woman's shriek cuts over the noise of the crowd.

'The chapel.'

My stomach drops. How have I forgotten? She's always insisted that anyone passing through the airport, whether coming or going, should go and light a candle in the church.

'Oh yeah,' I say. 'Yeah, of course.'

She leads me across the drop-off zone and through the entrance to the car park, explaining loudly that when she first came through the airport, for her honeymoon, the church was in a lovely spot, out on its own in green space. 'And now it's crammed in back here,' I say, finishing the story for her. She smiles.

'I've told you this before?'

I smile back. We've come through the far door of the car park and the squat church materialises on the other side of a zebra crossing. It's a dull day but the gold letters on the steeple gleam in what light there is. *God is Love.* We pass into the courtyard, where the roar of traffic seems muted, and I feel suddenly disoriented, like I've lost my place in time. I'm grateful to continue into the dim of the chapel, to drop my bags and sit down in a pew. My mother genuflects then kneels beside me. We don't speak. I count my breaths a while, longer out than in, letting the quiet bear down on me like a weight. I close my eyes and, quite suddenly, my mind stills for the first time in weeks. There's a trace of incense in the air and, breathing it in, I sink into a calm that's almost sleep. Time passes, maybe three minutes, maybe ten.

Eventually I hear a slight humming behind me and turn to see my mother already at the back of the church, having an almost noiseless conversation with an elderly Capuchin. As I stand up they allow their voices to lift, turning to smile as I approach. The monk's hand, when he reaches it out, is papery in mine.

'You're very welcome to Our Lady Queen of Heaven,' he says. 'It's always wonderful to see young people here.'

I smile, happy to indulge the Church's expansive definition of youth.

'It's beautiful,' I say, looking around. And I mean it. Though it's built in the blocky mid-century style, there's something elegant about the place. Shards of colour filter through the stained glass and spotlights illuminate the wooden altar. The friar nods and looks around himself, appreciatively.

'It was opened in 1964, by Archbishop John Charles McQuaid, of all people.' He raises his scant eyebrows at us. 'But the project was instigated and funded by the airport workers themselves. All of this paid for out of deductions from their wages.'

My mother sighs. 'Isn't that just amazing?'

The priest nods and starts clearing empty tea light casings from the votive stand. His habit hangs baggy from his shoulders and there's a lot of slack in the rope around his waist. Under his brown sandals he's wearing a pair of thick black hiking socks with neon stripes around the toes.

'They've certainly given us a great gift. And our hope, or mine at least, is to bring it back into wider use as a place of reflection, for those of all faiths and none.'

'What would Archbishop McQuaid think of that?' I interject, almost without thinking. My mother spins around.

'Jacinta!'

But the priest is unfazed. He gestures to her not to worry with a gentle dip of his hand, then smiles at me with a hint of mischief.

'McQuaid ran a church for his times,' he says. 'We've got to build one for ours.'

I raise my eyebrows, ready to respond, to get into it with him. But my mother hikes her handbag on her shoulder and shuffles her feet.

'We'll leave you to it, Father,' she says brightly and he nods. Though his cupped hands are full of burned-out candles he raises them towards us in approximate benediction.

'It's been a pleasure speaking to you, ladies. God bless.'

\*

'So the journey was all right?'

My father shunts in his seat, the way he always does when he needs to merge onto the motorway. I'm in the front – my mother insisted – and I can see his face tighten and then relax as he settles into the slow lane. It's the third time he's asked and twice I've told him that yes, it was fine.

'I was a little pushed for time getting to Gatwick,' I say. 'But otherwise it was fine.'

'Typical you,' says my mother.

'Is it?' I say, turning around.

'You're always late.'

'No, I'm not.'

There's silence in the car. I turn back around and take a breath. She is wrong, I'm hardly ever late, but it's not like it matters.

'And why did you tell us anyway?' she goes on. 'If you made it in the end.'

'I don't know, because Dad asked?'

She sighs loudly. The news comes on the radio and my father turns it up to listen. I lean back against the headrest and close my eyes, already exhausted by the effort of talking to my parents, of parsing every sentence for possible points of tension. As the presenter switches register for the sports news, my mother pokes me hard from behind.

'I need to get a few bits from Tesco. Is there anything you want?'

'I don't think so, thanks.'

'Do you want to come in with me? Just in case?'

'I'm shattered, Mammy. I was up at five,' I say, knowing that if I go in she'll take it as an excuse to have a look in the clothes section, to pick up glass candles and hold them out for me to smell, to linger in front of the tubs of hummus and olives and ask if there's any 'stuff like that' that I want. But I don't want anything other than to sleep, ideally alone in a plain, cheap hotel room on the outskirts of town. That's what I had in mind when I first agreed to come to Ireland, before I checked the room prices and realised there was nothing I could afford.

My father pulls up right outside the superstore and my mother swings her legs out. Halfway between the car and the automatic doors she breaks into a trot and I feel a spasm of worry that she'll trip and fall. My father watches her go too, not restarting the car until she's safely inside. It barely hums as it takes off.

'Have you gone automatic?' I ask.

'I have. The hybrids are all automatic.'

He drives a few hundred metres along the perimeter of the car park.

'There are plenty of spaces,' I say.

'She'll only be a minute.'

We pass four boys kicking a football against some wooden hoarding, violently, again and again. My father glances at them. It must be a relief, I say, not to have to worry about why they're not at school. He grunts. Nearly two years retired now, I'm surprised at how much my father has changed. His whole body seems to be collapsing in on itself; his shoulders slumped and his eyes hooded.

'You still haven't learned yourself, I assume?'

Gays can't drive, I think, but I tell him that it's on my to-do list. We're back at the front door now and with no sign of my mother, start a second lap.

'Mammy seems in good form,' I say. 'Full of beans.'

I watch for his reaction, wondering if he thinks, like I do, that she's a bit off kilter, too tightly wound. He glances over his shoulder to check again if she's come out. The car lists slightly and he corrects it with a jerk.

'We're well enough. Though I don't know where she's gotten herself to.' He raises his voice marginally. '"I only need one or two bits."'

He hasn't committed fully to the impression but still I laugh, trying to lift the atmosphere.

'I always remember coming here one day when I was little and it was still Quinnsworth. I was sitting in the front of the trolley and Mammy let me eat a whole container of jam doughnuts while she wheeled me around. Honestly, I thought I'd won the lotto.'

My father says nothing, drums his fingers on the wheel. A security guard has come to talk to the boys with the football and the smallest of them shouts something at him before they run away laughing.

'Are you looking forward to the weekend?' I ask.

'I am. And you?'

'It'll be nice to see some of the family,' I lie. 'It's been a long time.'

'You know that's not bad,' he says, looking towards the petrol station. 'One twenty-seven. Is there any sign of your mother?'

I crane my neck and squint at the front entrance. 'I don't think so.'

He doubles back at the roundabout. 'I'll chance it so.'

When he gets out of the car I close my eyes again, breathing in the smell of fuel. It's all too familiar, being dragged along on errands, cranky and bored, my father barely speaking. It's as though this endless circling of the car park, this dead time spent together, is still part of our routine. Then he knocks on the window and half mouths, half shouts through the glass.

'Do you want a paper or anything?'

I shake my head. He goes to pay. When he gets back into the car he says that we'll do one more lap.

'But if she's still not out after that, you might have to go in and extract her.'

I fold my lips over my teeth, wanting to tell him to park the car like a normal person and go find my mother himself. But then, as we arrive back at the entrance she appears through the sliding doors, braced against a shallow trolley that's piled high with food, none of it in bags. On the top, I can see a large container of pasta salad, balanced precariously on a twelve-pack of Tayto. My father sighs.

'Will you get out and help her put all that in the boot?'

I do, tensing against the wind, feeling tired and shivery. As soon the boot opens I start grabbing armfuls of stuff from the trolley and dumping them in. Vegetables, oven pizzas, sausages and eggs, cereal, fruit cake, bacardi and gin. My mother helps at first but then she stops, stands waiting for me to look up, a bag of potato smilies in her hand.

'Do you remember how much you used to love these?'

I pause to stare at her. They'd been one of the first things I learned to cook by myself and on evenings when she didn't feel able to make dinner, I'd eaten stacks of them with white bread and ketchup. I turn away, scoop up a tin of Roses, a packet of rashers, some new tea towels and a reed diffuser, dropping them on top of the rest before slamming the boot. My mother has already reclaimed her usual place in the front seat so I drop into the back and close my eyes. The drive home is only a few minutes but by the time we arrive I'm asleep.

# Chapter Thirteen

THERE'S A VASE OF lilies on the chest of drawers in what was once my bedroom and a wax burner on the windowsill. But the room is too bare for so much perfume; the effect is overpowering, like a funeral home or the inside of a showroom car. I perch on the edge of the single bed and look around, wishing my mother had put me in the spare room instead.

I don't remember ever clearing this place out, don't know what happened to all my tiny black tops, my books, my cheap calcified mascaras and carrier bags of CDs. I don't know when they painted over the eggshell blue of the walls and repaired all the damage I'd done by tacking up posters and prints. I only know that I was here for a long time and then I wasn't, that sometime in the depths of the financial crisis – when I was back from university and unemployed and the country was sinking so fast you could almost feel it sliding about under your feet – a friend texted to say there was a spare room going in a house her father owned in Sydenham, cheap for London, and would I like to try it for a bit. I left the following week on the overnight coach with one suitcase and one rucksack. My father insisted on driving me to Busáras though I told him it would be quicker to take the train.

In the car, I tried to reassure him that it wouldn't be for long. 'I only have enough stuff to stay a few months anyway,' I said, knowing he didn't want me to go. He hated London more than anywhere else in the world, would exhale in loud disgust every time its skyline appeared onscreen in a film. Filthy, he said. Polluted. Cold and inhuman.

The crossing to Wales was rough and by the time we landed in Holyhead – and were hauled off the bus to have our bags and passports checked – the rain was blowing sideways in sheets, soaking us through. I was twenty-two and for years, I'd been using Ferdia's death to justify the flatness at the heart of my life. I had done well in my Leaving Cert, getting far more points than I needed for Sociology and Portuguese at UCC. But once I was there, I struggled to get to lectures, spent too much time moping around the bars, picking up closeted gay girls for cramped encounters in toilet cubicles and dark alleyways (because neither of us wanted our roommates to know) and reading long, bleak Russian novels without even trying to remember the characters' names. I went home less and less frequently, spent weekends sleeping late in musty sheets, eating exclusively from the freezer. I drank most days, mostly with other people, and lived half the year without daylight.

But eventually my body started to rebel, fizzing and cramping, rejecting the slow, rolling, underground life I had resigned myself to after Ferdia's accident. When I lay in bed my muscles told me to get out and walk. When I walked they said, why not run? And when I ran the same tired routes around Cork or Maynooth, the electricity pulsing through my shoulders seemed to remind me how vast the world was and how little of it I had bothered to see.

When we arrived in London early the next morning, the city was blue-skied and wet with rain and even Victoria coach station, to me, looked radiant. Because I had made it out. Out of the bus, which had roared and rattled through the storm so that no one could sleep but the man next to me, who snored. Out of a country where the past, however terrible, was more comfortable than the future. Out of a house so saturated with a deep morgueish chill that many mornings I'd had to remind myself that in our family only one of us was dead. The streets thickened with traffic as I circled the station – bleary with exhaustion, not able to find my way to the Underground – but somehow the air tasted clean as the seaside and I was sure that in the bright watery light I could feel the glow of my brother's approval. I had done it. I was out.

\*

I go downstairs and into the sitting room, where china figurines teeter on their shelves and a bared heart of Christ throbs above the TV. I remember how sick I used to feel when I was a teenager and my mother suggested inviting my friends over for a birthday party or sleepover.

'You go to their houses so often,' she'd say. 'It's polite to invite people back.' And I didn't know how to tell her that my friends' houses were fitted with chrome and marble and expansive corner sofas, that there were original paintings by contemporary Irish artists on the walls, that they smelled of sea air and fifty-euro candles. In ours, there was a holy water font by the door and you had to angle your body slightly as you walked down the hall to avoid clipping the knees of a giant Crucifix. It smelled of boiled vegetables soaked into fraying upholstery, a single sniff of which would have shattered every illusion I'd tried to create about myself.

Hardly anything has changed since then. The only addition is a leather recliner where my father is stretched out watching cricket. It's far too big for the room and no matter where I look I can't quite escape the sight of his feet.

My mother appears in the door behind me. 'I can offer you soup and bread, if you'd like? Or rashers and eggs? Or one of the pizzas.'

I say that soup sounds lovely.

'And will you have a cup of tea?'

'Or a drink?' says my father, the first words he's spoken since I came in.

I'm standing in the middle of the room, half turned to each of my parents. Above the sofa are the portraits of Ferdia and I taken on our first communion days, each staring at the camera with the same dark ghostly eyes.

'Why not?' I say brightly. 'It's Patrick's weekend.'

My father stands up carefully, pausing once he's upright to check that his whole self has come with him. He bends over the lower cupboards of the sideboard, where he keeps one bottle of everything – whiskey, brandy, vodka, rum, gin – to cover all possible guests and eventualities. The whiskey he pours me is generous, three gulps for a nervous person.

'Sláinte,' he says, clinking the two glasses himself and then holding mine out for me to take. My mother has lit the artificial fire and turned on all the lamps. The room is warming up. When I sit down, the sofa sags under me. I feel a tweak in my right hip and have to shift around a little to ease it.

My father, back in his chair, stares at the TV.

'I've never been able to figure it out,' I say, gesturing at the cricket onscreen.

'It's actually very interesting,' he says. 'Very absorbing. Though this is just Twenty20 stuff, not as good as a full test.'

'Sure,' I say, as though I know what he's talking about, and we both look back at it. India is playing Bangladesh but I can't tell who's winning and turn, again, to look at my father. His mouth has opened slightly, his tongue sitting wet and pink on his bottom lip.

'Did you get to Lough Derg last year?'

'I did, thanks be to God.' He keeps his eyes fixed on the game. 'I did all right.'

'And was it the same as always?' I ask awkwardly. 'Or has it changed over the years?'

He sighs and shifts to look at me. 'It hasn't changed a bit,' he says. 'Time stands still on the lake. That's one reason I go, really. To step outside the whirlpool of modernity.'

The structure of his sentences is strange, choppy.

'Why else do you go?'

He shrugs. 'Habit.'

'Ah now, I won't let you off that easy.' My voice is loud, artificially upbeat, as though he's an old man on the train who needs the announcements repeated. I'm irritated with him for seeming so much frailer than I expected, for forcing me to think about how he'll be in five or ten or fifteen years, about what he'll need from me then.

He shrugs again. 'Well, in the early days it wasn't a particularly unusual thing to do. I first went in 1986 and back then there would be hundreds of people every week of the season. All ages and sexes and walks of life. And I just took it into my head one day that I'd like to go and see what it was all about.'

'And what was it like that first time?'

'It was tough going.' He looks upward and shakes his head, the bulk of his attention finally diverted from the TV. 'As a young fella you're not used to ever being deprived of anything. You barely know what physical discomfort feels like. So it was a shock to the system, I'll tell you that. But the camaraderie was something else back then. I remember in the middle of the night turning to a woman next to me – she must be long dead now – and saying, I think I'm in trouble here. I might not be able to manage.'

'What did she tell you?' I ask and he laughs, for the first time since I've arrived

'She told me to put my faith in the Rosary, to devote my pain and tiredness to the Blessed Lady.'

I laugh too. 'Did it work?'

'Well no, not at the time. But I still think of her saying it, often, and not just when I'm on the retreat. Because as you get older you start to understand that life is just the same. Bad sleep and back pain and sore feet. Grief. Disappointment. You're exhausted all the time.'

I watch as he reaches down to scratch his ankle. He's wearing blue and yellow striped socks, the pink of his skin visible through the soles.

'It's a lot quieter now, of course, you don't meet so many people. But still, I get a lot from it.' He falls silent a minute, hums slightly to himself, then reaches for the whiskey bottle on the roll-top bureau next to his chair. After topping up his own glass he proffers the bottle but I shake my head. He turns to the TV again and, thinking the conversation is over, I pull my phone out. But then my father speaks again.

'You know, we're very glad that you're here, Jacinta.' His voice is brusque, almost irritable, as though he's correcting something I've said.

'OK. Thanks.'

'I'm a man who likes to do things in the proper way. I took my work very seriously, I know that. Maybe too seriously.'

He pauses, as though to let me speak.

'We can all be guilty of that,' I say eventually and he nods.

'Yes, many of us can. But what you have to remember is that it's all superficial in the end. You can't bring any of it with you. So for me, the time at Lough Derg every year is an opportunity to sweep away all the detritus of life, you know? The doors of perception are cleansed.' He looks into his drink. 'The doors of perception are cleansed. Someone said that.'

'Blake,' I say quickly.

'I'm sorry?'

'It was William Blake who said it.'

He flushes. 'Of course. Yes, of course. Blake.'

\*

My mother brings me my soup on a tray with two pieces of buttered soda bread. It goes well with the whiskey and I watch the cricket while I eat, strangely soothed now by its mysterious patterns. Afterwards, I carry the tray back into the kitchen, where she's slicing apples for a tart, her body tensed over the counter top. I ask if I can help with anything but she says no, she's fine. Could I make a pot of tea at least? Her shoulders soften and she looks over at me.

'I would love a cup of tea,' she says, as though I've offered to pay off the mortgage on the house. I fill the pot so there's enough for us both, sit down at the table and ask about the family.

'Arrah, they're all all right,' she says, 'no one dead, thanks be to God, and no one engaged.'

She tells me that my cousin Gráinne is managing well with her new baby, my aunt Kathleen is getting a new kitchen, my uncle John is heading off to Turkey in a few days to watch Ireland play. More than a decade after my grandmother died, my grandfather is still going but not doing too well. It feels like they might be reaching the limits of what can be done at home but for now he seems happy enough so there's no need to rush the decision. Cousin Liam has a big new job and, though my mother wouldn't dream of being so crass as to pass it on, Kathleen has told everyone what the salary is and it's no wonder they can afford the new kitchen.

She pauses for breath, having spoken all this too rapidly for me to even consider asking a question. The apples have been swept into a bowl and now she's rolling out the pastry, flinging her whole body forward with the movement of the pin.

'Damian is working away on the farm, as always, and going to his meetings. And Maura's still feeding and clothing the lot of them, as far as I can tell, even though the arthritis is giving her real trouble. She does everything for Daddy. Absolutely everything.'

There's a long silence. My mother lowers the rolled base of the tart into a shallow tin.

'They all ask after you,' she says.

'Do they?'

She turns to look at me, takes a drink of tea. The pastry hangs over the tin's edges, like excess skin. 'They do.'

'And what do you tell them?'

'I tell them about your job and all your friends and the plays and things you go to.'

'Do you mean my girlfriends?'

I'm teasing but she flushes and turns back around.

'They were all very impressed when you did the half marathon,' she goes on and I feel a clenching in my chest. The half marathon was five years ago and I'm forced to imagine my mother nurturing her small scraps of information about my life, attempting to conceal how rarely we speak. I try to think of something new to tell her, a confidence to share. But now that her own racing chatter has stopped, I can think of nothing to say.

'Will you open the oven for me?' she says eventually, holding the tart in front of her on a draped tea towel. I jump up, glad to have something to do. The blast of preheated air makes my eyes water and fogs up her glasses. She slides the tin on to the middle shelf and I remember how astonished I used to be that something that went in so pale and chalky could come back out looking so beautiful, the sugar thick and caramelised, the hot apple bubbling around the edges.

'Is this for tomorrow?'

My mother is wiping her glasses on her apron, the same navy-striped and flour-encrusted one she's always worn. She blinks at me, her eyes small and watery.

'No,' she says. 'I made it for you.'

\*

After dinner – lamb chops served, for my benefit, with a pea and mint pilaf rather than potatoes – my father heads straight back to his recliner. I clear the plates and stack them on the counter but as I reach for the dishwasher door my mother bats my hand away.

'I'll do that,' she says. 'You go in to your father and I'll bring your sweet.'

She means the apple tart, served steaming with a brilliant brick of vanilla ice cream and one of the good spoons. I curl my feet under me on the sofa as I eat.

'I haven't had a dessert like this in a long time,' I say. 'Thanks, Mammy.'

She reaches out and squeezes the joint of my big toe. 'Well, it's not often I get the chance to spoil you.'

I smile but say nothing, knowing that it's dangerous to trust these shows of tenderness which, like spring showers, can lift as suddenly as they fall. Though she's having to lean half the length of the couch to reach it, my mother keeps her grip on my foot. I glance at my father to see if he's noticed, but he's transfixed by the nine o'clock news.

'I'm really sorry,' I say the moment I swallow my last bite of tart. 'But I think I'm going to have to go to bed.'

They look at me, surprised. 'I was going to offer you another drink,' says my father. I shrug apologetically. 'But young ones today can't stick the pace, I suppose.'

'I was just up so early for the flight,' I say. 'I promise I'll be in better form tomorrow.'

'You're all right,' says my mother, finally withdrawing her hand. 'He's only teasing you.'

I get up then linger awkwardly for a moment, wondering – though it's not something we've done in a long time – if I should kiss them goodnight.

'Right so,' I say, as the opening bars of the *Late Late* theme tune sound. 'See you in the morning.'

In the kitchen I deposit my bowl in the dishwasher and fill myself a glass of water, opening and closing the cupboard doors gently, running the tap at a trickle, padding down the hall in my socks and, without needing to think about it, stepping over the creaky fifth step on the stairs. I was a noisy child, everyone always said so, a storm of slamming doors and jangling crockery and laughing too loudly at whatever was on TV. But after Ferdia died I learned to move quietly. I picture the house, in those days, bisected like the stage set for a ballet, the three of us dancing silently inside.

On the landing, I pause and look at the closed door to my brother's room, cream like the rest but with small scab marks from the time he put up his Liverpool posters with Sellotape. I turn into my own room, put down my water and perch on the edge of the bed with my phone. Clem is out for an expensive meal tonight with his co-workers, posting ironic-not-ironic photos of all his food. Aisling, who I kissed in the garden all those years ago, is at home with her new kitten. Lindsay hasn't posted anything anywhere since I last spoke to her, nearly a week ago now. But I scroll through her feed anyway, back as far as her holiday to Madeira four years ago, with her ex-girlfriend. Her shoulders are bare, her teeth white against her tan. I feel a slash of desire and drop the phone quickly. I don't need that, not here.

As I brush my teeth I can hear the sound of the TV from downstairs. I step out on to the landing and carefully open the door to Ferdia's room. It looks just like it did in the years he was away at seminary: the bed made, a black jacket dangling from the back of the chair, a 'Radical for Christ' mug on the bedside locker. Everything is spotless and smells of all-purpose cleaning spray. I walk to his desk and see a Post-it stuck to the top, covered in his small careful print. The heading – *Books to Read:* – is what gets me, the intention in the two sharp dots of the colon.

'It's just as well we never cleared it out.'

I jump and a small burst of foam spurts down my chin. My mother is at the door. I gesture her out of the way, go into the bathroom and spit.

'What was that?' I ask, wiping my mouth on the hand towel.

'I've always been able to tell that people thought it was strange to leave his room like this. My sisters in particular.' She rolls her eyes at me. 'But I have the last laugh now. Because they'll need it all for the cause. His notebooks and letters. His computer.'

I touch my fingertips to the back of my head, the spot I once cracked on the corner of the windowsill. I understand now why sixteen-year-old Ferdia panicked at the sight of me wrapped in his duvet and I don't envy whoever's tasked with exploring the search histories of the saints.

'Already people are getting in touch asking for his clothes,' my mother goes on. She's picked up the sleeve of the black jacket and is running the fabric through her fingers. 'But Father Richter says it's best to hold off giving too many things away, that there's a process to be followed. He's spoken to a Carmelite prioress in New York who says that if we get some clothes and sheets and things shipped over then her sisters can make them into holy cards. They'll be able to make thousands with all that we have here. Tens of thousands.'

I glance around the room, imagining everything cut into tiny shreds and sent around the world, slid into prayer books and pinned to hospital headboards, passed from hand to hand, sold on eBay. My brother's old T-shirts and socks. The stuff of miracles.

'Do you not find it all a bit strange?' I ask my mother, tentative, and am surprised when she nods thoughtfully, as though she knows exactly what I mean.

'I worry about the house burning down before they've moved it all to a safe place.'

I reach out for the door jamb with my right hand, the reality of what's happening rushing through my body as a cold, rational ache. It's all so material here, in this house, among these things. My mother is looking around her, distracted, and though I don't want to, I remember the months after Ferdia died when I'd come home from school and find her in this room, searching the cupboards, crying on the floor, lying in his bed so deeply asleep that I would sometimes hold my hand in front of her mouth, searching for the warm mist of breath.

'It sounds like a lot of pressure,' I say.

'It's a privilege,' my mother replies. She steps forward and tugs at the duvet, smoothing out an imaginary crease, before looking up at me. The skin around her eyes has folded and sagged since I saw her last but her gaze is sharp. She ushers me out of the room and shuts the door gingerly behind her.

'Goodnight, Jacinta.'

She reaches up to rest her hand against my face. Her palm is soft. She smells of rosewater. I lean down to kiss her cheek.

'Goodnight,' I say. 'Sleep well.'

\*

That night I dream of her. We're at a wedding reception, held on a helicopter pad on the roof of a skyscraper. It's hot. Sweltering. My friends are there: Clem dancing provocatively, Cat wearing the face off someone, Ash doing shots. At the bar, Hannah and Lindsay are whispering to each other and they keep glancing at me, their faces full of malice. I pretend not to know any of them, afraid they'll speak to my mother and give something away. I want to go home, but no, my mother says she wants to dance too. And she does. Ancient dream lady though she is, her hair very white, she stands up and dances wildly, the loose flesh of her arms beating the warm air, her eyes wide and ecstatic as she moves. I'm angry with her. I'm embarrassed by her. I realise too late that she's danced herself close to the edge and, in the moment that I do, she trips backwards and is gone. There's no fanfare, everyone else dances on. Only I've seen what's happened and I run to the edge on heavy balloon feet and lie flat on my stomach to look down the dozens of floors. But she's so far away. All I can see is the white patch of her hair like a lost handkerchief on the pavement.

# Chapter Fourteen

THE WHEEZE OF THE hot tap in my parents' bathroom is so familiar that I can listen to it without waking. My bed is warm. It's early. There are low voices and feet shuffling on carpet. The six pips drift up from the kitchen radio and I sink back into sleep, not waking for real until I hear the slam of the front door and my mother's heels on the driveway. I remember her 8 a.m. blowdry. I know the date, and where I am, and why.

When I arrive downstairs, there's choral music on the radio. My father is standing by the kettle in a pair of plaid pyjama pants and a navy sweatshirt, reading something on his phone. I try to remember if he ever walked around like this when I was younger, feeling embarrassed by the sight of him. It's too intimate. We've seen so little of each other in the last few years.

I say hi and he looks up quickly and smiles.

'Oh, good morning. I wasn't expecting you down so early.'

I shrug, stay standing in the doorway. It's half past eight. My father puts his phone in his pocket.

'I'm making a pot of tea,' he says.

'Any chance of a coffee?'

He frowns and turns to open the cupboard above the hob, where the loose ends are kept, lifts out a half packet of pasta and an unopened jar of mint sauce.

'Will this do you?' He holds up a tin of Nescafé. 'It's been there a while . . .'

I nod, wondering why I didn't think of coffee yesterday when my mother asked if there was anything I wanted from the shops. I know neither of my parents ever drink it at home.

'Sure it's mostly preservatives anyway,' I say and he dumps a heaped spoon of it into a cup, splashes in the water and gives it a long noisy stir. 'Thanks.'

'And you know where the cereals and everything are. So have whatever you like.'

He stands looking at me, nodding, as though we're wrapping up a long conversation. And then, with his tea, he walks out of the kitchen and back upstairs.

I breathe in deeply, then out slowly. My coffee smells like stale battery acid but I keep it wrapped in both my hands as I walk through the back kitchen and into the garden. Forget-me-nots cluster in the cracks in the patio and, although the beds are thick with weeds, isolated heads of tulips and daffodils have broken through. I watch them dancing in the breeze. As soon as my mother gets back we'll be going, the three of us, to visit Ferdia's grave. I should be getting ready. I should eat something. But the coffee, undrinkable, has sapped my morale. Without even that small comfort, the day ahead feels like too much to bear.

\*

There's only one other person in the graveyard when we arrive, a woman. She's sitting on the ground in the front row of fresh graves, wearing a thin black jumper and yoga tights, an empty white wine bottle near her right hand. I glance at the small wooden cross next to her. Daniel Cunningham. Born eight years ago, died last November.

I walk a little faster down the path, wanting to protect the woman's privacy and to avoid my parents' faces. But then my father calls my name softly and I turn. He's stopped near the gates, waiting for my mother, who's kneeling next to the woman on the ground now, a hand resting gently on her leg. Through the gaps in the gravestones, I watch them exchange a few words. Then my mother looks up and beckons me in. My stomach clenches, wanting no part of this pain. But I walk forward and nod to the woman, who stares at me, realising, maybe in the same moment as I do, that we're the same age.

'We're all going to say a quick decade with Alison,' my mother says, pulling her beads out of her handbag. My father has moved close, shielding her from the bit of wind as she begins the Our Father. I stand silent; I haven't prayed the Rosary in years and I don't want to now. But then, as she moves on to the next bead, my mother fixes her eyes on my face, sorrowful and expectant.

'Hail Mary, full of grace, the Lord is with thee, blessed art thou amongst women and blessed is the fruit of thy womb Jesus . . .'

All three of them are looking at me. I crumble and pick up the thread, echoing my father's steady hum and Alison's wet mumble.

'Holy Mary, mother of God, pray for us sinners now and at the hour of our death.'

My mother nods, satisfied, and begins the cycle of call and response again, our voices layering and overlapping as she jumps back in with her section a fraction of a second before we've finished ours. It is comforting, propulsive, and Alison's voice gains strength as we go, the rhythm of the prayer restoring her purchase on the world.

'Glory be to the Father,' my mother begins, her voice higher now, stronger.

'And to the Son,' we follow. 'And to the Holy Spirit. As it was in the beginning, is now and ever shall be. World without end. Amen.'

'Amen,' my mother repeats softly and Alison takes her hand.

'Thank you, Margaret,' she says, so sincerely that I have to turn away.

\*

I'm surprised by how deep into the cemetery we have to walk to reach Ferdia's grave. I haven't been here in years and there are so many rows of headstones where before there was empty space, so many families with newer grief than ours. I worry that, without my parents to follow, I'd have struggled to find him at all. But then we turn into the row and, from a distance of twenty paces, I realise the grave would be hard to miss. It's covered in stuff and I slow down as we approach, trying to take it in. There are flowers, yes, in various states of health and decay. But it's the tat that shocks me: pillar candles printed with Ferdia's face, a rain-grimed blue teddy with halo and wings, rosaries like Mardi Gras beads hanging from the gravestone, garden centre angels, figurines of the saints. It's crowded. Chaotic. At the front of the plot there's a plastic suggestion box printed with the words "Prayers and Petitions", a few desiccated roses laid across the top.

I turn to stare at my parents.

'It looks well, doesn't it?' says my mother and I don't reply immediately, trying to figure out if she's being genuine. To me, there's nothing of my brother here, no space for him among the junk. But she does mean it; her eyes are glinting the way they used to when she looked at Ferdia himself, speaking at dinner time or serving mass. She steps forward to brush some imaginary dust from the stone then reaches down to lift a withered supermarket bouquet.

'Do you still come every week?' I ask and she nods.

'We never bring cut flowers, of course.' She gestures at the pots of daffodils and perennial shrubs. 'But so many other people come to visit now.'

'Do you run into them?' I ask and my mother hesitates.

'We try to avoid it,' my father answers firmly. 'You don't know what kind of problems people have and we're not trained for that.'

'But we have had reports, you know? Healings?' My mother bends, plucks a washed-out scrap of paper from the gravel. 'That woman in Baltimore with the diabetes . . .'

'It can do more harm than good,' my father cuts in. My mother's back is turned and he looks at me and shakes his head slightly, signalling that I should drop it. It's just like him to do this, to manage expectations, mitigate risks, never giving his own excitement a look-in. My mother steps backwards off the plot and I stretch out an arm, ready to catch her if she trips.

'Well, it's really something anyway,' I say and the three of us stand quietly for a while, the traffic outside the walls sparse enough that there are moments of silence between cars.

\*

There had been hundreds of people at the funeral home. Church people, lay people, town people, filing past in an endless procession of sombre faces and folded hands, all the usual pleasures of a funeral denied them because Ferdia was simply too young, was no age at all.

'I feel like I've lost a member of my own family,' says one middle-aged woman, squeezing my hands so tightly that her rings bite into my skin.

The removal to the church is scheduled for five but four thirty comes and goes and there's still a queue out the doors. As though it's a presidential primary, the undertakers agree that the coffin won't be closed until everyone who joined the line during the hours advertised in the funeral notice has seen the body. And so they keep coming, bursting with stories of all that Ferdia's done for them.

There are the elderly ladies he met as a teenager, flashing them smiles at weekday morning mass, and drawn young men he supported through their struggles with addiction, and teachers whose schools he visited as a seminarian and young mothers whose babies he prayed over. My friends from school are there with their parents, which means (and I think this over and over, though I know it hardly matters) that all my lies have been for nothing because they can see now, clear as day, that the man in the coffin isn't a trendy young Irish teacher, as I've told them. He's as good as a priest, dressed in vestments with a crucifix folded in his hands. But none of them say anything. They hold me in close, crushing hugs. They cry themselves.

A tiny nun who cooks at the Irish College and is afraid of flying has spent two days travelling from Rome by train and ferry so she can very quietly whisper her respects. A world removed from the loud German who came by plane to tell us about a visit to Lourdes when Ferdia had carried his stretcher.

'And I returned home cured,' he shouts, lifting his formerly injured foot for us to look at.

I smile, I nod, I crack my knuckles discreetly between mourners, glancing over the line of heads to gauge how many more could possibly be on their way. It's getting very warm with so many living bodies in here and I'm concerned about Ferdia. He's been dead for days now.

'You probably don't remember me?'

A red-cheeked woman with a Cork accent is standing in front of me. I shake my head, apologetic.

'Don't you worry, darling.' She squeezes my shoulders roughly with her two hands. 'I used to own the café in town where you and your brother came for iced buns. On Wednesday afternoons? Do you remember?'

'Oh, of course,' I lie and she beams.

'You know, I told him one day that I was really struggling to make ends meet with the café. My family had never wanted me to do it. They'd thought I was an awful eejit for even trying.' I smile, trying to ignore the bottleneck she's creating behind her. 'And then, the next time he came to the till and gave me this –' She opens her rough pink palm to show a small silver medal on a yellow string.

'Lovely,' I say but she lifts it higher, right under my nose.

'Do you see?' she asks, smiling so widely that I can see her fillings. 'Saint Jude. Patron saint of hopeless cases.'

I smile briefly then shake my head slightly, not knowing what she wants from me. A pressure builds in my skull. I want her to move on, want them all to hurry up and let us get on with things but at the same time I want to delay the moment when the coffin closes and the fuss dies down. I swallow and look around me and suddenly the woman collapses into violent wheezing sobs and hauls me into a damp hug.

'It's dreadful, pet,' she gasps. 'You poor girleen. Dreadful.'

\*

'Are you all right, Jacinta?' my father asks. 'You look a bit green around the gills.'

I nod and turn away from the gravestone to look around the cemetery. It's a perfect long rectangle, cordoned off and consecrated in the mid-twentieth century to accommodate Dublin's expanding suburbs and all their medium-density living and dying. I've always hated it, thought from the start that Ferdia deserved something grander. But that feeling is more complicated now. Like it or not, this is where we're from.

I turn back to my parents. 'I've been meaning to ask about the grave, actually. Is the plan . . . will it stay here?'

Neither of them answers immediately, leaving space for me to say more. But I don't want to express my worries fully, to acknowledge the holy relics that linger behind my eyelids late at night. Oliver Plunkett's leathery head, Maria Goretti smothered in wax, Jacinta Marto's small porcelain face. Even some of the newest saints have had their bodies put on display, shiny silicone masks pulled over mouldering skulls.

My father clears his throat. 'There are no immediate plans for exhumation.'

'No immediate plans,' I say. 'Right. So you're saying that down the line . . .?'

They glance at each other, confused.

'Well yes,' says my father. 'If the cause progresses past a certain point that's what's required.'

'Required by who?'

'By canon law,' he says slowly and I feel a rush of anger.

'There's no need to talk to me like I'm an idiot,' I say. 'No one has explained any of this to me. I don't know what's going to happen.'

My mother has been silent until now, she's still turned to the grave.

'Do we have to discuss this here?' she says quietly. 'Do we have to do it now?'

'Well yes, actually,' I say. 'I want to know now.'

She turns and I can see that she's getting angry too. 'All right then. According to the instructions of the Congregation for the Causes of Saints, there are two reasons for exhumation. One, the mortal remains of a Servant of God must be authenticated. And two, the holy relics must be protected and preserved to allow for veneration if and when the candidate is beatified or canonised. It's a formal and reverent process, the purpose of which is to protect the holy remains.'

She speaks with the quick neutral confidence of an expert.

'You mean the body,' I say. 'When you talk about relics and remains you mean Ferdia's actual body.'

My mother sighs. 'Yes. I do.'

'Well then surely *we* have rights of some kind? They can't just go around body snatching.'

'Well of course,' she says, frowning. 'But we've already agreed that when the time comes, we'll formally donate Ferdia's remains to the Church.'

I stare at her, stunned, and she glances around quickly as though she's afraid I'm about to make a scene. But my voice is small when I speak.

'Why didn't you ask me about it?'

She shakes her head. 'You've never had any interest. You've shown no intention of being involved.'

There's a silence. My mother and I look at each other and I remember what Brian said when we spoke, about how the canonisation process would show the distance between us. I hadn't fully understood what he was saying, I realise. But now I can see it in my mother's face, her complete certainty that what she's doing is right.

'Where will he go?' I ask, knowing that the argument is already lost. My parents glance at each other again and then my father takes a turn to speak.

'Well, the process does take some time, during which the . . . his . . . everything will be kept in a safe place.'

'And after that?'

'That's not decided,' he says. 'But something we have been conscious of is how devoted Ferdia was to Knock.'

I sigh. It's true, of course. When we visited my grandparents as children, I always wanted to be out in the garden or running around the fields, exploring a world that seemed so much wider than the housing estates at home. But instead we'd pile into the back of the car for a nauseating drive to the depths of County Mayo where, in 1879 and apparently with nowhere better to go, the Blessed Virgin appeared to some fourteen villagers.

'So he'll be buried again in Knock?' I ask my father.

'Not buried,' he says. 'The resting place of a blessed or saint should be above ground. But yes, there is consideration of a shrine at Knock, if we get to that point. Though of course it would depend on various discussions between the archdioseses of Dublin and Tuam.'

Tuam. The word startles me, globular and bulbous, metastasising in his mouth.

'Surely Tuam has enough bones already.'

I say it very quietly but still my father flinches and I'm glad, satisfied to have landed a blow. Have they just forgotten it all, I wonder, in the excitement? Otherwise, how do they live with the idea that the saints can't be left underground because they're too precious, but the tiny babies of unmarried mothers can be left anywhere? I'm lightheaded with anger and I open my mouth to speak again, but I can't find the words. I look at my mother, with her newly done hair and the smudges of dirt on her tights where she knelt next to Alison, and a sandy darkness closes in. Like on the day of the funeral, I feel dizzy. I stumble and brace for a long fall into blackness. But this time my father is ready, his hand firm on my elbow.

'You're all right,' he says softly. But the dizziness doesn't pass and I lurch towards him, resting my hand on his chest. He wraps his other arm around my shoulders, his body warped as an old tree, steady in the wind.

'Just sink your feet into the ground there,' he murmurs. 'Can you feel the earth under you?'

I do as he says and as the world reconstructs itself from the bottom up, my breath slowly settles. The grave is in front of me again, solid and sealed. I pat my father's shoulder.

'Sorry about that, Dad.'

'Not a bother,' he murmurs and gingerly I step away from him. My mother looks pale too, almost grey. She catches my eye and I wait for a flash of frustration but it doesn't come. Still, I'm embarrassed.

'Could probably have done with a bit more breakfast,' I say. 'Sorry.'

She opens her handbag and I think the moment is over. I feel shivery now and I pull my jacket closer around me, turn to look at the grave once more before we head back to the car. And then my mother taps me on the arm. She's holding out a small biscuit in a red plastic wrapper, the kind you get free with your coffee.

'You're still stashing these away?' I say, taking it off her. She smiles.

'I know it's not much.'

I unwrap it and take a bite. 'Thanks,' I say. 'It'll help.'

# Chapter Fifteen

WE ARRIVE AT SAINT Patrick's College half an hour before the mass is due to start and still my mother shuffles in her seat as my father parks, checking her watch and her phone, craning her neck to look towards the entrance. I'm anxious too; left to my own devices I'd have arrived with seconds to spare, no time for pre-chat, no option but to slide into a seat close to the door and far from the family. But instead we're here first. The morning has closed over and the hulking grey stone bully of a church blends with the clouds. It's deserted outside but for one priest in a black suit and trench coat, standing next to the doors and typing on his phone. My mother raises her hand high above her head and waves. And only then, as he looks up and walks towards us, do I realise it's Father Richter.

'Margaret.'

He takes both her hands and squeezes them.

'Brendan.'

A firm, masculine shake.

'And Jay.' We nod from a safe distance of two metres. 'It's wonderful that you could make it.'

His smile seems triumphal and I want to tell him that he shouldn't take any credit for my being here. But my mother is looking at the two of us, beaming, and having already started an argument in the graveyard, I don't want to do the same now.

'Nice to see you again, Matthew,' I say and we watch each other a moment longer before I look away.

As the three of them talk, people begin to arrive in ones and twos, slowing down as they pass us by. My father doesn't seem to notice. My mother smiles and nods at anyone who catches her eye, though I can't tell if she knows them or if she's just being polite.

'Are you expecting a big crowd?' she asks and Father Richter shrugs.

'I've had a fair few responses to the email about it and to my posts online. So a good number, I suspect.'

'We'll be heading to the hotel for a meal later,' my father says. 'You'd be very welcome to join us.'

'That's kind of you, Brendan, but I think I'll have lunch with the community here, if that's all right. I still think we can find a way to wring a bit more support out of them.'

He winks at my mother, she chirps that there's no rest for the wicked and I glance at my father, thinking that it can't be easy to see your wife flirting so transparently with someone else, irrespective of their sworn vow of celibacy. But he doesn't seem to be paying attention, is looking the other way.

'Margaret,' he says softly, and nods in the direction of the car park. We both turn. Her brothers, John and Damian, are striding towards us in tight shirts and baggy jackets. And behind them, my aunts Kathleen and Maura are walking slowly on either side of my grandfather, grown tiny in the years since I've seen him, his body curled low over a walking frame.

'I can't believe he's come,' my mother whispers and, eyes shining, she reaches for my father's hand. He squeezes it and they smile at one another briefly.

Then John and Damian are on top of us, shouting hellos, rubbing their whiskered faces against my cheeks.

'It must be a special occasion if we've got royalty over from London,' John bellows, sticking his hands deep in his pockets and rolling his hips, delighted to find himself on a day out, with a free meal and a decent feed of pints in prospect.

'I like to ration my appearances, John,' I say. 'It maximises impact.'

Father Richter, out of the spotlight now, gestures goodbye to my parents and disappears into the church. Damian asks if I'm back for long but I don't answer because I'm focused on my grandfather and my aunts, who have finally reached us.

'Well, look at this woman,' Maura calls from his right side, beaming at me.

'Isn't she gorgeous?' Kathleen adds, speaking to my mother.

I smile at them, then step forward and stoop to be close to my grandfather's ear.

'Hi, Granddad.' I rest my hand on his shoulder, brittle under the loose serge of his suit. He looks up. Frowns.

'Isn't it great to see Jacinta, Daddy?' shouts Kathleen and he nods, but still looks confused.

'I'm just having a bit of trouble with my eyes,' he tells me, his voice wavering, and I realise that he doesn't know who I am but is trying to hide it.

'That's all right,' I say softly and pat his hand, fighting a wave of guilt.

My grandmother didn't last long after Ferdia died. When she forgot her shoes for the funeral and had to borrow a pair of mine, everyone thought the shock had thrown her temporarily and that she'd be back to her old self soon. But the recovery never came. After a month, though she still went to the shops by herself, by the time she got home she'd have forgotten what she wanted to do with the food she'd bought and would stand in the middle of the kitchen, shouting at anyone who tried to help. After three months she'd stopped eating anything but toast and biscuits. After four she had an episode in the dairy aisle of the supermarket, insisting someone had spilled a whole carton of milk and trapped her there. And then she tripped over the edge of a carpet at home and gashed her forehead, had to go into hospital with a possible concussion and, between one thing and another, never came out.

I remember sitting behind them at her funeral – my grandfather, John, Damian, Maura, Kathleen, my mother and Breda – looking at the backs of their heads lined up like bowling balls in a rack and realising they were all on borrowed time. I prepared myself for everyone I knew to die, one after the other, until it was just me left, alone. But my grandfather has surprised everyone. Despite never seeming all that bothered about life or the living of it (unlike Granny, who was livid near the end, kicking and squalling, twisting knots in the hospital blankets), he's kept on, year after year, threatening and then refusing to die so many times that by now no one seems to believe it will ever happen.

'Arrah, he's mighty, he'll outlast the lot of us,' Damian says now to no one in particular. I feel a clutch of irritation, wanting to remind him that my grandfather can't outlive all of us because some of us are already dead. I feel tense, jittery. Though I knew they were all coming, still there's something surreal and unsettling about being with them again, back in the fold with all of us pretending I've never been gone. They're loud, shouting and laughing to each other, and a bubble of panic rises in my chest. But then someone touches my shoulder and I turn to see my aunt Breda. She opens her arms and I sink into a hug, breathing in her fresh citrusy scent.

Breda is my mother's closest sister, the person she called first when Ferdia had his accident, who stayed with me in the days after he died. I remember being surprised at the choice because she had no children, no husband. She wasn't accustomed – as my mother's older sisters were – to looking after anyone but herself, and I had absorbed the family view of her as a sort of perpetual teenager, pitiable but reprehensible, lonely but selfish.

As it turned out, my aunt's quiet, solitary habits were manna and balm in those long, empty days. She fed me consistently and simply, without regard to established mealtimes, seeming instead so attuned to my moods that whenever the slash of grief cut the air she blunted its edge with hot buttered toast, scrambled eggs, or a starchy spicy soup she claimed was minestrone. We'd go for a walk by the canal at least once each day, in the afternoon when the sun was brightest and the early-returning birds were loudest, their calls interspersing with the pad and crunch of our feet.

Beyond a sad, straight exchange of facts whenever my parents called – they were struggling to arrange the repatriation of the body – Breda and I didn't talk about what had happened. But at night, when I woke up sobbing, she'd perch on my bedside and stroke my hair.

'I know,' she'd murmur. 'I know.'

Other family members called constantly, of course, and seemed convinced that I was being terribly let down in my moment of need. Maura wanted me to come and stay at her house, Kathleen thought I'd be better off back at school, my grandmother was convinced that I was ill and should be fed more, given supplements, brought to the GP. But Breda rebuffed them all.

'We're doing fine,' she'd say on the phone. 'We're just taking it as it comes.'

I realised later that her whole life was built on this sort of quiet, dignified resistance to the family's expectations. After the funeral, I thought our closeness would last, that we'd become like the aunts and nieces you saw in films, tactile and solicitous. I had a fantasy of her inviting me to come and live with her in her tiny one-bed on Mountjoy Square. But though she was kind and we met for coffee more often than we had before, she kept her distance, was careful never to tread on my parents' toes.

'Thirteen years,' she says now, the first person to make any reference to Ferdia, keeping an arm around my shoulders as she turns to my mother. 'Can you believe it?'

My mother shakes her head. They don't speak. Even after forty years living apart they can still fit a full-blown conversation into a look. I watch, jealous.

'Are you all right?' Breda asks her very quietly. 'You look—'

'I'm fine,' my mother says abruptly. 'It's great to see Daddy.'

'Right.' Breda doesn't seem convinced and I look at my mother myself. She's still smiling, but almost too brightly, her eyes darting about as different people try to talk to her. A lot has already happened today, for her as well as for me, and she hasn't had any time to herself.

'Will we go inside?' I ask and my mother looks at her watch.

'We're still expecting Sean and Gearóid, and Gráinne and the baby . . .'

I glance around, expecting to see my three cousins coming around the corner in a pack, the baby stepping in for the fourth, Liam, who's living in Australia. Split evenly between Kathleen and Maura, these four were always as close as siblings, forever huddled together at family events. Though Ferdia was the same age as them he was never included and would float around the edges instead, speaking to the adults, pretending not to notice.

At the meal after his funeral, they had all gotten very drunk very quickly, sitting together on tall stools. When it was time to leave, Gráinne had grabbed me in a tight, almost hysterical, hug and whispered that I had her number if there was 'any single thing' I needed. She called me babes and gave me a pasty kiss on the cheek.

'Let's just head in,' says Breda now, decisively. 'They know the way.'

\*

The inside of the college chapel is dimmer than I remember. The pews here run parallel to the walls instead of perpendicular, so that the two halves of the congregation are facing one another. It's much fuller than I expected and, as we walk to the front and arrange ourselves into stiff, inhospitable seats, I can sense we're being stared at from the rows opposite. I don't look back. We wait for the choir and the arrival of the priests.

This has always been my favourite moment of mass, the pause before it all kicks off. On the whole, I hated Sundays growing up. The dresses, the thick bobbly tights, the smell of boiling ham that rubbed itself against every wall in the house. But there was respite, at least, in this moment, in the shared intake of breath. No one to talk to and nowhere to be. The altar bells jangle. The organ changes key. The pews rumble and creak as the congregation stands to greet a procession of two altar servers, three deacons and five priests, including Father Richter, all of them in white but for the presider, whose cream and emerald chasuble sways about him as he moves up the aisle. He holds back as the other men make their prostrations and take their places, before stepping forward and bowing low to kiss the altar. Through the rest of the opening hymn he stands with his hands hidden in his sleeves, eyes upwards. When the music stops, he stays in position, unspeaking, for a long time. Someone coughs. The priest stays quiet a further fifteen seconds, as though to prove a point, then heaves in a breath.

'The grace of our Lord Jesus Christ, the love of God and the fellowship of the Holy Spirit be with you all,' he booms out, his voice nasal and reverberant.

'And also with you,' I reply automatically, smiling at two children opposite who've broken into giggles. Then I realise, too late, that everyone else has said something different. The words changed years ago, they've already caught me out.

'Today's mass is offered for the repose of the soul of Ferdia Devane, late of this parish and a seminarian of this diocese who studied at the Pontifical Irish College in Rome. We are very pleased to have many of Ferdia's family and friends here with us today as we remember once again his life of faith and service.'

The priest inclines his head towards us and my mother lifts a hand to her heart and makes a small bow. The entire congregation twists to look at us. I keep my eyes fixed on the oak of the pew.

'Let us acknowledge our sins.'

The movements and responses of the mass are still so instinctive to me that, like with the Hail Marys in the graveyard, I find it easier to go along with them than to resist. But the penitential act is my one exception; I've decided in advance that I won't even mouth along. I dip my head so no one will see and against the backdrop of droning voices, think suddenly of a Swedish woman I slept with in Barcelona, three summers ago on a holiday with Clem. She and her friends had invited us to join their table and we all got drunk, first on enormous jugs of Sangria then on fishbowl gin and tonics. It was long after midnight when we moved on, Clem disappearing into a dark underground club, the woman and I teetering into the hot night, first for baguettes stuffed with generous wedges of Spanish omelette, and then on to the tight white sheets of her hotel bed, the room dark, the filmy curtains pulled back so we could see the thousand orange lights of the city. She was so beautiful and it was such a perfect evening that I left early the next morning, before there was any chance to talk about breakfast or exchanging phone numbers or anything else that might, eventually, take the shine off. But I hadn't really wanted the night to end and so, when I saw the vast half-cut towers of the Sagrada Família, I'd walked along the block to get a closer look, then tacked myself on to the queue for mass inside. I'd learned, the day before, that by the time he began the basilica, Gaudí had been working for years to break the restraints of church architecture, pushing against all that was tight and fixed in the gothic, encouraging it, tweak by tweak, to soften and splay. And that morning – listening to the voices of the choir floating high and light through the overstory of branching stone – I felt that he had done it, that there was something about the lines of his achievement, the muscles and bones of the place, that meant I could stretch out in the cool blue-stained light and think (against the rumble of the psalms) of the hours I had spent fucking the night before.

Behind me, Kathleen and Maura sigh heavily as their children arrive, ten minutes late. I look up and wave discreetly at my cousins. Gráinne takes her daughter out of the pram, lifting her chubby little arm and waving it back. Around me, the whole family makes small adoring sounds, distracted entirely from the mass. I smile. Gráinne doesn't have a partner and no one's told me exactly where this baby came from. But they've never said a bad word about the situation either, and clearly have nothing but love for this child, born out of wedlock at the right time in history. She squawks cheerfully as we stand for the gospel and all around the chapel people turn and smile indulgently, including the priest who's stepped forward to read, a young red-haired American.

'A reading from the Holy Gospel according to Matthew,' he says, in an accent so thickly Boston Irish that I think it must be put on. I make the three small crosses with my thumb, on my forehead, my lips, my heart.

'Glory to you, oh Lord.'

'Love your enemy and pray for those who persecute you,' the priest begins. 'For if you love those who love you, what reward will you get? Do not even the tax collectors do as much?'

He stops and looks around, as though checking that the words are landing the way they should, his face gleaming with the effort of investing each one with the meaning and power it deserves. And suddenly I feel a pressure building in the air around me, a pressure on my shoulders, on the top of my head. Pray for them, Ferdia would tell me when I complained about bullies at school. Pray for them, he'd tell my father as he grumbled in front of the evening news. It was completely insufferable then, but I still hear it sometimes when I'm being unkind, or impatient, or gossipy. And I hear it now, like real sound, the words of the gospel in my brother's voice. 'Be perfect, just as your heavenly Father is perfect,' he says and I look up, trying to control my feelings as the priests chant their second set of Hallelujahs. I know this is a secular epiphany, that what I'm remembering is Ferdia's kindness, his patience, his generosity to other people even when they were cruel or ignorant. And still, looking up, part of me expects a sunbeam to burst through the stained glass.

When I turn back to the altar, the presiding priest has replaced the young American at the lectern. He clears his throat, but just as he does a scream unfurls from the body of the church. Gráinne's baby has had enough already. The man sighs, irritated, then starts to speak.

'Some years ago, I was asked to lead a retreat at a school a few hours from here. A long-established school, run by the Jesuits, not at all different to Belvedere College, the one I attended myself. So I admit that I was looking forward to it. To a day out of town and a nice drive through the country. Perhaps even a chance to relive my – by then – very distant youth.'

Along with everyone else in the chapel, I release an obedient puff of laughter. The priest nods his big head and goes on, his voice rising and falling in uniform waves as he tells us, in exhaustive detail, about the road he took to get to the school, the biscuits he was served when he arrived, the presentation he gave to a class of well-fed and well-bred fourth-year boys. I let the words wash by me, thinking that in another twenty-four hours I'll be through all of this and on my way back to London. I imagine myself with Lindsay, watching a film, her legs sprawled across me on the sofa, but then quickly push the thought away. The priest's tone has altered a little now, it's querulous as he tells us about a group of three young lads who sat in the back corner of the classroom, smirking and exchanging notes. He had tried to ignore them, he said, but they kept on. And when it came to time for questions, they pounced, took turns sticking their hands up, asking about the Church's teaching on the sanctity of life in the womb, on the ordained roles of men and women, on the parameters of normal healthy sexual life.

On all sides I can hear people shifting in their seats. The priest has a high colour now, red and quite shiny as he tells us how agitated he felt driving home after his encounter with the teenage boys.

'But thankfully,' he goes on, 'it's always been my experience that at times of disquiet, the Lord will provide. And that evening, I happened to find myself walking into the refectory with a visiting seminarian, an exceptionally talented and thoughtful young man, blessed with an extraordinarily powerful faith. And since he was only a few years older than the schoolboys I'd dealt with that day I had him sit next to me at dinner and I told him what happened. And I admit that I half expected that he'd soft-shoe me, give me the "Yes, Father Mannion, no, Father Mannion, sure isn't that terrible, Father Mannion?". But no, he reminded me of the message of today's gospel, the importance of praying for these young people, who were growing up in a time of such change and confusion.' The priest leaves a long silence then, looking up and down the banks of seats. 'And as I'm sure many of you will have realised by now, the young man I was speaking to was Ferdia Devane.'

There's a ripple of genuine feeling around the chapel and my family members sigh and hum appreciatively. Father Mannion smiles in our direction and I massage the point of my jaw, which has been clenched since he mentioned the sanctity of life.

'As some of you might have seen in the media, though it hasn't been as widely covered as it might have been, the archdiocese of Dublin is now launching a campaign for Ferdia's beatification and, in the months and years ahead, we will be asking for your support in the way of prayers, letters of endorsement, social-media posts and other practical contributions. And my hope is that the story I've shared with you today shows why we believe that Ferdia may one day be counted among the number of the Blessed.'

There's a moment's silence before a single clap sounds like a shot, then is picked up by the whole congregation, the noise gradually accumulating, filling the chapel. I look at my mother, who smiles with the shy delight of the top prizewinner in a raffle. But as the applause continues and intensifies, she covers her eyes with one hand and her shoulders begin to shake. My father reaches an arm around her. Breda, sitting behind, leans forward and gently kisses the top of her head. Father Mannion, too, seems taken aback by the strength of the response. When the clapping finally tapers off he opens and closes his mouth a few times, his mic picking up the wet click of tongue on back teeth.

'The last thing I'll say is this. I don't want you to walk away with the idea that Ferdia wasn't as troubled as I was by what those young men had to say. As those who lived and studied with him attest, he was a powerful proponent of the Church's culture of life. Opposed to euthanasia, to abortion –' he's lifted his right hand and is counting the points off on his fingers '– and to the undermining of the traditional family based on the marriage of one man and one woman.'

I feel cold, clammy and at the same time filled with a rising, burning heat. Looking at the other priests on the altar, I can see pursed lips and sideways glances. I want to believe that Father Mannion has gone off message, that he's lying. I'm desperate for him to stop speaking and for the mass to be over, but instead he takes a deep breath, like a swimmer perched on the edge of a pier, and plunges back in.

'What Ferdia could offer me that day was the perspective of someone from the same generation as those young men. And I have often thought since his sad death, how desperately we could do with his guidance and influence, with regard to the forthcoming referendum on the Eighth Amendment, for example. Because what Ferdia Devane reminded me that day was of my duty to protect and uphold the faith, not with anger but, just as Matthew the evangelist exhorts us, with love.'

He falls silent. Around the church people glance at one another, cough, wondering if he's finished. I don't look at my parents. I consider walking out. Eventually the congregation stands to recite the creed, but their voices sound strange, distant, like the boom of approaching artillery.

For the rest of the mass, I haul myself about as expected: standing, sitting, kneeling. But I've lost my grip on the service. The words I briefly found so comforting have turned rough and rigid, so that when the time comes for communion and my parents rise, I stay seated, shuffling my knees to the side and waving them on. My mother's eyes widen and she tilts her head, imploring me not to embarrass her. I know how she feels. I'm embarrassed myself, understanding now that the whole church is probably watching, that these people know who I am, that they've likely googled me. I want to go to the front and take the wafer, to blend in as much as I can. But I can't do it. I don't move.

'Sorry,' I whisper to my mother and she closes her eyes, as though in pain. 'Not for me.'

# Chapter Sixteen

THE HOTEL WHERE WE'RE having lunch is a short way from Saint Patrick's and all through mass I've been looking forward to the walk. The break from my family, the fresh air, a chance to recalibrate after Father Mannion's sermon. But when the chatter outside the chapel has died down and everyone is dispersing, I see that my aunt Maura has ended up alone with my grandfather, and is struggling to help him into the car. I go to join her, holding the passenger door steady as she manoeuvres him inside. She's breathless by the end of it, sweat gathering around her temples, and I wonder where my uncles have disappeared to.

'Thank you, Jacinta,' she says, patting my hand where it still rests on top of the door. 'You'll come over with us, will you?'

I hesitate but Maura doesn't pick up on it, just smiles vaguely as she waits for me to answer, the car keys bunched in her hand. She looks tired, old.

'A lift would be great,' I say. 'Thanks.'

On the way she asks about London. Have I seen any good shows recently? What sorts of things are in the shops? Is Covent Garden still as nice as it used to be? Maura has lived on the Leitrim-Roscommon border her whole life except for one halcyon summer in her early twenties when she worked as a junior orderly in Moorfields Eye Hospital and spent her days off drifting wide-eyed around the West End. Now, past seventy, she runs both her own house and my grandfather's, dropping in twice or three times a day to feed, clean and care for him, and for her brothers as well. People tend to be quite voluble about how hard this is for poor Maura, without showing any inclination to shoulder some of the load.

'I was in the Royal Opera House recently,' I tell her. 'Just before Christmas.'

'Wow,' she says. 'Now I've been lots of places but I've never been there.'

'It's amazing. There's this outside balcony up on the top floor with the best view over Covent Garden.'

'I'll have to go one day,' she says. 'If I ever find the time.'

'Absolutely,' I agree and then add, surprising myself, that we should go together.

When we arrive at the hotel a few minutes later, inching my grandfather through the automatic doors, Maura's son, Sean, is in full flight, circling each carload as it arrives, determined to show off by getting the first and biggest round.

'Right,' I can hear him shout at the barmaid, 'one pint of Budweiser, one Guinness, a glass of shandy, two pots of tea . . .'

John and Damian are sitting at the closest table, but Maura has to call to them twice before they pay her any attention.

'John! Would you get a chair for Daddy?'

'Allow me,' says Sean, coming back with the first of the drinks. He swings a sturdy-backed chair up and over everyone's heads. 'There you are, Granddad, sir. And I assume you'll have a Paddy?'

'Yes,' says Granddad, suddenly focused as we lower him into the chair.

'No,' says Maura. 'You know it doesn't agree with him.'

Sean and John wink at each other. Maura wipes her face. I glance at my watch. My father has booked dinner for one thirty but it's only twenty past twelve. The day stretches long ahead of us.

'And I suppose it'll be tequila shots for you, Jacinta,' Sean says.

I force a smile. I know he's trying to be friendly but it's been so long since I've seen any of them that they're talking to me like I'm still nineteen. I consider refusing a drink, proving some kind of point by asking for a Diet Coke. But I want a gin and tonic, and that's what I say to Sean.

'Slimline?'

'No.'

I sit down and look around. The place is just the way I remember it: shiny wood and brass, bright lights on the rows of bottles behind the bar, all of it a bit artificial-looking. The velvet on the seats is crumpled and thin, the tabletops traced with white rings. I remember when the hotel opened, one of the first big investments of the nineties, when Maynooth was beginning to be absorbed into the Dublin property boom. We came here for my communion and confirmation, and to celebrate my Junior

Cert results (6 As, 5 Bs, better than Ferdia's). When I imagined running away from home, I used to think I could come here for the first night, splurge my savings and figure out my options.

We also came after Ferdia's funeral, of course. A boy I knew was working behind the bar that day and served me three vodka shots on the run, which I downed and then threw up before they'd gone anywhere near my bloodstream. No one noticed, except a young nun, a friend of Ferdia's, who was in the bathroom at the time.

'It's the stress of the day,' she said tactfully as she dabbed a small patch of vomit off my dress. 'Probably a good idea to drink plenty of water.'

When my G&T arrives, I try not to slam it. I'm nervous, afraid of the questions my family might ask me. But to begin, the conversation is dominated by the people who see each other most. John and Damian shout about the weekend's football. Kathleen plays with her granddaughter. Gráinne drinks a glass of white wine and answers Maura's questions about how the baby is feeding (well) and sleeping (badly). She sounds exhausted, close to tears. Sean yells questions at my grandfather, who looks confused but does his best to answer. It's easy for me to sit quietly, buffeted by the noise. Every few minutes I take out my phone, swiping automatically into the apps I most often use, reading whatever's onscreen without even the intention of taking it in. I feel sad that no one has texted to see how I'm getting on, then have to remind myself that no one knows I'm here, apart from Lindsay. And that I've pushed Lindsay away. So I sip my gin and look at my phone and let it all wash over me until suddenly, as the men at the far end let out a blast of laughter, everyone hushes. My parents have arrived. I half expect the table to burst into cheers, like they're newlyweds.

Eventually my father speaks into the silence. 'Do you all have drinks?'

'We do,' says Sean, jumping up to take another two orders: my father's, a sparkling water, my mother's, a hot port. Then my father disappears again, muttering something about the hotel manager and the meal. There's a free chair near the middle of the table and I expect my mother to sit there, anticipating that she'll avoid speaking to me for the rest of the day, as punishment for my conscientious objection to the Eucharist. But instead, she makes straight for the empty chair next to me, squeezing my shoulders as she walks past, saying something to everyone about how happy she is to have 'her girl' at home. I don't react, don't really know how to.

'Thirteen years,' says Breda again. 'Can you believe it?'

My aunts and uncles shake their heads slowly.

'Do you know,' says John, 'there was a clue in last week's crossword that I just could not get. Blessing given by . . .' He falters, suddenly confused, looks at Damian. 'What was it?'

'Blessings attributed to Jesus at the Sermon of the Mount,' says Damian, picking up his glass of Coke.

'That was it,' says John. 'And honest to God, my first thought was: I must ring Ferdia. And do you know, I bet he'd have got it.'

'Well, any of us could have told you it was beatitudes,' Maura cuts in coldly.

'Even still,' says Damian. 'Ferdia did have some brain. Didn't we always say how lucky the Church was to get him when he could have done anything?'

'He'd probably have been Ireland's youngest bishop by now,' says Sean. 'And those of us with any notions of our own success would have been put to shame.'

I take a few deep breaths, irritated. They don't always talk like this, only morphing into a J. M. Synge cast when they're discussing someone dead. My mother is humming softly in the seat next to me, delighted as always to be listening to people say nice things about Ferdia.

'So kind,' says Breda.

'Nothing he wouldn't do for you,' agrees Kathleen. 'Isn't that right, Daddy?'

'Who?' my grandfather says, his glass of whiskey half-lifted and his head bent towards it.

'Ferdia, Daddy,' she says.

'I've never heard of him.'

There's a long, painful pause then. Maura looks at Kathleen, Breda at my mother. John and Damian pick up their drinks.

'And I'll tell you what,' Sean says, lunging forward in his seat, desperate to move things on. 'He wasn't a bad footballer eith—'

Before he's even finished the sentence his eyes are wide as plates and the table, again, is deathly quiet. I don't look at my mother, at anyone. And eventually Gearóid, who hasn't spoken a word yet, leans over and claps his brother's shoulder.

'Well, boy. Looks like the second round's on you too, and you've only yourself to blame.'

Everyone laughs, loud and relieved.

'Mine's another port, Seanie,' my mother calls in a high, teasing voice and, though it's a joke, Sean jumps up, his face now a painful, boiling red, says he'll get everyone the same again.

The conversation is slow to restart. My father comes back, sits down in the middle of the table. A rising smell of soup suggests it must be nearly time for lunch.

'Well, it was a nice mass,' says Breda.

'It was,' says my mother.

'He's some priest though, isn't he?' says John. 'One of the old school.'

'The sort of fella you used to dread landing in front of for confession,' Damian agrees, and I expect these comments to split the table. It's the kind of joke my parents used to bristle at, but now everyone laughs.

'He obviously takes it very seriously, the poor man,' says Kathleen, looking to her sisters, who nod sympathetically. My mouth is beginning to taste sour.

'But can't you just imagine him bombing along the dual carriageway,' Damian goes on. 'Absolutely hopping about those young fellas. Seething.'

'And then poor Ferdia having to placate him when he got home,' says Breda. 'Probably didn't get a chance to eat a bite of his dinner.'

Everyone laughs again. I look around. Like seals on a rock, the siblings are starting to relax now and it's impossible to think of them as children, arguing over toys or the biggest piece of cake. They're on the edge of being elderly and they've settled into a collective equilibrium, a lazy harmony that allows neither closeness nor distance, precludes conflict but at the cost of any real connection. My gaze settles last on my mother. Her eyes are closed and she's smiling vaguely, her glass of hot port lifted right up to her nose so she can breathe in the steam of sugar and cloves.

'Wasn't actually funny though, was it?' I mutter. My mother opens her eyes, shoots me a swift, worried glance.

'What's that, Jacinta?' Damian calls, already laughing again, thinking I'm in on it.

I raise my voice for him. 'I'm saying that I don't think a sermon like that is something to laugh about.'

Damian frowns. 'We're just making fun. No one means any harm.'

'Yeah, but what's the joke?' I ask. 'That the Church is actually still really homophobic? That they still really hate women?'

Heads fall like dominoes around the table, my aunts and cousins suddenly very interested in the contents of their glasses. John, who's managed to magic up and finish off a third pint, rolls his eyes.

'Here we go,' he says and, on either side of him, Sean and Damian laugh loudly. I flush. There's a bank of tears gathering in the back of my head and I'm afraid to say anything in case my voice breaks. I take a deep breath and grab the edge of my seat, trying to compose myself. And then, out of nowhere, Gráinne speaks.

'Would you grow up, the lot of you,' she snaps. 'Jacinta's completely right.'

'Right about what?' Sean asks.

'About what's happened in this country. All the Church did for years. The lives they ruined . . .' she falters, but only slightly. 'And the people they killed.'

'Ah now . . .' Damian begins, but she waves him down.

'Yes, I do mean killed. I remember Savita even if you don't. And all those babies in the homes.'

As Gráinne says the word babies, her voice high and stiff, she reaches out for her own daughter. The table has gone very quiet and I look at Breda, Kathleen and Maura, but their faces are blank.

'Listen, ladies,' says Damian, in a voice he clearly thinks is diplomatic. 'I appreciate that you both feel strongly about this. But can we agree to just leave this stuff at the door, the referendums and all the rest. Politics shouldn't come between a family, especially today.'

'But it's not politics,' I say, emboldened.

Damian sighs, throws up his hands. 'You can't win.'

'No, Damian, I'm serious. What we're talking about with these issues is people's lives.' I take a deep breath. 'Like, the marriage referendum, that was *my* life . . .'

I trail off, my voice disappearing into a profound silence, a vacuum of embarrassment. I can hear my mother's breath and I know I've committed a cardinal sin, that the only thing worse than talking about politics is talking about feelings. I avoid looking at anyone. And then John laughs loudly and calls down the table:

'You're not telling us you're *like that*, are you, Jacinta?'

The words hit me as one compact force, like a sonic boom. The noise of the bar is drowned out by the ringing in my ears. I stare at John through the haze, can see that he's smiling stupidly, nervously, not understanding what he's done. He just doesn't know, I think, and suddenly my body flashes from cold to raging hot, the shame boiling then evaporating away, leaving a pure white anger, a perfect clarity. I turn to my mother.

'You've never told them?' I say, with barely enough breath in my chest to get the words out. She won't even turn to me, stares into her lap with tears quivering in her eyes. I keep watching her, not looking at anyone else but feeling the weight of their mortified silence and hoping she feels it too.

'Jacinta,' my father says eventually from down the table, his voice level. I snap my head to look at him. 'We can talk about this later.'

I push my chair back, pull on my coat. Only Gráinne looks at me, her face white and strained, as though she's worried all this is partially her fault. Everyone else has averted their eyes, waiting for the discomfort to pass. I want to punish them, want to lift each of their glasses in turn and hurl them against the walls, to smash their pathetic, fearful complacency.

'Jay,' says my father. 'Come on. Please.'

I shake my head, glance down once more at my mother's big blow-dried hair. The real shock isn't in finding out what my parents have done, or being reminded that they're still embarrassed by me, it's in knowing that I've let them take me in, with their apple tarts and their tiny shows of physical affection. I feel like a fool for believing, even for a few hours, that there might be a way to let them back in, to make my peace.

'Honestly, Dad,' I say, my voice controlled and cold. 'You can get to fuck.'

# Chapter Seventeen

WHEN I LEAVE THE HOTEL I walk towards the train station, thinking that I'll go into Dublin, lose myself in the Patrick's Day crowds. But the board says there's no train for half an hour and my father has already called four times. I assume, not having had an answer, that he'll soon come to the station himself. The idea that my family will continue on with their meal, that they won't want to waste the money or disrupt the day any further, doesn't even occur to me. But that's exactly what happens, I find out later. My father pauses his chain of calls to go and eat his soup, spooning it up stoically, ignoring my mother's panicked glances around the room. She's asked the waiter to leave a bowl for me. 'My daughter will be along in a minute,' she says far too brightly. But my cream of vegetable goes untouched, as does hers. The rest of the family chatter on loudly, as though it's a kindness to pretend nothing has happened. My father tilts his bowl away from him to scoop the dish clean, then returns to the lobby at the same time that I start walking along the canal towpath by the station. My phone buzzes again and I stare at his name onscreen for a moment before switching it off. It's then, hearing the premature cut to voicemail, that he understands I'm not coming back.

This section of the Royal Canal is shallow and tangled with weeds. On either side, scraggly trees shield rows of semi-detached houses from the noise of the railway. I've been coming here since I was a baby in my pram. We'd walk the path as a family sometimes, on Sunday mornings after mass. I walked here with Breda in the week after Ferdia died. And in the long days of the summer that followed, I covered this stretch nearly every day, alone, walking the four miles to Leixlip and the four miles back. I didn't want to be in the house. It felt poisoned, sick and I was on edge there, always, afraid of running into my parents, of having them look at me with their strange flat eyes while I tried to make conversation.

I walk quickly now, building up a sweat, trying to push the scene in the hotel from my mind. The terrible quiet after John's expectant laugh. The expressions on my aunts' faces that told me they had all suspected and said nothing. My mother's refusal even to look at me. It's textbook really, the almost inevitable product of generations of silence and secret-keeping, of a whole country of us witnessing the meat and bones of human life through cracks in the door, reduced to prying and poking around, pressing our ears to the bedroom floor, scrabbling for some hint of what we weren't being told. But times are supposed to be changing, everyone says so. We're living in a new Ireland. So why are they still like this?

First, I wish I had never come. I imagine the weekend I could be having in London: the year's first swim in Hampstead Ponds, a pint afterwards in a warm pub, a night out somewhere low-ceilinged and grungy. Then I think I should have sat and said nothing, let them laugh, saved my energy. Ripples begin to appear on the canal, spots of rain. My feet are burning slightly in my loafers but still I press on, even faster, until I'm breathing heavily, almost running. I feel guilty, like I should have gone further, called John out the way I would any bigot on the bus. Or I could have challenged my parents instead of running away, forcing them to explain why they've insisted that I come all the way to Ireland to celebrate every fibre of Ferdia's life when they're not willing to admit the most essential components of mine. I kick an empty beer can off the towpath and into the weeds. Do I know that Ferdia would have been any different? That we'd have stayed close through his ordination and my coming out, like I've always assumed? Maybe Father Mannion was right and Lindsay was right and there's no middle way when it comes to the Church, no escaping the bad and hateful, even in the people you love most.

I slow down, that thought piercing something deep in my chest. I feel the sting and wait a moment before my body buckles under a wave of grief so intense that I have to stop and stand very still, let it roar through me. This happens less often now than it used to. A loss, which at first fills your life like water, eventually diminishes. The pressure eases. But there are still moments like these, each one worse than the last specifically because more time has passed and it's still true. They're still dead. They've been gone so long that you have no up-to-date stories, no running jokes, no shared friends. Early on you can imagine their alternative life so easily, where they braked an instant sooner, or tested the balcony before stepping out, where the boot had landed slightly differently. For a little while, the two worlds run exactly parallel, like when you pull out of the station and can see into another moving train next to yours, the people inside fussing with their bags, just like you are, arranging their books and sandwiches and cans of beer on the little fold-out tables. But then time passes and the tracks fork, the trains hurtle further and further apart.

I start walking again, but slowly now, barely lifting my feet as I move towards a metal bench in the distance. The surface is wet but I sit down anyway and pull out my phone. I'm desperate to talk to someone, to connect myself with the other world, my real world, where I exist as the person I've chosen to be. But this isn't the time to speak to Lindsay, launching straight back into the conversation that drove us apart. And it would be too much to land on Brian.

I scroll through my contacts. I know I need to talk to Clem. And he answers immediately.

'All right?' he sings down the line. 'What's happening?'

I don't reply at once. He's out somewhere, walking, and immediately, at the sound of his slightly breathless voice and the background noise of London, I feel better.

'I'm in Ireland,' I say eventually.

'Ah, OK,' says Clem. 'I didn't realise.'

'Well, that's because I didn't tell you.'

He picks up on my tone now and his own shifts, becomes serious.

'Has something happened?' he asks. 'Are your parents all right?'

'My brother died,' I say, my voice breaking, and there's a stunned silence. 'I mean, not today. He died when I was sixteen.'

Clem doesn't answer for a moment. There's less noise on his end of the line and I think he must have stopped walking, moved somewhere quieter.

'I'm really sorry to hear that,' he says. 'I mean, obviously I am.'

'Thanks.'

'But why have you never told me about it?'

I don't answer. Clem sounds hurt and I think of the days when I first met him, when we worked in the café together and we talked and talked, our words filling the crevices in the morning rush and the long lulls in the afternoons. We gossiped about the regulars, inventing fantastical lives for them. We talked about his family, and about queerness and race and what austerity was doing to the city. One day on my lunch break a woman had asked me for money and when I said I didn't have any she pulled her boob out, there on the high street, to show me that her milk had dried up. I had pushed past her, shocked, but then I'd thought of Ferdia and taken my second-last twenty from an ATM. But I couldn't find her again and I arrived back in the café with the note still crumpled in my hand. When I dissolved into tears Clem wrapped me in his arms and made soothing noises. I cried harder and above my head he mouthed to customers that they'd just need to wait outside a minute. It was the first hug he ever gave me and it made me realise how special he was. In the years since, we've gone to each other with more problems than I can count.

'Are you angry?' I ask quietly, braced for another argument. Clem's my best friend and I've lied to him. I loved Lindsay from the second day I knew her and still I let our relationship grow around a secret.

'Well yes, I am a bit,' he says and I say nothing. Two women with a dog are walking on the towpath and they glance at me as they pass, bent low on this damp bench. I swallow hard to stop myself from sobbing. Clem sighs.

'But anyway, we can talk about your weird neuroses another time. What's going on?'

I laugh. Tears and snot drop on to the ground. 'I just didn't want you to know how bizarre my family is. I didn't want to tell anyone.'

'Why would I have cared?'

'Well, my brother was training to be a priest when he died.'

Clem barely pauses. 'All right, and?'

'And now the Catholic Church in Ireland wants to make him a saint.'

This time there's a beat of silence.

'Like, a literal saint?'

His tone has altered again, our usual hint of irony slipping back in. I'm glad. It's easier to talk about it in this register.

'Yeah,' I say. 'Saint Patrick, Saint Francis, Saint Augustine. That kind of saint.'

'I didn't realise they were still even a thing?'

'Yes, well, they are,' I say, realising that this is an explanation I'm going to have to give, again and again, for the rest of my life. 'Actually, the last three popes have created more saints than all the others combined.'

'Wow.' Clem says, then whistles softly. 'Must be quite the mindfuck.'

'Yeah, it really is. I feel like an absolute nutcase even saying it to you.'

He laughs. 'OK, so I'm caught up on the essential background. But what's occurring in Ireland right now? Why are you there?'

I sigh. 'Well, it's a long story. But basically I've stormed out of a family commemoration thing because some homophobia happened and now I'm sat on a park bench by a canal trying to figure out what to do next.'

'Are you cold?' he asks.

'I really am.'

'Well maybe stand up then, walk for a bit.'

I do as he tells me, hesitating a moment before turning back towards Maynooth.

'OK, so option one, you just come home.' Clem says. 'Right now. I can book you a flight.'

I smile, both at his generosity and at how easily he's introduced the word home into the conversation. Meaning London. Our home.

'No, I left my passport in my parents' house like an idiot.' I sigh. 'But I just don't know if I can face them.'

'I can imagine,' says Clem. 'And I am sorry to be the bearer of bad news but it doesn't sound like you have much of a choice.'

I laugh. Just speaking to him makes the prospect of going home less menacing. The other world is real. I'll be there tomorrow, whatever happens. I pick up my pace a little bit. For a minute or two, we don't speak.

'Are you still there?' I say eventually, realising that Clem must have been on his way somewhere, that he's stopped in the middle of his day to be here for me.

'I am,' he says. 'What did he do, if you don't mind me asking?'

'Who?'

'Your brother. What did he do that means he gets to be a saint?'

I'm confused. 'Well, nothing really. He was just a holy guy.'

'Oh.' Clem sounds disappointed and I realise he expected a story of heroism, martyrdom, of fainting in rapture or speaking in tongues. 'Is that really all it takes?'

'Well, he'll have to perform some miracles at some point. But yeah, all you have to do in your lifetime is achieve complete moral perfection.'

'Tough act to follow,' he says.

'Yeah,' I agree quietly and there's a pause.

'Did it feel that way when you were kids?'

'How do you mean?'

'Well . . .' Clem hesitates. 'Did they prefer him?'

Down the canal I can see a train approaching, heading towards Dublin. The rumble builds to a roar. No one's ever asked me this question before, not outright.

'Yes,' I say when the noise has subsided. 'They did. Always.'

He makes a small sound, almost drowned out by the crackle of the wind on the line. We don't speak for another while and I watch a scatter of ducks drift by slowly.

'Honestly, I thought this would bother you more,' I say eventually, thinking of Lindsay, of how quickly she flipped when I mentioned it.

'Why would it bother me?'

'I mean, the Church is pretty awful, right?'

Clem laughs softly. 'Why are Catholics always like this? You think we're all as obsessed with your Church as you are.'

I bristle unexpectedly. 'Well, it is the most powerful religious institution in the world.'

'Yeah, and?' says Clem. 'Not my circus, not my monkeys, babe. I've got my own homophobic religion to be getting on with.'

'Well, how do you deal with that then?' I ask, suddenly embarrassed that I don't actually know this detail about Clem's family. Are they Baptists? Anglicans? I decide to hedge, for now, then do better in future, to stop letting my own baggage blind me to everyone else's. 'Your family are still practising, right?'

'They are.' He exhales heavily down the line. 'And the answer is, I just put up with it.'

'Why?' I ask and the question sounds childish, simplistic. But I look up to Clem, he's bold in his queerness in the way I want to be, so his compromises confuse me. There's a short silence and then he says it's because they're his family and he loves them.

'But doesn't it hurt?' I ask and he sighs again, loud and exasperated.

'Of course it hurts. But that's life, isn't it? It's not simple. So I take it to my therapist and we talk about the fact that their faith isn't actually a rejection of me, any more than my queerness is a rejection of them. It's just who they are.'

'Do you actually believe that?' I ask and Clem doesn't speak for a long time.

'On good days,' he says eventually. 'On good days I believe it.'

The light over the canal is beginning to dim, the sky draining to white as the water turns yellow and glassy.

'I should let you go,' I say, speeding up. I don't want to get stuck on the towpath in the dark.

'OK,' he says. 'Call me when you're back, if you fancy a drink.'

'I will,' I say. 'And thanks. I love you.'

\*

My parents and I went on one last holiday together after Ferdia died, to an expensive-but-rustic resort in Naxos. I think of it now, on the walk back to Maynooth, cold and hungry.

'It's not one of those all-inclusives,' my father explained again and again, as though he was worried

I'd be disappointed. 'But we'll have a small kitchen area and a terrace where you can sit and eat, and each day, if we want, they'll deliver food for breakfast. Fresh fruit and bread and yoghurt.' Inexplicably, for the duration of the holiday, he pronounced 'yoghurt' the British way, with short bouncy vowels.

We fly into Athens, planning to spend four full days there before catching the ferry on the morning of the fifth. The travel agent recommended a hotel an eleven-minute walk from the Acropolis and we set off almost immediately after arriving. But it's the end of July and so hot that before we make it halfway my mother sits down on a wall and bursts into tears, two dark half moons of sweat soaking through the front of her dress. We take her back to the hotel and I wait in the lobby for half an hour, reading the translation of *The Odyssey* I've brought with me, but holding the book almost flat on my lap so that the Greek delivery men coming in and out don't see what a cliché I am. By the time my father comes back down it's past one and the streets outside are slippy with heat. Three times I skid in my cheap flip-flops, losing my temper the third time. He asks if I would rather go back to the hotel too and I say yes. My father calls the travel agent and moves our ferry tickets forward to the next day. We never make it to the Acropolis.

'It'll be cooler out there,' he promises. 'We'll be closer to the sea.'

'Was it really expensive?' I ask and he smiles.

'That's my problem, not yours.'

On the sailing, my mother and I are both seasick, spend hours spitting bile into candy-striped paper bags. My father buys cans of soft drinks and cups of tea, which we drink and then throw back up until eventually an elderly Greek man with refined mid-century English tells him that if he asks at the desk they'll probably give him some seasickness tablets. He does and within minutes we're cured.

'I should have thought of that sooner,' he keeps saying to my mother.

As promised, it is cooler on Naxos and that evening, after my mother and I have slept for a few hours, we go out for dinner. The light is low and pink and she's enchanted by the whitewashed buildings of the town.

'Let's start again,' I say brightly and they smile. In less than two weeks, the day after we arrive home, I'll get my exam results. Two months after that I'll leave for university in Cork, which is part of the reason for the trip, to spend some time together before I go. On the walk through town my father constantly offers to buy me things: an ice cream, a go on some rickety waltzers, one of the hundreds of rings a local woman has laid out on blankets on the footpath, the kind I know will turn my fingers green. I shake my head and he shrugs.

'Well, just be sure to make the most of it,' he says. 'You'll be counting every cent once you're a student.'

I've tried to convince my parents that, though the arts curriculum in Cork isn't the highest-ranked on the league tables, it is the best-suited to me because they offer courses you can't find anywhere else. They've always nodded along, asked a few polite questions – 'have you always been interested in Portuguese?' – but I know they can see the truth, that Cork suits me because it's the furthest away from them.

We go for a drink before dinner, a bottle of Greek white that tastes of apples. For a few minutes we chat and watch people going past: families, honeymooners, rich and loud Brits in their twenties. Then my father reaches into his pocket and takes out a pack of cards.

'I know it's been a long time,' he says, 'but do you remember how to play rummy?'

He's a good card player, from a card-playing family, and his shoulders relax as he shuffles, his hands light, birdlike. We play a few hands, sipping our drinks, enjoying being together without having to speak.

'It's really time you learned bridge,' my father says when it's his turn to deal again. 'It's just a shame there aren't four of us.'

Time catches then. Silence drops over the waterfront and I can hear my mother's shallow breath, can hear the cards falter and crash in my father's hands. I've read that in traveller families, when someone dies, they mark a day of mourning in every month of the first year. It seems like a good custom to me, a recognition that death doesn't visit your home briefly or leave it quietly. By the time we went on that holiday Ferdia had been dead a year and three months and still we were locked in the horror of it. Later that same evening, when a middle-aged restaurateur called endearments to my mother and I – 'Beautiful sisters, come for dinner' – my father turned and shouted at him to leave us alone, his lips wet with fury. The next day my mother bought herself a small leather coin purse in sunshine yellow but an hour later became convinced she'd been tricked into paying more than it was worth and threw it in the sea.

Still, for the first week I try to make the best of it, getting up early each morning to swim in the sea before breakfast, when the beach is quiet and the water cool. But then I get my period and go to bed for three days, long enough to finish *The Odyssey* and move on to *The Iliad*, not so much because I'm in pain as because I'm glad of the excuse and know neither of them would question it.

On the morning we're due to fly home, my mother starts to cry over breakfast and doesn't stop.

'We'll get a taxi,' my father says, but she goes on crying in the taxi, silently, the warm air from the open window whipping the tears diagonally from her eyes to her jaw. By the time we get to the airport her face is so swollen that the woman at the check-in desk keeps glancing nervously at her over the top of the passports. When my parents pick up their hand luggage and turn to go, she leans over the tall desk and grabs my shoulder.

'Is everything OK?' she asks in a whisper. 'Do you need any help?'

I smile and say no, everything's fine. I smile and nod at the security staff and at the woman who brings us our tea in the departure lounge and at the man who checks our boarding passes at the gate, until I feel as exhausted by smiling as my mother must by crying. I'm relieved when, sitting down on the plane, she leans across me and asks if my father could get her 'something small' from her carry-on.

He frowns. 'Are you sure?'

But then her eyes flood again and he stands and reaches into the overhead bin, passes her a blister pack of tiny pills. I watch her swallow one quickly, without water, and her eyes start to dull now, her face goes blank. I take out *The Iliad* and begin to read about the funeral games of Patroclus, wanting to finish the book before we get to Dublin. After a few minutes, before we've even heard the security briefing, I glance over at my mother and see that she's asleep, her head lolling over her right clavicle, her cheek hanging loose and open, exposing the pink of her inner lip.

I notice then, the way you might suddenly see a piece of furniture in a dark corner of the room and be surprised at having missed it, that I despise my mother. As her head droops closer to my shoulder I feel physically repulsed by it, want to force it away with the flat of my hand. But I'm trapped between her and my father, whose left arm reaches into my airspace as he frowns into his free newspaper. I despise them both and my disgust, once acknowledged, grows beyond reason or control in the four hours we spend on that plane. I stored up those feelings. I've lived off them for more than ten years.

# Chapter Eighteen

MY PARENTS' HOUSE IS DARK when I arrive back. I scan the windows, afraid they're still out. Though my anger has faded away now, I know I can't face a return to the hotel, to a drunker, less inhibited version of the gathering I left. But then, just as I lift my finger to press the bell, my father opens the door. I jump.

'Christ, Dad.'

He lifts a finger to his lips. 'Your mother's asleep.'

I frown, shuffle past him and turn into the dark sitting room, grateful for its stuffy, enveloping warmth. 'But it's only half-six.'

'She was very upset.' He speaks quietly, his hand on the door. 'Already, in the hotel. And then we got home and you weren't here . . .'

There's blame in the shape of his words and I narrow my eyes. 'So has she taken something?'

'That's her business,' he says, crossing the room to switch on the green desk lamp by his chair.

'Does she often pop pills in the afternoon?'

With a heavy rush of breath, he lowers himself into the chair. 'It's been an extremely difficult day,' he says. 'For you too, I know.'

I slide back on the sofa and fold my legs under me. The room is shadowy and unfamiliar in this light, the pictures clouded over, the china figurines glinting like spirits. After a minute, my father picks up a few sheets of paper from the bureau next to him, neatly folded into thirds.

'I'd written down a few words. Just welcoming everyone, remembering Ferdia. But I couldn't read them, in the end.'

I close my eyes briefly, resisting guilt. He'll have spent weeks working on it, I know, leaning in close to the desktop screen as he typed. A few little jokes, a heartfelt middle section, a simple toast to close.

'Can I have a look?' I ask.

He doesn't reply immediately, reaches for his glasses and studies his own words in silence. I watch him read and something in his body, closed and guarded, tells me that the words on the front sheet aren't about Ferdia, they're about me. Then he shakes his head and tucks the pages down the side of the chair.

'It's not important,' he says and my guilt turns to frustration at another door being closed in my face. I gather up my coat from next to me on the sofa, move to stand up, to go to bed myself.

'Hang on, Jay,' my father says quickly. 'Just wait, listen a minute.'

I pause. He sounds nervous. 'OK.'

'I think there's been some crossed wires. The thing is, when you told us, your mother and I, about your ... relationships, well, we took it as a confidence. We didn't think it was something to be shared with others.'

I stare at him, trying to gauge if he's being genuine, if it's possible for him to be so out of touch.

'I'm sorry, Dad, but the whole point of coming out is for people to know. What you're saying doesn't make sense.'

He flinches. 'Well, I apologise for not making sense. Maybe I'd have the chance to learn if you ever spoke to me.'

'I'm sorry, what?' The pitch of my voice lifts. 'You've never brought it up with me. You've never asked a question.'

'And when have I had the opportunity?'

'What does that mean?'

'You never come to see us.'

'Oh, come on.' I shake my head. It's so absurdly peevish. 'When have you come to see me?'

But now there's a long pause and when my father speaks again his voice is low and insinuating.

'Your mother came to see you. Do you not remember that?'

The breath goes out of me, I don't reply. It was six or eight months after I'd moved to London and I'd tried to dissuade her from coming. There would be nowhere for her to stay, I pointed out, no space in the small semi-detached house I was sharing with five other people. But she said she was happy to stay in a hotel, that she'd already booked the flights. We arranged to meet at Waterloo station early on Saturday morning, under the clock. But then I went out with my housemates the night before – to a pub, to a late bar, to a stranger's living room. I ignored my alarm when it went off, lay in the hungover stew of my sheets for another three hours, trying not to vomit, not even answering my mother's calls until after midday and then inventing some confusion about the dates. She had told me not to worry, though she had stood under the clock, she said (now breathless with relief) for more than two hours.

'That was a long time ago,' I tell my father, though my skin's crawling at the memory.

'You humiliated her. You can't imagine the state she was in when she came home.'

I try to remember the rest of the weekend. We went to a show in the West End, ate in an overpriced bistro off The Strand. She was effusive about everything: the Christmas lights, the festive buskers, the grey cashmere jumper she bought me in a small white shop in Seven Dials, which I destroyed the first time I washed it, chucking it into the machine with the rest of my clothes.

'She seemed fine to me. We had a nice time.'

'She didn't get out of bed for over a week.'

I stare at him, struggling to attach this new detail to the memory. It's not that I don't believe it; I've seen my mother take to her bed enough times to know that that part is true. But still a sound escapes from my throat, a strangled cough, because if it is true then what he's saying strikes at something fundamental in the way I understand my life, that I'm a victim of my mother's depressions and not a cause.

'Why didn't you tell me?'

'She asked me not to,' he says. 'She said you had seemed happy in London and she didn't want you to worry.'

I take a few deep breaths, the high ground slipping away from under me.

'Well, to be honest, this brings me back to my original question. About Mammy. About how . . . distressed she gets about things.'

'Well, she hasn't had an easy time of it,' he snaps back, though I've tried to be delicate. 'Losing a child—'

'Yeah, of course,' I say, cutting him off. 'But it didn't start when Ferdia died, did it?'

In the quiet that follows, we both look away. I press my fingers to my jaw, cracking it, trying to work out the tension. When I turn back to my father, he's doing exactly the same and I almost laugh, wondering how I've never noticed it before. Eventually, he stands up and goes to the drinks cabinet, takes out a bottle.

'Will you have one?' he asks.

'Sure,' I say, allowing him this diversion. 'A small one.'

The drinks he pours aren't small but it doesn't matter. It's good whiskey in the good crystal and, as we drink, I think of sitting in this room on the night before Ferdia went to Rome, remembering the weight of the silence, the almost unbearable pressure of all the things my father didn't know how to say. He stares into his glass now, like he did then, opening his mouth to speak and then closing it again. I say nothing, trying not to show any impatience, and eventually he starts to talk.

'After your mother and I got engaged, we went down to Roscommon to tell everyone. It was a Friday evening and we'd left straight from work but the traffic was so bad that we didn't make it until after eight. I was tired and a bit nervous and I suggested to your mother that we wait until the following day to make the announcement.' He smiles. 'But she was having none of it.'

I smile too, imagining the two of them sitting in the dark car outside my grandparents' house, whispered plans, my mother sliding the ring off her finger and hiding it in a secure pocket of her handbag.

'We'd managed to arrange it so that everyone was there. Your mother had already told Breda and asked her to come down too. Maura and Kathleen had dropped over for the evening, John and Damian stayed home from the pub. And you would not believe the volume when we told them. The shrieks that came out of your aunts.' He shakes his head, the small grin still on his face. 'It transpired they'd all been waiting for me to take the leap for quite some time. Your grandmother had two bottles of champagne in the fridge for months.'

He takes a sip of his whiskey.

'It sounds lovely,' I say and he nods.

'It was. A perfect moment, really, and just what your mother wanted.' He coughs. 'But then your grandfather asked if he could have a word with me in the other room. And everyone was whistling and jeering. But not your grandmother, I always remember that. She didn't laugh at all. And I thought to myself that they were traditional people and I hadn't asked their permission because your mother thought that was too old-fashioned, so I knew this was my chance to show your grandfather the kind of respect he'd anticipate.'

I nod. I can picture him so clearly, young, broad and serious, standing in the good sitting room with my grandfather, in the middle of the big Persian rug, their hands in their pockets and the air so cold – because no one ever goes in there – that their breath mists in front of them. The sounds from the other room are muffled by the heavy walls but you can hear the giggles as my mother passes the ring around and my aunts swirl it on their fingers and make wishes.

'And then, without any warning, he told me that your mother hadn't left the convent by choice, that they'd asked her to leave. An hysterical episode was how he described it.'

The scene is still in my mind and I watch as the younger man recoils then forces himself straight again.

'Dad,' I say. 'That's . . . that's awful.' I shake my head. 'What did he expect you to do?'

My father shrugs, tilting the liquid in his glass from side to side. 'I think he probably believed it was only fair. He was giving me the option of walking away.'

'And had Mammy told you anything before then?'

He sighs. 'Yes and no. She had told me she wasn't able to hack convent life, the rigour of it. I could see she felt ashamed, but it was very common for postulants to leave. It was a harsh life in those days. A lonely life. And, of course –' he glances up at me with a shy smile '– I was secretly very pleased that she wasn't a nun.'

I try to smile back, sensing that he wants me to reassure him somehow and then move on. But the details of the story are still developing in my mind.

'Can I ask what he meant by an hysterical episode?'

My father's face clouds over and he takes a drink. 'My understanding then,' he begins, enunciating every word very clearly, 'was that she tried to take her own life. Or at least that she was harming herself and they were afraid she might.'

He looks away. I suck in a loud breath and then another, filled with a burning childlike fear, with a desperate need to run upstairs and see my mother, to check that she's breathing. I want to jostle her awake and climb into her arms and make her promise never to leave me alone. My fingers shaking a little, I take a drink of whiskey. It goes down the wrong way. I splutter and cough. And yet, though it's shocking to hear it said out loud, this story doesn't actually land like a revelation. It has the leaden familiarity of something I've known my whole life, in my body if not my mind, in the terror that always accompanied my mother's illnesses.

'I've never told Margaret about that conversation,' my father goes on. 'And I'd appreciate it if you didn't either.'

'Has it been that bad again?' I ask. He shrugs.

'You know yourself. She has her ups and downs.'

'Has it been that bad again?' I repeat and he sucks in his cheeks, then puffs them out with a sigh.

'There was a very difficult period after you were born. You wouldn't remember, of course, but between them,

Breda and your grandmother were here for nearly the entire first year.' I nod, thinking of Granny's rough hand on my forehead, of how easily Breda read my mood in the days before the funeral. My father goes on: 'We had difficulties, you know, in the years before that.'

'You mean the miscarriages?' I say and he starts.

'You know about . . .?'

I nod but say nothing. I do know, though no one has ever actually told me. In this dim light it's easy to remember midnight mass each year, being pulled from the warm sitting room so late on Christmas Eve and transferred to a packed pew and the faint sweet scent of booze filtered through skin. When the mass ends, the moment the priest is down the aisle and out the door, my father jumps up and leaves. To warm up the car, he says. But the rest of us stay in place, my mother and Ferdia and I. The rows around us empty and the music stops. The singers pack up their stands and chat about their turkeys, and the church, so magical when it was filled with candlelight and carols just a few minutes before, seems commonplace in the glare of the big lights. Eventually, as the last festive shouts are carried off by the wind, we stand and walk to the back left corner where the candle racks are. My mother takes four coins from her purse and drops them, clanging, into the collection slot. With steady hands she takes four tealights and places them on the stand, lighting each one from the flame of the last. Then, the year that Ferdia died, it was five candles.

'Did she get any help?' I ask my father. He shakes his head.

'It wasn't really the thing.'

'Even when you were dealing with a new mother with a history of self-harm?' I keep my voice low but the edges of the words are sharp. I can feel my anger building again, gradually, like heat in coal.

'Things were different then,' my father says. 'Your grandmother was very insistent that it wouldn't be right for her.'

'And you were powerless, were you?' The anger is burning now. Like sun and rain, my grandmother had said about Ferdia and me, and everyone had let me believe it was my fault, that I was born difficult, bad-tempered, out of place. My father closes his eyes a moment and tips his head back.

'No, I wasn't. And I'm not proud of how I behaved, but I wasn't in a great way myself, if I'm entirely honest.' He looks up, with a quicksilver tilt of defiance. 'You're not the only person to ever lose a brother, you know.'

It's like a slap in the head. My father never talks about my uncle Ambrose and I was hushed anytime I asked about him as a child. I don't know what to say. But then he coughs and rubs his eyes.

'I don't know why I brought that up,' he says, seeming genuinely dazed. 'Sorry. What were you saying?'

'Well, I was just going to ask if Mammy's getting help now,' I say. 'But if you'd rather talk—'

'No,' my father cuts in. 'It's not something she wants. She has the tablets for when her sleep is bad.'

I'm confused now, the conversation seems to be cracking up, pulling us in different directions.

'But that's not how it works,' I say. 'If she's been having depressive episodes for more than forty years they're clearly not going to go away on their own.'

'I keep an eye on her,' says my father.

'Do you?' I ask softly. 'Because that's not how I remember it.' He tries to reply but I raise my voice over his. 'No, seriously. I don't remember you being here when she couldn't get up to bring me to school. Or when Ferdia had to go and sit by her bed and talk to her all evening. And I don't remember you "keeping an eye" on her when he died and I was here on my own for hours every day, afraid I'd find her hanging from the light fittings.'

At these last words, my father flinches hard, turns his head away and gestures for me to stop.

'Please, Jay,' he says, sounding like he's in pain.

'Please what?'

'Can't you understand that I had to work? Someone had to hold things together.'

'I was sixteen, Dad.' I'm close to tears now. 'And there was no one to look after me. I felt like I didn't exist.'

'Jacinta.' His voice is so low now it's almost a whisper. 'Let's keep this in perspective.'

'No, Dad, don't do that. This is my perspective. And you're still doing it, by the way. You're both so desperate to make Ferdia a saint that you've clearly never even considered what it's like for me.'

'Fine.' He almost spits it. Something has flipped and he's suddenly as angry as I've ever seen him. 'What is it like for you? Enlighten me.'

'Well, I'm having fucking nightmares for one thing, about his body being dragged out of the ground, about what it'll look like when they open the lid . . .' My voice is shrill with tears. It's painful even to speak these thoughts out loud but as I do I realise how consuming they've been, that all my feelings about the process are wrapped up with this fear, with the thought that one day I'll see a silicone-wrapped version of Ferdia on the news. 'Do you not worry about it, at all?'

My father seems to deflate then, his anger dissipating as quickly as it rose. He watches me for a minute, his lips pursed, his brow a little crumpled. Outside, a group of drunk young men are making their way down the street, roaring insults at one another. I take a final sip of my drink, feeling lightheaded. I haven't eaten since the handbag biscuit my mother gave me in the graveyard. My father picks up the bottle. I shake my head. He tops up his own glass then sits with it, quiet.

'It bothers you that much?' he says eventually and I look at him, thinking he'll answer his own question. But he's speaking in earnest, he really doesn't understand.

'Yeah, Dad, it does. I feel like the Church is stealing Ferdia from us. And I hate it.'

'You *hate* it?' He blinks a few times, so genuinely bewildered that I'm struggling to hold on to my anger. 'We just assumed you'd be proud.'

'Well, you could have asked me,' I say and sigh. 'Why can't we talk about anything like normal people? Why does everything need to be a secret?'

He's still looking confused. 'I don't think I know what you mean.'

'I mean everything that we've just been talking about. That I couldn't tell you I was queer and then you couldn't tell anyone else. That no one can ever just say that Mammy has depression and that maybe she needs help with it and that there's nothing actually wrong with that. That none of us could bring ourselves to have an honest conversation about Ferdia's cause. That I didn't get to see him before he died because I was so terrified of you finding out that I'd had a drink at a party. That I don't even know, since you brought it up, I don't even know what happened to Ambrose.'

I stop, breathing heavily. My father shakes his head.

'What do you mean?'

'I don't know how he died,' I say and my father blinks, incredulous.

'Really?'

I nod. All I know about my uncle comes from the photos in the big album in the study upstairs. Him and my father together on their bikes, in their football jerseys, in the uniform of their Catholic boarding school. They were Irish twins, Dad born eleven months after Ambrose, and they looked almost identical as children. But as they grew older my father became broad-based, sturdy, while his brother was tall and reedy, with a narrow face that was almost all smile. Except in the last picture of them together, where they're both frowning and serious. It was taken at my father's graduation from teaching college. He's in a navy suit while Ambrose wears a baggy brown jumper and torn bell-bottom jeans, his face covered with a long untidy beard.

My father takes a drink now, clears his throat. 'Ambrose died of a heroin overdose.'

'Oh,' I say, taken aback. This was never one of my theories and it doesn't fit with the image I've always had of my uncle. 'Had he been struggling with it for long?'

My father sighs. 'It's hard to know. We saw so little of him in the last few years, after he stopped coming home.'

'That must have been hard,' I say, thinking of how unhappy my father had been when I first moved to London.

'It was.' He clears his throat again. 'At one point your grandparents sent me over there to look for him, to try and talk some sense into him, and I brought your mother and your brother on the ferry.' His words are tumbling out, slightly disjointed. 'It was a big trip to take with a child in those days, but Ambrose loved Ferdia, lit up when he looked at him. So I thought that if anything might, you know, bring him back . . .'

He breaks off, shaking his head. We sit quietly for a minute or two.

'What happened?'

He takes a long breath, stretches his palms out on his lap and looks at them, then speaks so quietly that I have to lean in to hear. 'He was in such a bad way. So thin and sick and his eyes . . .' My father swallows. 'Just completely gone.'

'I'm sorry,' I whisper, shocked at how quickly he's transformed, sinking under the weight of this pain I've never seen before. 'That's awful.'

He looks into his glass. 'I was planning to bring him back to the hotel to see Ferdia but I just couldn't. I thought he'd frighten him. And, to be honest, I was afraid of . . . the risk, in those days. So I took him for a meal instead but he barely touched it. And I asked if I could see where he was living but he said no, that it was a long way out of town and he didn't want to take up my time. He was getting jumpy by then anyway and he said he had to leave and I said to him would you not just come home, let me bring you home and we can sort it out.' His voice wavers, comes close to breaking.

'What did he say?' I ask, and my father looks up at me, his eyes wide and frightened.

'He said: "I wouldn't go back to that haunted country if God Himself tried to drag me there."'

I feel a tugging in my chest, pulling tight with each beat of my heart. But I force myself to hold my father's eye.

'You don't know what he meant?'

'I do not.' He shakes his head. 'I never asked anyone else about it. And I never saw him again.'

We sit in silence for a long time before my father tips the last of his whiskey down his throat and looks at his watch.

'Dad, I'm sorry,' I burst out before he can move. 'But does that not . . . what happened to Ambrose, does it not make you question Ferdia's cause? Getting involved with the Church like this?'

He rubs his eyes. 'You're assuming a connection that might not exist.'

'It seems fairly credible.'

'It's easy to draw correlations with thirty years of hindsight, but we don't know.'

'We know it happened at schools like yours. And no one ever wanted to believe it was their child.' My father repeats his gesture from earlier, lifting his hand, signalling for me to stop. He looks bone-weary but I press on. 'And even if it wasn't Ambrose, it was thousands and thousands of other kids. How can you live with that? I mean, you didn't even want Ferdia to be a priest.'

There's a pause and my father frowns. 'What makes you think that?'

'I remember. You weren't happy about it, you tried to talk him out of it.'

His mouth twists into a smile. 'Nothing got past you, did it?' he says, and there's warmth in the question.

'So I'm right, then?'

He shrugs. 'I had my worries about it, yes. I wondered if for Ferdia the priesthood would be a sort of retreat from life. That and . . . well, the way things were then, I suppose I was afraid about what kind of life it would be for him. The way he'd be seen, the things he might encounter . . .'

'You're talking about clerical abuse,' I say, though I know he won't like it being made explicit. He nods heavily and I don't speak for a bit, letting the thought settle before I ask him what changed his mind.

'About what?' he says.

'Well, you didn't want him to be a priest but you do want him to be a saint. What happened in between?'

'Ferdia convinced me,' my father says, a smile flashing across his face and then fading. 'During his years in the seminary I came to understand the depth of his faith, the strength of it.' He looks at me. 'I really believe your mother and I have a duty to do this. It's not simple and you're right that it's not easy, but I believe we've been called.'

I feel uncomfortable but try to keep my voice even. 'Can you tell me why?'

'Because we were given a child so much better than ourselves, who shone so much brighter than anyone around him. There has to have been a reason.'

Bitterness floods my mouth then and, though I know it's so much less important than the real point I'm making about the crimes of the Church, I find myself muttering: 'You had two children.'

'Yes, of course,' he says.

'So when you say he was better and brighter than everyone else . . .' My voice catches. 'That includes me? You believe he was better than me?'

The silence that follows is like a skein of wool unravelling in the dark.

'We love you, Jacinta,' my father says eventually. 'You know that? We love you just as you are.'

I turn away. This is the first time my father has ever told me he loves me and it's filled my chest with a horrible shifting agony. After a minute or two, he hauls himself out of the chair. He's still wearing his brown suit trousers and white shirt, though he's undone the top two buttons and wisps of grey poke through.

'I understand that none of this is straightforward. And I will think about all that you've said, I promise. But right now I can't do any more. I'm sorry. I have to go to bed.'

I stare at him, fighting an urge to grab his sleeves, his trouser legs, to stop him from going. We've never had a conversation like this before and somehow I know that, once he leaves, we never will again.

'I can't be involved, Dad.'

'You mean with . . .?' He really is exhausted, his voice flat, his shoulders stooped.

'The cause. I just can't get behind it or give my testimony or any of it. I thought maybe . . . I came this weekend to try and understand it more, to get some clarity.'

'And you have?' he asks. 'Got clarity?'

'Yes,' I say. 'I thought that maybe I could do something to support it. Or I thought maybe I could stop it. Now I realise I can't do either. I'm sorry, I just don't think it's right.'

He sighs and murmurs something I can't quite hear, then reaches his arm out slowly and rests his hand on the top of my head. I'm surprised, but I close my eyes, feel the weight of his touch. We stay there for a long moment, frozen, before he straightens and walks out of the room.

# Chapter Nineteen

I WAKE EARLY the next morning. The room is cold and, but for its usual murmurs and clicks, the house is quiet. I stay under the covers for a few minutes, running through all that happened yesterday, feeling tender, over-exposed, the way you might walking through an unfamiliar airport the morning after a rough and frightening long-haul flight.

Already, the day's recurring floods of emotion seem strange and embarrassing, disproportionate to anything that actually happened. I feel foolish, like I've let something get the better of me, and awkward too, at having seen my parents lose control, at the shocking gush of my father's revelations. I get dressed in the jumper and jeans I was wearing when I arrived, less than two days ago, then quietly pack the rest of my things into my small backpack. Swinging it over one shoulder, I look around the empty room, drab and lustreless in the white morning light. The heads of a few lilies have dropped from their stems and they lie on top of the chest of drawers, beginning to crumple.

As I cross the landing, I rest my fingertips very lightly on Ferdia's door. But the gesture feels false. I lift them swiftly and continue down the stairs, skipping the noisy fifth step. Though I know it's cruel, I want to slip away without saying goodbye. I know that as soon as I see my father again the significance of last night's conversation will drain away, any sense of catharsis collapsing under the weight of making breakfast and acting like nothing has happened.

But still, reaching the hall, I hesitate. The chill of the morning has slid through the Chubb keyhole and the gaps around the front door. I take out my reusable cup, deciding to make myself some tea, to delay a few minutes before facing the cold. It's early still, before seven. But the kettle is old, it rattles and gushes, waking my mother and also drowning out the sound of her footsteps on the stairs, so that I jump when she speaks from the doorway.

'Are you leaving already?'

I close my eyes a moment, breathe, turn to face her. She's wearing a white hotel dressing gown, turned grey after too many washes, and she has the drowsy, persecuted look of a newly woken child. 'I thought your flight wasn't until this afternoon.'

'They moved it. I only got the email late last night and I didn't want to wake you.' I turn back to the counter, pour boiling water over the teabag. The lie is so blatant that I haven't bothered to put any energy behind it. 'Are you feeling any better?'

She rubs her eyes. 'I thought we'd have some time together today. A chance to talk.'

I shrug. 'They didn't give a reason for the change.'

'Can I drive you to the airport at least?'

I shake my head. 'That's OK. You had a long day yesterday.'

'But I want to speak to you.' She steps further into the room. I lift the teabag from the cup and, holding it with my fingernails, open the cupboard under the sink and drop it in the bin. What drew me into the kitchen was the thought of tea like my mother makes it, strong and milky, but now there isn't time and I know I shouldn't have bothered, should have gotten out while I could.

'I spoke to Dad,' I say briskly, clipping the plastic lid onto the cup and taking three quick steps to the kitchen door before I turn. 'Last night, when I got home. We talked a lot of things over.'

My mother's eyes fill with tears then. She sags slightly and I expect her to crumple. But instead she places her palm flat on the table and draws herself a little taller, the dressing gown wrapped close around her slight knobbly body.

'You know, I have things I'd like to talk about too,' she says, her voice thin but each word carefully weighted. It takes me a moment to understand what's happening, to recognise that she's calling me out, not as a cranky child or a sulky teenager, but as a woman who should know better than to wave another woman aside. I'm thrown by this sudden shift in our positions and I don't know what to say. So I keep standing in the door, staring, stupidly conscious of the cup of tea in my hand, and of the fact that I didn't make one for her. My chest tightens. The prospect of another day like the one we've just had, filled with messy, overspilling emotion, is too much for me. I feel trapped in this house again, just like I did when I was a teenager. But now I know the alternative, know I can escape into the calm and control of my own company, my own life.

'I've got to go,' I say eventually, my voice hoarse. 'I'm sorry.'

And my mother does crumple then. Her pale knees poke out of her dressing gown as she sinks into a chair and, walking down the hall, I can hear her sobbing, can hear my father moving upstairs as I pick up my bag. I speed up, pulling the door hard behind me, walking quickly through the garden and down the street and around the corner, not letting myself slow or stop, trying not to think. The streets are quiet, almost deserted, and I have a strange temptation to scream at the curtained windows, to shake my one-time neighbours from their sleep, to punish them for their indifference after Ferdia died, for the way they always blithely go about their own lives no matter what's happening in ours.

I walk even faster, my rucksack rising and falling with each step, a slick of sweat spreading across my back. There's no reason to hurry. If my parents wanted to follow me, they could jump in the car and beat me to the bus stop. But I know that they won't. Because to people like us, running away – to England, to the pub, to your bed – is more than just a tradition, it's an institution symbiotic with the family itself, necessary to the functioning of society, insulating us from the realities we're not prepared to face.

When I reach the bus stop, there are already four people waiting, students, their padded coats bright against the dawn-grey sky. I join them under the shelter, my breath coming quick, my skin scratchy with indecision, with the possibility of turning back. But the bus comes on time, small and red, its lights cheerful. I get on and pay, feeling as though I'm going on a school tour, sitting alone by a window near the front and curling inwards so that the others can't see the bright tears that flood down my cheeks as we pull away, so they won't know that I'm frightened to leave my mother. They're all so young, I think defensively, they probably don't even realise that anyone can die at any moment. The last glimpse I ever had of Ferdia was through the back window of a taxi. Or it should have been. But I missed it. I was fussing with my bags.

And Ferdia ran away too, I remind myself, as the bus passes through Leixlip village. The first few shops have opened now, and a scattering of people are out walking with their buggies and dogs, newspapers tucked under their arms, cartons of eggs. From the time he could walk, my mother told me, he would find places to hide, disappearing into wardrobes and bushes and under beds, a tiny anchorite searching for a cave. He had a mystical experience in one of the kitchen cupboards, she insists. While she was frying sausages he felt a hand resting on the crown of his head, was surrounded by warmth and light. And that was where it all began. In retreat. By the time he escaped to Rome, what did any of us really know about him?

I think of my conversation with Brian, of my quiet hope that Ferdia had been secretly fucking men all along. I think of him hugging Paul, the boy with the sick mother, or holding an old woman's hands as she rattled towards death, or shouting at football on TV, or watching porn, or dancing, or losing his temper, or sleeping. I want to crawl inside my brother's skin and know what these moments felt like, in his muscles, his bones. Already, the saintly stories are colonising Ferdia, overriding my memories, like a film adaptation of a favourite novel, scrubbing out his voice, his smell, the strange intensity of his eyes when he looked at you. I want there to be something that only I know, some mystery, some part of my brother that I can unfold now like an old letter, or hold close to my skin like a pearl. My brother. Mine. Not a being made of light but a living boy, a body like the rest of us, made of flesh and blood and sex and hunger and subject to death and decay, yes, and before his time, and missed every day, but isn't that the beauty of it?

When we hit the M50 I take out my phone. I want to text Lindsay, to ask if we can meet. I don't want to delay, don't want to let the feeling slip away, the clarity about what matters. I can see now that after Ferdia died, when my mother took to her bed and my father disappeared into his work, I held fast to that night in the starlight with Aisling, to the queer, flickering promise of another life. It was what saw me through the worst years, reassuring me that like a light tracing a dark coastline, I was going somewhere.

But with my phone in my hand, I wonder again if I should call my mother. There would be time for her to follow me. We could have coffee in the terminal, take advantage of the strange liminal freedom you get in airports. I stare at the screen. I put it away. Better to use that space for myself, to buy a paperback and drink coffee alone in the departure lounge, watch dozens of planes take off and land. It'll be out of my hands once I'm through security. The decision will have been made.

And still I dawdle when I get off the bus, hovering on the footpath, getting in the way of bleary Americans just off the red-eye, their voices strained and tired, their suitcase wheels rattling like gunfire across the lanes of concrete that were once green fields.

*

Though it's Sunday, the chapel is empty and still. Outside, the low clouds are beginning to burn off and the morning sun glints through the windows in green and blue. I walk to the votive stand, digging in my wallet for coins. I light one candle and set it down, my brother's face burning bright in my memory. And then, slowly, I light four more, trying to feel what each of them means to me, but really just thinking of my mother, of all she gave, sharing again and again the gifts of her body. And for what?

I reach into my pocket, feeling for the weight of my phone. It hasn't passed yet, whatever strange power has filled this weekend, as though Ferdia's anniversary is already his feast day, his carnival, when normal rules don't apply and barriers wear thin, where the dead draw near and the living are closer too, easier to reach. The anger I've cultivated for so many years, the disgust for my parents that I've cosseted and nourished, that's driven me forwards and outwards, is draining away. I've seen them too clearly this year, their hopes and disappointments, their scars.

I shake my head, turn to face the empty church. 'What would you do?' I call softly into the quiet.

And then I wait, my heart loud in my ears. I sit down in a pew and stay there, silent, for nearly an hour.

But my brother doesn't respond.

# Part Three

# Chapter Twenty

THEY SAY THAT Matt Talbot was a well-known character in early-century Dublin, but when he collapsed and died on his way to mass one Sunday morning in 1925, none of the bystanders knew who he was. An ambulance was called, though there was nothing to be done for the heart failure, and he was brought to Jervis Street Hospital where the sisters, undressing the body so it could be washed, found the chain wrapped around his waist and the cords twining his arms and legs.

Born in the North Docks in 1856, Matt was the second son of twelve and left school young to work as a messenger boy for a wine merchants. That was where his trouble began. He started sampling the product, then visiting various public houses with his brother and friends. By thirteen he was known as a hopeless alcoholic, the kind who sold his own boots to pay for drink, who'd steal a fiddle from a blind fiddler. But then, somewhere in his twenties, after waiting a whole night outside the pub and finding no one willing to stand him a pint, he took himself to a priest, made his first confession in years, and pledged to go three months without a drink. After that, he upped the pledge to six and after six took it for life. A great triumph, in the eyes of the Church, a show of courage, abstinence and repentance, and an example to sinners and drinkers everywhere. They didn't mind that he starved himself, or that he slept on a wooden board and wore the chains and cords under his clothes, kneeling for hours each night on the bare floors of his small room, to pacify his longings and mortify his flesh. All of that seemed completely fine and normal to the archbishop of Dublin who opened a sworn inquiry into Matt Talbot's life in 1931. And to Pope Paul VI who in 1975 declared him Venerable. And to Pope John Paul II who, as a young man, wrote a biography of Matt Talbot in Polish and was, they say, very keen to beatify him. But unfortunately, nearly a century after his death, Matt has yet to come good with a miracle and his candle is starting to flicker. Ireland has changed. It's been voted on and we're compassionate now, modern, not interested in those old austerities. This is the risk with causes for canonisation, that the process is so long and arduous that would-be saints fall out of step with the times. A reputation for holiness might be maintained for fifty years but waver before it reaches a hundred, in that strange darkening window when the last of the people who knew you get old and die.

But then, suddenly, it can all turn around, like it does for Matt Talbot in the summer of 2018 when Pope Francis visits Our Lady of Lourdes Church on Sean McDermott Street in Dublin and prays in front of his bones, singling the holy drinker out among all the Irish saints and candidates as worthy of veneration.

Reading about it, I try to convince myself that the reason I'm so livid is that Sean McDermott Street is also home to an old Magdalene Laundry, which kept operating longer than any of the others, only closing its doors in 1996. And while Francis has been willing to stretch his schedule to include a drive by Matt's tomb, he wouldn't cross the street to pay his respects to the women who were tortured and died in his Church's name. Of course, my solidarity is with them, and with all the survivors and women and queers who are protesting the visit, who embarrass the bishops by booking thousands of tickets to attend mass in the Phoenix Park and then leave the seats empty, joining a demonstration on O'Connell Street instead.

Because by now I've picked a side. I've announced to my family, and to myself, that I don't believe in the process of canonisation. I've written to Father Richter to tell him that I don't agree with the bishops using my brother's name and memory to paper over their own history, their own crimes. And so, if the whole cause is a charade and a con, it shouldn't matter to me that the pope has chosen to honour someone else instead of Ferdia. But the truth is, I'm furious. I open the livestream of the final mass of his visit and am glad that Francis, personally, has been humiliated, that only 125,000 people have shown up in a rainy field laid out for 500,000.

'Do you think it's a good idea to watch that?' Lindsay asks from behind her book. I look up, surprised. We're lying in her bed, our legs touching, but I've angled the laptop away from her to hide what's onscreen.

'It's a free country,' I say and she smiles, shuffles across the mattress to watch with me, stroking the back of my head as the camera pans across old women waving Vatican flags and children in sodden gold baseball caps.

'More than a million people were there in 1979,' I say. 'In the same spot.'

She drops her arm around my shoulders, her fingertips tracing patterns on my upper arm as onscreen a bearded priest valiantly fires jokes into the drizzle, trying to warm up the crowd.

'Your parents are there?'

'Yeah.'

I close my eyes and focus on the feeling of having her near me, trying to ignore the image of my mother and father sat near the front in their good clothes and plastic ponchos, my mother's joints complaining in the damp. On the evening I got back from Ireland I came straight to Lindsay's flat and, like a needy man in a film, told her I loved her and wanted to be with her.

As we lay together later that night, she began asking more about Ferdia, about the material reality of him. How tall was he? What did his voice sound like? Could he dance?

'Surely he didn't eat spaghetti the same chaotic way as you?' she said, over a meal we'd thrown together from her cupboards. 'He'd have been kicked out of Italy.'

There are some questions I know the answer to without thinking, and others that I never knew the answer to and never will. And then there are some that, with a little thought, I can work my way through. Could he drink coffee in the evenings?, asks Lindsay, and I remember a specific meal when he was home one Christmas, in the only restaurant in my grandparents' local town, where he had ordered an espresso after dinner and then turned slightly green when he tasted it.

'But he didn't say anything,' I tell her. 'He'd have drunk a pint of dirty coffee sooner than embarrass my grandparents by complaining.'

She nods, says that makes sense. Slowly, our conversations are growing into something more than an exchange of information. Ferdia is becoming a real figure in our life together, someone Lindsay knows. She starts talking to his picture on Liverpool match days, convinced the club should make him patron saint.

Onscreen, they switch to a clip of the 1979 mass, the field bathed in sun and dark with people. I shake my head.

'My parents were there that day too,' I say. 'When my mum was first pregnant. Isn't it kind of impossible to get your head around? That so much can change in the span of, like, an ordinary adult life. That you can see whole worlds fall apart.'

'Yeah.' Lindsay squeezes my shoulders. 'But they'll be all right, you know? Christians actually love to be persecuted, same as gays. It's easier to feel elite and glamorous when the majority hate you.'

I laugh, shutting the laptop as I lean in to kiss her. 'Can we go out somewhere? I could use a distraction.'

She nods and jumps out of bed. She's wearing a grey tank top and nothing else and I watch as she picks up her clothes from around the room. She's been cycling a lot this summer and her legs are tanned and muscly, her upper thighs and ass white.

'Is it weird how obsessed I am with your hamstrings?'

She turns around and smiles, letting go of her armful of clothes as she crosses the room. Then she steps onto the bed and drops to kneel across my hips. She feels warm and strong and, although we've already fucked twice today, slightly wet.

'I thought you wanted to go out.' She rests a hand lightly on the right side of my neck, just below the jaw. My breath catches and I lift my hips into her. 'Don't you?' She presses very slightly harder, begins to move her hand down my throat. 'I was planning to take you for a nice walk in the park, buy you a lemonade.'

I shake my head.

'What do you want then?' Her hands are at my chest now, palms barely grazing my nipples.

'I want you.'

'You want me to . . .?'

'I want you to fuck me.' She grins and presses down hard. 'Please,' I breathe. 'I want you to fuck me, please.'

Lindsay goes back across the room to the chest of drawers and takes out her strap-on. I touch myself softly as I watch her put it on, looking solemn and reverent.

'Move that,' she says, nodding at my laptop, and very briefly I think again of the crowd in front of the white cross, the sad mass in the rain. But then Lindsay is back on the bed and telling me to kneel and all that's left in the world is the grip of her hand in my hair and her fingers against me, slick and cold. When she slides into me, my eyes water and I let myself cry out. I've been surprised by how this second act of our relationship has gone, how more honesty about our lives has flooded everything – meals, jokes, sex – with a new richness. The wildest things flash through my head when she fucks me like this. I want her to marry me, to buy me houses or cars. 'Can we get a dog?' I imagine myself saying as she adjusts her hips to improve the angle and, noticing me grin, she tells me, between short breaths, to stop laughing. But I can hear a smile in her voice too. And then we're both laughing and she's moving into me harder and my body fills with light and air, is expansive as an empty cathedral.

Lindsay drops to my side and I slide my hand below the dildo and feel her grind against it, already close. I love her like this, fully in her body. Her eyes are closed but she wraps a hand around the back of my head. She comes quietly, looking vulnerable and fierce.

'Thanks,' she says, a minute later and I ruffle her hair with still-damp fingers.

'No, thank *you*.'

We laugh again. There are hours of daylight still stretching out in front of us. I kiss the top of her head as she drifts into a nap, certain we have nothing but time.

# Chapter Twenty-One

IT'S NINE MONTHS LATER that I run into Brian Fallon, at the junction between Stoke Newington Church Street and High Street. We're both walking quickly, heads down, and we nearly collide. I laugh when I realise who it is. I'm excited to see him. It's the May Day bank holiday and he's dressed for a day off, endearing in a pair of slouchy black tracksuit bottoms and green sliders over yellow socks. But when we hug, his arms are loose and he lets go quickly.

'Where are you off to?' he asks, and I launch into a story about Lindsay's birthday, which is coming up, and the Clarice Lispector novel I'm on my way to buy for her. The weekend has been warm and sunny. I've just been swimming in the reservoir nearby and I feel fresh and happy, enthralled with my own little world.

'Have you read it?' I ask brightly, because Brian has read everything.

'Yeah, it's good,' he says. But his voice is flat and he doesn't look at me when he speaks.

'What about you?' I say, slowing my words down. 'Doing anything exciting?'

He shakes his head. 'Just needed a bit of air.'

I don't reply immediately and I watch Brian in the pause. There's a tremor in the air around him, a dullness in his features. I want to ask if he's all right. But before I can formulate the question he notices me noticing and laughs, trying to cover it up. 'Tristram has decided to re-curate the garden. I've been lifting pots around all morning.'

I laugh too. 'Well, I could walk with you for a while, if you'd like the company?'

Brian hesitates, glances at his watch. I try to smile reassuringly. 'It's not a problem if it doesn't suit.'

'No,' Brian says. 'No, of course that would be great. How about you go get your book and I'll grab us some coffees? I'll meet you at the gates of the cemetery in ten minutes and we can walk in there?'

I agree, happy to have the chance to spend time with him. Though we stayed in touch after our first meeting, I haven't seen Brian in months, not since near the end of last summer, when he invited Lindsay and I over for a barbeque.

I'd felt strangely nervous about it, as though I was introducing her to a family member. I baked cookies but threw out the first two batches because I didn't think they were good enough. Then I slept badly the night before and snapped at Lindsay while I was getting dressed, because she seemed half-hearted when I asked if I looked OK. And then, inevitably, we had a lovely time. The day was hot and Brian and Tristram waltzed around in baggy shirts and espadrilles, serving us icy glasses of mint, lime and soda – 'not to be referred to as *nojitos* under any circumstances,' insisted Tristram, who was older and camper than I expected.

Brian and I had agreed that the afternoon would be purely social, without any saint talk, and we only spoke about Ferdia if he came up naturally, like when Tristram and Lindsay got into a discussion about the medical use of LSD and Brian told us that, in their second year of seminary, Ferdia had become briefly obsessed with finding some for the two of them, believing it would help them achieve spiritual transcendence.

'But then he backed out at the last minute, the poor wee lamb. Decided he was close enough to God already.'

We all laughed and, for a moment, it felt that Ferdia was really a part of the day, planning to come along and meet Lindsay too, just running late, maybe, or gone to get more ice. But as our laughter died down, Tristram reached casually from his chair and took Brian's hand. Brian squeezed it and there was a shadow in the glance they shared. And then Tristram went to check the vegetables on the grill and Brian refilled our glasses. The moment passed.

He's waiting for me now when I get back to our meeting place, reading the information plaque outside the cemetery gate.

'Did you get it?' he asks, handing me my coffee.

I lift the zebra-striped paper bag with the book inside. 'I did, thanks be to God.'

We pass through the gates, watching our feet on the uneven flagstones.

'What date's her birthday?' asks Brian.

'The tenth,' I say. 'A Taurus.'

'Like himself.'

I nod. Ferdia's thirty-ninth birthday was two days ago. I've been thinking about him more than usual, and I suppose Brian has too.

'Do you come here often?' he asks and I look around. It's a garden cemetery, large and so dense with growth that already, just a few steps from the entrance, we're in a dim greenworld, the noise of the city absorbed by the trees, the air mulchy and organic. Everywhere, tilting headstones are being claimed back by nature: ivy crawling across their faces, a shag pile of old leaves breaking down at their feet.

'I do, actually. I find it so peaceful.'

'Me too.'

We walk on, the dirt track soaking up the sound of our footsteps. Every few metres, narrow desire paths spiral off through the undergrowth.

'It's a shame they can't take new burials,' says Brian softly. 'I wouldn't say no to a spot.'

'You wouldn't want to be buried in Donegal?' I ask. 'Bás in Éirinn?'

He shakes his head. 'I might consider having my ashes scattered off Errigal on a windy day, but not a chance I'd let them put me under Irish ground.'

He probably intends it as a joke but it lands heavily and I think of my uncle Ambrose. They did bring him home after he died in London, buried him in an empty family plot, where his parents joined him within a few years. I shiver, suddenly wishing we were back out in the sunlight.

'Any update from your folks?' Brian asks eventually. 'On the process, I mean.'

'Not really,' I say. My parents and I are speaking more regularly now, but they've respected my decision to step away from the cause, giving me occasional highlights rather than a running commentary. 'Though I did get another call from Father Richter a few months ago, looking for any emails or letters I have. So I guess they're still going through his writings?'

'Yeah, that makes sense,' says Brian. 'He contacted me too.'

'God loves a trier,' I say and laugh. But Brian doesn't join in, just stares darkly at the ground in front of his feet.

'He's some prick, isn't he? Richter.'

I stop, startled by the venom in his voice. I've never seen Brian in a mood like this before and it's hard work. To avoid answering, I step off the path to look more closely at a monument, an elaborate angel carving on top of a plinth. Amelia Buxton was her name, and she fell asleep (as the stone puts it) just short of her twentieth birthday. Her little sister is also buried in the plot, having died the same year, aged eleven months.

After a minute, I hear Brian's steps in the undergrowth, stopping just behind me.

'Where were their miracles?' I ask, gesturing at the inscription. But this joke fails too. My voice sounds bitter. I feel bitter. The energy between Brian and I is strange and morbid.

He steps forward now and runs his long fingers across the mossy grooves of the angel's wings. 'My problem with the doctrine of miracles is that they take the form of people being saved from death.' He turns to me. 'But it doesn't serve us to treat death as a catastrophe, does it? As something we should all hope to be saved from. That's the promise of the pharmaceutical industry, it shouldn't be the promise of the Church.'

Though he's looking in my direction, his voice is low, his eyes unfocused, as though he's speaking more to himself than to me. He turns from the grave and starts to walk again, his sliders scuffing the dust, his empty coffee cup dangling from his left hand. When I catch up I take it from him and drop it in a bin.

'Are you all right, Brian?' I ask.

'I've always believed I'd have to pay,' he says, as though it's an answer to my question.

'What do you mean?'

He stares upwards, through the canopy and into the clouds. 'For what I did to Ferdia.'

My throat constricts and I swallow hard. This is territory we've always avoided and I'm shocked that he's brought it up so bluntly. For a moment, I wonder if he might be drunk.

'That's not how it works,' I say eventually.

'But it's how it feels,' he snaps. 'A life for a life. You don't realise how deep that instinct is until you come up against it.' His voice cracks and he coughs, angrily. 'And all those years when I was drinking and using, all I wanted was to die. It felt like what I deserved.'

'Brian,' I say softly.

'And then in recovery, one of the hardest things to accept was that actually there's no such thing as cosmic justice. I just have to fucking live.'

There's a long pause.

'No one ever blamed you,' I say tentatively, but immediately I know it's the wrong thing.

'Yes, I know. But that only made it worse. You want an angry family, a crusade for vengeance. And instead everyone was just so charitable.'

I say nothing, not knowing what else I can say. From the beginning, my parents' response to the accident was so consistent that I've never even thought of it as a choice. Ferdia hit his head playing football, they tell people, rarely even acknowledging that there was a second person involved. Just one of those awful things, they say, and I feel suddenly proud of them.

'I guess I hadn't thought of it that way,' I say to Brian.

He nods, his jaw clenched. I check the time on my phone. The conversation seems beyond redemption and I'm trying to figure out an excuse to leave. There's an older couple walking towards us now, their grey lurcher galloping around ahead of them. Brian stops to rub the dog's head and cradles its face between his palms. The owners stop too and Brian tells them that his grandfather trained greyhounds. After they move on, his gait seems a little looser. He runs a hand through his hair and sighs.

'You've caught me at a bad moment, Jay,' he says. 'I'm sorry. I was actually just on my way to a meeting when I ran into you.'

'That's OK,' I say, feeling a rush of relief that he's said something and that his mood isn't because of me. 'I'm sorry, I should have just let you go.'

'No, not at all.' He pauses. 'I've actually been meaning to get in touch with you, to be honest.'

'Oh yeah?' I say and he nods but doesn't say anything more for a few seconds. He pulls a hand over his eyes and takes a deep breath.

'The thing is ... well, I wanted to tell you that I am now considering giving my testimony.'

I turn to stare at him. 'Sorry, what?'

'I've told Matt Richter I'll think about it.'

'But why?' I stutter on the words. 'You were the person who convinced me to have nothing to do with it.'

'I know,' he says. 'I know I did. But you're a blank slate to them, they don't have anything on you. Whereas for me it's different. I've already said things about Ferdia, you know? I've put things down in writing that ... well, I don't want them to be used out of context.'

I shake my head. 'I don't understand what you're talking about.'

Brian walks to a bench and sits down, resting his head very briefly in his hands. I stop too, but stay standing. My heartbeat is vibrating strangely through my arms and legs. He looks up at me.

'So this is probably something else I should have told you before. But I think I hoped you already knew.'

'OK.' I'm on high alert now. Brian clears his throat.

'So, you know that I was there the whole time Ferdia was in hospital, right? I arrived with him in the ambulance and put out the word to your parents, to everyone?'

'Yeah, I know that.'

'OK.' His voice is soft. 'And do you know that when I spoke to the rector of the Irish College, I insisted that he had to find a cardinal to administer the sacrament of the sick?'

I frown. 'I knew there was a cardinal there, yeah, but I didn't know who arranged it.'

'Well, it was me. I was adamant we had to find someone. It took until the next day but I kept chasing it.' He stops and looks up at me. 'Do you know why? Do you understand what I'm saying?'

I pause, trying to figure it out. I shake my head and he takes another deep breath.

'In its teaching, the Church holds that saintly bodies can have a particular quality at the time of their deaths. You might have heard of it – the odour of sanctity?'

'I think I've heard the phrase,' I say, wanting to understand.

'Historically it was understood as an actual smell, usually of flowers. But over time that was refined a bit and it was more commonly understood to mean a state of grace that could present itself in different ways, maybe through a smell, but more commonly through the appearance of light around the dying person's body.'

'So it's like incorruptibility?' I say. 'A physical indicator of holiness?'

'Exactly that,' he says, then pauses again. I feel stupid now, can tell that there's something he's pleading with me to understand without his having to say it explicitly. He looks towards the treetops, shakes his head, then looks back at me and speaks very slowly.

'And if the odour of sanctity were to be observed by a very authoritative figure – a prince of the Church, say – that would probably carry a lot of weight in any future cause for beatification or canonisation.'

The breath squeezes out of me as he says this, like I'm being crushed by a crawling truck.

'That's why you called for a cardinal?' My voice is hushed.

'Yes.'

The cemetery feels claustrophobic now, the overgrowth sinister and suffocating. I wonder why we've come here, why I didn't leave earlier.

'You started all of this?'

'It might have happened anyway—' he begins, but I scoff and turn my back to him, not wanting him to see the emotion in my face.

'OK, yes,' says Brian. 'I told the head of the Irish College that I believed Ferdia was dying in the odour of sanctity. He arranged for the cardinal to come and perform the sacrament. The cardinal expressed his agreement. And then the Dublin archdiocese asked us both to confirm what we'd seen in writing.'

'Did my parents know this?' I ask.

A silence. I turn around again, Brian is leaning forward on the bench, his elbows on his knees. He nods, and I feel both hot and cold, furious and stupid. Of course they knew. And of course they didn't tell me.

'I know it's a lot to process,' Brian says.

'I don't even know how it would occur to you to make those calls,' I say, the words tumbling out fast and high-pitched. Brian has been my ally in all this, the person I've trusted most, and now I have to deal with this new image of him, not sitting by Ferdia's bedside but pacing around the hospital on his phone. Strategising. 'I find it pretty sinister, to be honest.'

Brian nods and rubs his eyes. 'I can appreciate that.'

'Well then why the fuck did you do it?'

I don't intend to shout, but two women in the distance look towards us. Brian straightens up, gazes directly into my face.

'It was because I believed it,' he says quietly.

I drop on to the bench then and press the heels of my hands into my eye sockets. He reaches out to touch my back but I jerk away.

'Jay,' he says, his voice low and even. 'I am sorry. I thought your parents would have said . . .'

'Well, that's hardly a safe bet, is it?' I mutter. And then, after a second, my own sarcasm makes me smile, draws me back from the edge. I sit up. Brian is watching me, his face full of worry.

'I was absolutely frantic that night, you know? I was really trying to keep a handle on it. For your mother and father, at the very least, I wanted to be calm. But underneath, I was hysterical. Seeing Ferdia like that . . . when they brought him out of surgery . . .'

His voice disintegrates into a sob. I don't react immediately. Though I do feel sorry for Brian, I'm also jealous that he got to be there, to see Ferdia at the end. My palms are slippy with it. But I force myself to reach out and touch his shoulder, and he smiles at me through his tears.

'It's hard to know what to make of it all now,' he says. 'But I swear I can still see it so clearly. I can see him lying there, surrounded by light.'

'But you were in a pretty unsteady state,' I say. 'You've just told me so.'

'I know that.' He nods. 'But that doesn't necessarily mean that I was wrong. If a client came and told me this story I wouldn't dismiss the reality of what they'd seen. I wouldn't pathologise it.' He pauses. 'There's a lot I don't understand, Jay. But like I told you before, if there is such a thing as a saint, religious or secular, I believe that Ferdia was one.'

'So is that your testimony?' I ask, trying to keep the harshness out of my voice. 'You're backing him for canonisation now?'

'No, of course not,' Brian says. 'I just feel that since I was the one who started it all, I don't get to turn my back. And I'm afraid that if they don't hear from either of us that they'll get away with changing Ferdia's story, that they'll turn him into some kind of hyper-conservative.'

'Yeah,' I say. 'I worry about that too. But you told me that it wouldn't matter what I said or did, that they'd do what they wanted with Ferdia's story and all that would change is that I'd never be able to get any closure.'

Brian closes his eyes and sighs. 'Well, do as I say, not as I do, I suppose.'

I don't reply. I feel tired beyond possibility now, every part of my body sagging under the weight of the next. Just as on the afternoon of Ferdia's funeral, some force is both dragging me towards Brian and forcing me away, as though some time long ago we were hit by an enormous wave and have been tumbling together towards the shore ever since. I press my hands to the wood of the bench, ready to stand, to walk away. But in the same moment Brian heaves in a terrible, gasping breath and begins crying like a child, wailing almost. I freeze, shocked, a little scared, embarrassed.

'Fuck, I'm sorry,' Brian whispers between sobs.

'It's OK,' I say. 'It's OK.' And as I speak something rises up behind me, like a surging current or a gust of wind. I slide along the bench and wrap myself around Brian as best I can: one arm over his shoulders, another hooked across his ribs, my chin pressed awkwardly into his neck. He sobs harder. I feel my own eyes fill and hold on to him more tightly. He turns towards me, buries his face in my shoulder, and we stay like that a long time, clinging to one another and crying, paying no attention to the people who walk by and stare.

When we finally let go and look into each other's faces, we both laugh immediately, rubbing our eyes like children who can't remember now what they were so upset about. We stand up and start to walk, following the track to the main entrance. I want the path to stretch on longer.

I want more time. But the trees are thinning out over our heads now, the noise of the traffic surging through the gates to meet us. We stop just inside the threshold and face one another.

'Maybe run into you again sometime?' I say. Brian nods. We can both see that there's no other way, not yet. The pain is too much stronger than anything else we might share. We hug, swift and close, and then Brian pulls his hoodie tight around him and walks away, skipping quickly through a gap in the traffic, blending into the stream of people on the far side of the street.

# Chapter Twenty-Two

THE CROWD ON THE PLATFORM at Earl's Court goes through seven or eight cycles before my mother arrives. A few more years have passed and a week ago she emailed to say that she was going to Birmingham for a meeting but that, if I was free, she could fly into Heathrow and meet me for lunch before travelling on. Though I can't see much evidence that Ferdia's cause is progressing, it's keeping her busy at least. During lockdown she appeared at more than forty virtual parish halls in Britain and North America and, now that things are opening up, they've started inviting her back in person.

As each train pulls in, I stare through the windows, trying to catch a glimpse of her. She should have arrived about ten minutes ago and I'm afraid that she's gotten lost, though I've tried to make it easy by coming to meet her directly off the Piccadilly Line. She gets nervous at airports and on public transport, and was always much happier when we took our holidays in Ireland or Wales, where we could all just get in the car, drive for several hours on the correct side of the road and then get out somewhere breathtakingly beautiful. She barely even made an exception for Ferdia; we only visited him once in Rome, a few months before he died. I still cringe when I think of arriving into Ciampino, where the luggage was slow in coming and the staff were tetchy, refusing to speak to my father in English when he asked what was going on. He got flustered and then angry. Neither of them cope well with the small inconveniences of being abroad.

A rush, bleeps, opening doors. I take a few steps back to get a better look at the crowd but she isn't there. Even if she has gotten on the right train, I worry that no one will have offered her a seat. The day is hot. What if she's fainted? An image of her shoes poking out from a crowd of concerned travellers, her hair (she'll have had it cut and coloured for the trip) pressed against the filth of the platform at Acton Town.

'Excuse me?' I jump, look down. A small northern couple about the same age as my parents. 'Do you know which direction for Leicester Square?'

I point forwards, indicating that they're on the right side of the tracks. The man thanks me and the woman smiles. They're both carrying backpacks and have string pouches for their water bottles hanging from their necks. I watch as they walk a few steps and join a small cluster of commuters. As the next train pulls in the man keeps glancing around for his wife, checking she's still with him. The train leaves. I look away. And my mother is there, her eyes already fixed on me as she makes her way from the far end of the platform, pulling a small wheelie suitcase. When she realises I've spotted her she raises her handbag arm in a quick, excited wave and I have to swallow hard at the sight of her, beaming but alone.

My father died on a Sunday afternoon, early in the first wave of the pandemic. A funny time to go, the afternoon. Once someone makes it through the night you think you're in the clear for another day, at least. He had been in the hospital for weeks. At first, he told me not to bother coming home. And then, after they put him under, my mother said it was only a precaution. It was so difficult to travel then and they didn't want to put me through the stress of quarantine. They were afraid I'd get infected on the flight. But there came a point when I had to make my own decisions, when I called the hospital and spoke to a nurse who told me that nothing was ever certain but that if it was her father – 'and it could be, you know, one of these days, it could be anyone' – that she'd be getting on a plane. So I did. And after I'd obeyed all the rules to the letter, I managed to see him, once, the morning of the day he died.

'He was waiting for you,' my mother said, as soon as the hospital called with the news.

'He was a devoted father to the very last,' said the parish priest at the sad sparse funeral mass. 'Not ending his struggle with this terrible and cruel virus until his daughter, Jacinta, was finally able to come and see him, to say goodbye.'

With only ten of us in it, the church was deathly quiet and everyone could hear the gasp that escaped me then. My mother slid a little way along the pew and took my hand. Though we knew it was probably in breach of the rules, I had gone to stay with her, and after I broke social distance to prop her up while she took the call from the hospital, we had stayed close.

In the days after the funeral, the house really did feel like a bubble. We could see the world but not quite hear it, and everything had a faint oily distortion. I tried to be for my mother what Breda had been for me when Ferdia died, a place of calm. I cooked for us both, tidied, kept a running shortlist of TV shows and films for her to choose from. She spent a lot of time in the garden, which that spring looked the best it ever had. We didn't speak much and I tried to resist thoughts of how and if I would ever get back to London, convinced that she needed me there, that I was holding back the dark tide.

But in the end, as shining spring turned to hot summer, my mother told me it was time to leave.

'Surely Lindsay is missing you?' she said, in the haze of a slow May sunset, when we were sitting out in the garden after dinner, drinking tea and getting cold but reluctant to go inside. The house felt enormous now. My father's empty recliner squatted miserably in the living room and Ferdia's room, after sitting untouched for so long, was suddenly bare, Father Richter having swept through the previous year, gathering his possessions and putting them, according to my mother, in plastic sandwich bags.

I nodded. Lindsay was missing me. Though she barely spoke about it, not wanting to intrude on my grief, in the long silences that punctuated our nightly video calls, I could sense how much she was struggling with the weeks spent alone in our flat, speaking to no one, delivering her classes to dozens of mute blank boxes.

'But what about you?' I asked, and my mother shrugged.

'I'll just have to find my way, won't I?'

When we hug now, she smells different, her usual rosewater overpowered by something spicy and expensive she sampled in the departure lounge.

'You look fantastic,' she says, taking a step back, and though I don't entirely believe her, I appreciate the compliment. I've ironed my best white shirt for the occasion but worn it, as normal, with jeans and boots. I wondered about taking out one of the summer dresses that I haven't worn since before the pandemic. But I decided against, not wanting to see the look on Lindsay's face when she saw me. She's going to join us later and I'm nervous. She's never met anyone in my family before.

'So do you,' I say to my mother. 'I like your shoes!'

They're a pair of supportive navy Skechers and she pops her foot to give me a clearer look.

'My first ever runners.'

'And how do you find them?'

'I can't believe what I've been missing out on all this time. I bought them for my walks during lockdown but now I wear them everywhere. They make travelling so easy, don't they?'

I nod, trying not to laugh, but she sees it in my eyes.

'Am I being a daft old woman?'

I do laugh then and she smiles, pleased. I reach for her suitcase and she lets me take it, though today, for the first time in years, I'm surprised at how young she seems. She's upright, energetic, shining.

'Are you ready for some lunch?' I ask.

'I'm famished.'

We patter happily enough on the short walk to the restaurant. My mother is delighted with everything: with being able to use her contactless for the tube rather than worrying about an Oyster card, with the weather, with the arrangements of alliums she sees in a florist's window. There's something so exciting, she says, about coming out of the Underground and finding yourself right there in the heart of things. It's only when we sit down to eat, in a Lebanese café I've only been to once before, that we become a little shy of one another.

'So what's the set-up here?' she asks, looking at the menu. 'Do I just get one thing? Or is it tapas?'

'We can do either. But it might be nice to share?'

'Lovely.' She puts down her menu. 'I'll trust you to choose.'

I order simply. Hummus, stuffed vine leaves, falafel, grilled halloumi, tabbouleh, batata harra, a green bean stew, a large bottle of sparkling water. Between lockdown and moving in with Lindsay, I've stopped eating meat almost completely. I was hoping my mother wouldn't notice but she's frowning at the menu as I speak. She looks up at the server.

'Will that definitely be enough for two of us?'

'Yes, it should be plenty.' The woman glances at her notepad to confirm, then nods again. 'Is it a special occasion?'

'Well, it is for me,' my mother says. 'I don't get to see my daughter very often.'

Smiling, the woman rests her hand on my shoulder. 'Make the most of it, this mama time.'

I smile. There's a note of longing in her voice that I recognise.

'So how's work going?' my mother asks.

'Good,' I reply. 'Really good, actually.'

'You prefer it to the old job?'

I nod. It's been a few years since I trained as a language teacher, starting out with English and then, after a month-long intensive program in Lisbon, adding beginners' Portuguese. Initially, I had intended the job, at a small language school in Lambeth, as a stop-gap, a way of getting myself out of marketing and keeping some money coming in while I figured out what I really wanted to do. But I've been happy. I have no plans to leave.

'It's just nice to show up every day and do something tangible for people, something immediate. Does that make sense? I mean, if I go in and I'm tired I can see that the lesson doesn't go as well, that my students don't get as much out of it. But then the flip side is that if it does go well, I know I've made a difference, I've helped them to achieve something they wouldn't have achieved otherwise.'

'I never had that feeling with teaching,' my mother says and for a moment she flattens, drifts into the past. 'You must be good at it.' I shrug. She smiles. 'And you like your students?'

'Yeah, I do. Obviously lots of the ones studying English are people who've come here to work, so they're really focused on improving and they're brilliant students. The Portuguese gang are a bit more chaotic. We get lots of Brits with Brazilian partners, or people who've just booked holidays, or retired women who love languages and are looking for a challenge. I like watching how they all engage with each other though, over the course of the term, how they start to tease each other, or help each other out.' I pause. I feel like I'm babbling but my mother watches my face closely as I speak, nodding along. 'At the end of term, I invite them all to come for some drinks and food at a little Portuguese bar near the school. The owners hosted a port tasting for us last time . . .'

'That sounds fantastic,' my mother says. 'I wish I could sign up myself.'

I take a mouthful of water, feeling myself blush a little.

'I mean, I know it's not translating in Strasbourg,' I say, which was what my father had always hoped I'd do with my degree. 'And there aren't really that many options for progression.'

My mother shakes her head. 'You can't think that way. None of us knows what we're going to get called to do, that's what I think. You've just got to follow your instincts.'

The server arrives with our hummus and flatbreads. I tear some off quickly, slightly overwhelmed by what my mother's just said. She watches me do it, then tentatively copies me, scooping up a tiny pat of hummus. I worry that I've made a mistake with the restaurant, that I'm going to have to spend the next hour pretending to believe her when she pretends to like the food. But when the server comes back with our vine leaves and falafel, my mother grabs hold of her forearm.

'This is absolutely delicious.'

The woman glances at me, bemused. 'You haven't had hummus before?'

'I have,' my mother says. 'But I didn't know it could taste like this.'

The woman laughs then, but kindly. 'Well, I'm very pleased that you like it. And I hope everything else tastes as good.'

'I'm sure it will.' My mother is still hanging on to her arm. 'Can I ask your name?'

'Sahar.'

'Is that like Sarah?' The woman's face freezes and I think I should say something, but my mother gets there herself, lifting her hand quickly to her temple. 'Oh no, I shouldn't ask you that. I'm sorry, Sahar.'

Sahar laughs again, not knowing what to make of us. 'That's all right . . .?'

'Margaret.'

'Nice to meet you, Margaret.'

My mother nods and lets her go. She tears a larger piece of bread and takes a wild swipe at the hummus, scanning the other plates as she does.

'This was a great recommendation, Jacinta. Thank you.'

I consider correcting her but decide not to.

'What's bringing you to Birmingham?' I ask instead, casually, assuming it's a visit to a church or an Irish community centre. I watch clips of her speeches every now and then. It still makes me slightly queasy, hearing Ferdia's life story being re-tooled for the cause. But she's become very good at it, by turns funny and sombre, always confident. Now though, she hesitates.

'Well, it's actually Wolverhampton I'm going to. Have you ever been there?'

'No, I haven't.'

She nods. Sahar comes back with the potatoes, halloumi, green beans.

'Thank you,' my mother says and smiles appreciatively at the food, then at me. But her face is strained.

'What's in Wolverhampton, Mammy?'

She takes a breath. 'Well, there's a girl there ... no, actually, let's not start with that. There's a woman there who's from Kildare originally but she came over more than fifty years ago now to work in a hospital. All of her family have stayed in that area and they've always been very involved in the Irish community ...' She looks up at me, inviting a question.

'That's nice,' I say, stabbing a stuffed vine leaf with my fork and putting the whole thing in my mouth. It's cold and claggy, the flavours gone sour.

'It is, yes. She seems like a very nice woman though I haven't met her yet. We've spoken on the phone.' She pauses to eat a few bites, chewing slowly. 'But then, well, this is very sad, but a couple of years ago her granddaughter was diagnosed with a glioblastoma. That's a type of—'

'I know what it is.'

'Right,' says my mother. 'So you'll know then that it's untreatable. Well, incurable I should say.'

I nod, my heartbeat high in my chest. 'How old was she?'

'She was fifteen at the time. She's seventeen now.'

I reach for more food rather than replying. And instead of going on, my mother quietly refills her own plate. For a few minutes, we sit in silence. I cut a falafel in two and eat half of it with a scoop of green beans. But the combination of crumbs and oil feels obstructive. I swallow and it all goes down in a painful lump.

'And how is she now?' I ask. But still my mother takes her time answering, dabbing at the corners of her mouth and sipping some water, before she looks me dead in the eye.

'She's fully recovered.'

Though I knew it was coming, I still feel breathless, a bit sick. 'And there's a connection to Ferdia?'

'Yes. The grandmother wrote to us early on and asked for some prayer cards. They had one on the girl's headboard and the two of them prayed to him every morning and evening.'

There's another few moments' silence. I wipe my mouth, done with the food.

'I mean, obviously, I'm glad she's better,' I say.

'Of course.' My mother smiles. Her voice is gentle. 'But it is a lot to take in.'

'Yeah.'

I take a drink of water. She goes on picking at the share plates. The café is fuller now, with a line of office workers stretching out the door, waiting to order takeaway wraps. It's noisy and I'm struggling to think.

'So sorry, why are you actually going?'

My tone is sharp and my mother grimaces slightly. 'Well, the grandmother was the one who submitted the account. We have a form on Ferdia's website, you know? Where people can report favours? Anyway, the grandmother submitted it and the girl agreed. But the parents aren't entirely certain. And because she's only seventeen ...'

She doesn't finish. I breathe out slowly.

'You're hoping to chivvy them along?'

My mother sighs. 'We just thought it might be nice for me to meet them.'

'We being ...?'

'Father Richter and I.'

'Right.'

'He does think it's very promising.'

'I'm sure he does.' The sarcasm is loud in my voice now and my mother looks away. Sahar returns to the table.

'Are we all done?' she asks, slightly apprehensively.

'Yes, I think so.' My mother smiles at her. 'And it was all delicious, thank you.'

She asks if we'd like teas or coffees. My mother orders breakfast, I ask for mint.

'We have fresh or peppermint?'

'Fresh, thanks,' I say, not really considering the choice, trying to get my thoughts in order. There's something I've been chewing over for a while, probably since the day I met Brian in the graveyard.

'OK, so I have a question,' I say to my mother. 'And I mean it genuinely, even if it sounds a bit ...'

She smiles, nods encouragingly. 'Go on.'

'Do you really believe it? I mean, do you really in your heart of hearts believe that Ferdia personally intervened to save this girl?'

She looks down and drums her fingers on the tabletop. Though she doesn't look angry, still I'm worried I've offended her. Sahar comes back, with the tea and a few squares of baklava on the house. My mother thanks her profusely. Then, still without speaking, she lifts the lid of the teapot, peers in, stirs, squeezes the bag with her spoon.

'I don't believe it in a purely literal sense,' she says finally, as she pours. 'I don't think that Ferdia can just pick up the phone to Our Lord and ask for an intervention and . . . you know . . . ba da bing ba da boom.'

This phrase is so unexpected that I laugh. My tea is halfway to my mouth and it spills over the table. My mother moves fast to mop it up with a napkin.

'Sorry.' I smile and she shakes her head indulgently. 'You were saying?'

'Well, of course, I believe that Ferdia is in heaven, and your father too.' She lifts her cup and puts the soggy napkins down on the saucer. 'But I believe that heaven is completely incomprehensible to us, it's greater than anything we could know or imagine.' She takes another sip. 'So the answer to your question is yes. While I'm not entirely sure about this specific case, I do believe in the possibility of miracles being performed through Ferdia's intercession. But how that actually works? I mean, the logistics of what's happening in heaven? That's not something I'll ever understand, or try to. That's the mind of God.'

I say nothing for a moment. She gives me a little smile, shrugs.

'You've obviously thought a lot about it,' I say.

'I have. And I've read a lot and spoken to people as well, academics and experts in sanctity.' She pauses. 'I loved theology, you know, when I was with the order. I thought that prayer and contemplation would be my favourite part, but it turned out that was the struggle.' She drifts off and I don't know what to say. I've never heard her speak about this before. 'I should have done it for my degree, really. But Mammy and Daddy thought it would only remind me of the convent, so I gave it up altogether.'

'I'm sorry,' I say quietly and she looks at me.

'I used to be so jealous of Ferdia when he was in seminary. When he came home and told us all he was learning, him and Brian. I'd feel almost sick with it.'

She pours some more tea, tar-dark now.

'What happened at the convent, Mammy?'

She shakes her head. 'I spent so many years wondering about that, you know, searching my conscience, trying to figure out why I wasn't good enough.' She glances around the restaurant. 'And now I think I was just sick. You know, I was young and I had never really been away from home and it all got on top of me. People get depressed sometimes. But no one was willing or able to help me. It was easier for them to send me away.'

'And did you really . . .?' I begin, my voice small and uncertain. 'I mean, did you really want to end everything?'

After a tiny pause, she reaches out and takes my hand.

'To be honest, I don't know,' she says. 'I don't know what I really wanted, only that I was in such terrible pain and no one seemed to notice.'

I nod, thinking about myself at eighteen, lonely, grieving, resentful. 'You must be furious about it.'

'Well,' she says softly. 'You've got to be grateful for the life you have, don't you?'

'Do you?'

She smiles at me. 'I can't imagine having lived my life without you or Ferdia. It's not hard to feel that this was what I was supposed to do.' She squeezes my hand. 'Though I know I haven't always gotten it right.'

I look down, trying to hold back tears. The skin on her hands is stretched and thin, mottled with the faint beginnings of age spots. There are so many arguments I've been waiting to have with her, accusations I've been rehearsing in my mind for years. But what is it I want her to say? What's left to gain?

'You did your best,' I say. Her hand squeezes mine again.

'I don't think I did, not always.' There's a very long pause. 'But I am trying now.'

'OK,' I whisper, and she nods, begins fussing with her handbag.

'Let me get it,' I say, patting my pockets for my card. 'You're visiting.'

'Not at all, it's my treat,' she says, opening her purse and taking out two pristine fifty pound notes, fresh from the Maynooth post office.

I shake my head. 'No one uses those. Your new friend is going to think you're a drug dealer.'

'Who's to say I'm not?' she says and we laugh. But there's a lull then while we wait for the change, a lingering awkwardness.

'Can I ask you one more question?' my mother asks. 'While we're on the big topics.'

'Sure.'

'Do you not believe at all?' She says it almost absently, looking at a picture on the wall, a faded photograph of a town on the Lebanese coast. When I don't reply she turns, with an effort, to look at me. 'Not at all?'

I shake my head slowly. The prospect of this question, from anyone in my family, has always terrified me. When I was younger, whenever I moved into a new flat, I'd visit the nearest Catholic church and learn the name of the parish priest, just in case anyone asked. But now I feel calm.

'No,' I say quietly, holding my mother's eye. 'No, not at all.'

'All right then,' she says quickly, and starts counting out coins for the tip.

'I'm sorry,' I say and I mean it. Though rejecting the Church was easy, it took me a lot longer to let go of the message, to accept that, for me, the meaning had drained away. But my mother smiles and shakes her head, blinking rapidly.

'At least we know where we stand now.' She looks down at the coins in her palm, frowns, then abruptly drops them back into her purse, leaving a ten-pound note instead. We rise from the table and she takes a big breath.

'So. Where to now?'

\*

When I wake up on the first morning of that trip to visit Ferdia, my hotel room is gauzy with winter sunshine. I pull back the net curtains to look outside and, from three floors above street level, can see the yellow and pink glow of the buildings, the traditional shutters and tiny, ornate balconies.

'This is *Rome*,' I say aloud, as purely sixteen as anyone has ever been. We're meeting Ferdia in a café nearby and I'm so excited to see him that I'm first down to the lobby, first to step through the heavy door and into the cold air, to see the old woman who's standing opposite, leaning on her stick in a silk scarf and a double-breasted navy coat that falls almost to her feet. She looks so elegant, so perfectly Roman, that I can't stop staring. I don't notice the young man standing a few metres further along the street until he shouts, 'Ciao!' in such an overblown Italian accent that I think he must be catcalling me. My friends, who've been taking Continental holidays since they were in the womb, have warned me about the men here. But then I look over and realise it's a priest. He steps away from the wall and begins walking towards me. And only then do I understand that it's Ferdia.

He doesn't look different, that's not the issue. It's that he moves differently here, as he shepherds us across lanes of traffic, placating the crazed drivers with smiling priestly waves. His shoulders are softer than at home, his hips looser. He walks ahead of us through the streets, shouting over his shoulder that we're going to a beautiful little piazza for breakfast, that he comes here all the time.

'Padre! Buongiorno!' call the waiters, gorgeous in white shirts and short aprons. And Ferdia lifts an arm in a flamboyant wave, shouts back:

'Ciao ragazzi! Como state?'

Though it's cold, he insists we sit outside – 'great people-watching to be done' – and my mother glances at me quickly, a gleam of triumph in her eyes. We had a disagreement on Thursday evening about what coat I should pack, her arguing for my padded school one and me for my black trench coat. I held my ground but as soon as we sit down I can feel the cold metal of the seat bleeding through the PVC. I'm angry with her about it, though later she'll stop outside a boutique window and insist on buying me a black quilted jacket, more expensive than anything else I own.

Ferdia leans backwards in his chair, stretches, then grins at us.

'Now remember you can only drink milky coffee in the morning here or you'll show yourselves up.'

My father laughs. 'Well, your sister only drinks hers black now. Very sophisticated.'

I smile. Though we often go for coffee on Sundays, after mass, I'm surprised he's noticed.

'Gennaro!' Ferdia waves to the nearest waiter and orders for all of us.

'You're doing very well with the Italian,' my mother says. Like me, she's shy with Ferdia, thrown off balance by all the small ways he's changed, by the weight he's put on since we last saw him and the way his eyes shine happily over the crescents of his cheeks so that, brushing his curls out of his face, he looks like the kind of good-looking young priest you'd see in a black-and-white film: delivering sacraments on his moped, drinking espresso in dusty bars and slapping old Italian men on the back.

Now he laughs. 'Hello, how are you?, a bottle of wine, please – that's about the sum of it.' My mother frowns, not sure if he's joking or not, and he sighs. 'Our lectures are in Italian, Mother. I wouldn't get very far if I didn't have enough to order a coffee.'

She flushes. There's a painful silence, then my father speaks gently, helping her through the moment.

'It's easy to forget what an educated man our son is.'

She smiles at him, blinking rapidly, and nods. Then the waiter arrives with our coffees and four enormous cream buns.

'So, I'm thinking that today we can wander around some of the ancient stuff. Forum, Colosseum, Pantheon . . .' Ferdia checks the sights off on his fingers as he speaks, playing it casual. He wants us to think he barely even notices the Colosseum now as he passes it, but he can't suppress the little smile. 'Then tomorrow I'm on duty in the college chapel. But you might prefer to catch mass in Saint Peter's?'

My mother shakes her head violently. 'Oh no. We'd much rather come to your mass, wouldn't we?'

She looks at me and I nod in agreement. My father grins.

'We've seen the fella from Saint Peter's before anyway.'

'Well, only part of a mass,' my mother adds and they smile at each other fondly, almost romantically. I look away, embarrassed.

'The poor Holy Father isn't saying that many masses these days anyway,' Ferdia says quietly. My mother leans forward in her chair at the prospect of some Vatican gossip.

'His health is as bad as they say?'

'It's only going one way,' Ferdia replies. 'You might keep him in your prayers.'

My mother's hand travels to the gold cross at her throat. 'I still think of the day he was shot. I just couldn't get you to go down for a nap that day so I took you out in the buggy instead and we walked for hours up and down the canal. And then I stopped into the shop for some milk on the way home and the woman asked if I'd heard the news . . .' Her eyes fill at the memory.

'Terrible,' says Ferdia, and my mother looks at him so intensely that he seems to struggle to hold her gaze.

'I can still see your eyes watching me, wide awake,' she says. 'Like you knew what had happened.'

Ferdia doesn't reply. There's another long silence.

'I suppose it'll be strange for you two,' my father says eventually, 'when the time comes. Never having known another pope.'

'But we're lucky to have only known such a saint,' Ferdia says. He looks at me and I make a low non-committal sound. Though the old man is part of my mental furniture, I don't feel much towards him, whereas Ferdia speaks about John Paul II like he's a special uncle, a mentor. It occurs to me for the first time that, secretly, my brother probably dreams of holding the top job himself, of making cardinal at the very least.

'Who do they think will replace him?' I ask. Ferdia shoots me a glance then looks ostentatiously over both of his shoulders, gesturing to me to keep my voice down. I feel hot, ashamed, then quickly irritated. Who does he think he is?

'Sorry,' he says. 'We're just not encouraged to talk about it.'

'Say no more then,' says my father, with his teacher's regard for the rules. But, ignoring him, Ferdia continues in an undertone.

'The word is that it'll be someone already established in the hierarchy. They won't take any risks this time, I don't think. They'll want to steady the ship.'

He lifts his eyebrows knowingly, but then quickly takes such an enormous bite of his bun that his cheeks get dusted in icing sugar.

'Stay classy, Ferdy,' I say, and he looks at me. I laugh and so does he, then we get giddy and laugh harder, until he's struggling even to chew. The smug priest is finally gone, we're giggling like children. He leans over the table, covers his mouth with his hand.

'Oh my God, are you going to spit it out?' I say, my voice hushed with mock horror. 'That will be so embarrassing for you!'

He lifts his metal chair and turns it to face away from me. It clangs back down on the cobbles and he chews rapidly for a few more seconds before swallowing and then grinning at me over his shoulder.

'You don't visit me for six years and then as soon as you're here I get nothing but grief.'

\*

Standing in Kensington Gardens, in front of the Albert Memorial, Lindsay looks a bit like a bouncer. She's wearing her heaviest boots, faded jeans and a men's canvas overshirt unbuttoned over a white muscle tee. Her fists are jammed deep into her pockets and, though I've been nervous on the walk over – trying to hide it, playing the tour guide – my body goes light at the sight of her.

'There she is,' I say.

'Ah,' my mother says. 'Lovely.'

Lindsay ambles forward to meet us, pausing to avoid a couple of skateboarders. She sets for the handshake too early and has to walk a long way with her arm outstretched.

'Nice to meet you, Mrs—'

'No, no. Please. Margaret.'

They shake hands. Then Lindsay turns and kisses my cheek.

'Hey.'

'Hey.'

My mother has looked away, is studying the monument. 'And this is?'

'Prince Albert,' I say. 'Queen Victoria commissioned it in his memory.'

'Oh right,' she says. 'Do you think I should get one made for your father?'

I laugh. Lindsay clears her throat.

'I was very sorry for your loss,' she says, and to me it sounds forced, outside her normal register. But my mother nods, appreciative.

'Thank you, Lindsay.'

I start walking, steering our awkward little group around the monument. Lindsay takes the handle of the suitcase. I haven't planned anything besides a walk through the park, towards Marylebone, where my mother is getting the train in a few hours' time.

'But just let me know if you need a breather,' I say, turning to her, thinking she'd seemed slightly winded on the walk from lunch. 'There's lots of nice little cafés and things.'

'Not at all. It's nice to be out.'

'Great,' I say, glancing from her to Lindsay, who's intently focused on her suitcase duties. I'm desperate for one of them to ask a question.

'So what brings you over?' Lindsay offers eventually and my stomach drops. It's far too soon for the miracle story. But my mother just shrugs, says something about a meeting.

'I've already bored Jacinta with the details,' she says. 'And you? Have you been working today? You're a lecturer, isn't that right?'

'Yes. Politics,' says Lindsay, then gives a longer than necessary explanation of how she structures her working day outside term time.

'Sounds like it's flexible,' my mother says.

'But a lot of work,' Lindsay clarifies and I can tell she's afraid my mother thinks she's slacking. 'Too much really.'

'Well, that's a shame.'

We walk on. As we approach the meeting of two paths, a couple of children rocket by on push scooters, nearly hitting us. Their grandparents, trotting thirty metres behind, call out an apology.

'Do you have many older students?' my mother asks Lindsay. 'I mean my age. OAPs.'

'Oh yeah, a few each year. Are you thinking of going back?'

'Jacinta and I were just talking over lunch about . . .' She looks at me. 'Well, about missed opportunities, I suppose.'

'Mammy always wanted to study theology.'

'You should!' says Lindsay and I love her for being so effusive. 'We all adore mature students because they really appreciate the opportunity to study. Not like some of the little shits.'

There's a pause and Lindsay glances at me, panicked at having sworn. I roll my eyes at her, laughing silently.

'Well, thanks for your encouragement,' my mother says. 'But it's just a notion. I probably won't go through with it.'

'You should,' I say. 'She's right.'

'We'll see.'

We all drop back into silence. I look at my watch in agony. Two-and-a-half hours to go. And then, apropos of absolutely nothing, my mother says:

'I'm actually seeing someone.'

The suitcase hits a bump, there's a loud bang of plastic on tarmac. Lindsay lunges to keep it under control.

'I'm sorry?' I say.

'I know.' My mother giggles. 'I've been trying to find a moment to tell you all afternoon but I kept losing my nerve.'

My mouth drops open. I look at Lindsay, who's barely containing a laugh. Suddenly the vibe of the whole day has clarified. My mother's energy, her charm, how young she looks. I stare at her and she frowns, suddenly worried.

'You don't mind, do you?'

'Well, that depends. Who is he? Where has he come from?'

She smiles. 'Do you remember that at the beginning of the year I started going to a poetry workshop in the library?'

I nod. She had told me about it over Christmas and I'd been pleased. 'But I didn't think . . .'

She laughs. 'Well, neither did I! And the group was nine women and him the only man. So how I ended up with him I don't know.'

She blushes and, watching her, I can't help but smile.

'What's his name?'

'Marcus.'

'Is he Irish?'

'Yes.'

'Is he religious?'

'In his own way, yes. We go to mass together sometimes.'

'And what does Father Richter think?'

I keep up my ironic tone, but still I feel guilty. It's a cheap move, outsourcing my own doubts to the priest.

'What Father Richter doesn't know won't hurt him,' my mother says and actually winks at me. It's too much. I look to Lindsay for help.

'That's great, Margaret,' she says. 'Good for you.'

My mother smiles. 'This is some impression you're getting of me, Lindsay. This isn't my typical behaviour.'

'No.' I interject. 'No, it isn't.'

'All right, Jay.' Lindsay pokes me in the ribs. 'Not like you to be such a prude.'

I laugh and shake my head. The conversation goes on and I keep smiling and nodding but I don't follow what they're saying. I feel disoriented. Ferdia's gone. My father's gone. And of course I want my mother to be happy, but if she moves on, what's left of the family? We're passing the Italian Gardens now and I look away from the two of them, taking in the ornate fountains, the marble animals. Garish Victorian borders swim slightly sickeningly in the corners of my vision and I blink a few times, rub my eyes.

'Jacinta?' My mother takes my wrist. Her grip is delicate, her skin soft against mine. I look at her and she nods towards the café on the garden's edge. 'Will we let you have a breather?'

Though her tone is teasing, there's genuine concern in her face and I smile, wanting to reassure her, to clear the strange shimmering mist that's settled between us.

'I think I need a drink,' I say and she smiles.

'Even better.'

We sit on the terrace. The afternoon is beginning to fade to evening but there's still warmth in the sun and my mother tilts her face to catch it. Lindsay stays standing, rests her hand just over my shirt collar, her palm dry and comforting against my neck.

'What's everyone drinking?'

My mother reaches for her purse again. 'A glass of red for me.'

Lindsay looks at me and I nod. 'Same.'

'In that case, you'd better get a bottle,' my mother says, producing another fresh fifty.

I watch Lindsay as she walks inside, then look around the terrace. Most of the tables are full. Two women in smart summer dresses look over a document. A young guy with a ponytail writes in a notebook. A straight couple our age clutch at each other's forearms over the tabletop. My mother clears her throat softly.

'I hope I haven't upset you,' she says and I turn to look at her. 'Truly.'

I shake my head. 'No, of course not.' But my voice is rough with emotion. I blink and tears I hadn't even noticed break down my cheeks. My father's absence is suddenly everywhere, like sand carried in on a gust of wind.

'It's just that . . . he's gone, isn't he?'

She doesn't say anything, just nods and looks out over the gardens. I think we're done speaking about it and I close my eyes, turn my head towards the orange glow of the sun. I'm surprised when I hear her voice again, low and insistent.

'For a long time I felt that my life was too long. After Ferdia's accident, the years seemed to stretch on and on in front of me. And I just wished I could get it over with. Not that I wanted to end it myself, that wasn't it. I just wanted it to speed up, you know? Or I wanted a pill I could take so I could shave a few months off sometimes.'

My jaw has clenched. I take a breath. I want to tell her that she did take time off, that she disappeared for months on end, and that the years she wished away were her one chance to see me grow up, to understand who I was going to be.

But, 'That sounds awful,' is what I say instead, trying to control my tone. And when she looks at me her eyes are so full of pain that I realise she already knows, she understands in her bones the magnitude of what she's missed, but the words aren't there to express it.

'It was,' she says quietly. 'But then your father died and suddenly I saw the reality: that I am actually getting old. That most of my life is behind me.' She plants her palms on the table. 'And I'm desperate to live what I have left, to really live it.'

I look around for Lindsay. She's already got the wine but is hovering inside the doors, waiting for us to finish. Again, my eyes fill with tears.

'I like her,' my mother says and I smile.

'Thanks. Me too.'

'She'd get on great with Ferdia, I think.'

'Really?'

She shrugs. 'It's just a first impression.'

I gesture to Lindsay that she can come back. After she's poured three generous glasses, she digs in her pocket and pulls out a fistful of notes and coins. But my mother shakes her head.

'Keep it,' she says. 'Then you can buy yourselves another drink once I'm gone.'

I roll my eyes. 'You know I'm in my thirties, Mammy?'

'I know. So you're old enough to humour me.'

I smile. Lindsay sits and we all clink glasses. For a while, we're silent, sipping our wine. I'm still getting my emotions under control and keep having to pat my eyes dry.

'I've never actually been here before,' Lindsay says. 'It's nice, isn't it?'

'Gorgeous,' says my mother. 'You could almost believe you were in Rome.'

'Have you been often?' Lindsay asks. 'To Rome?'

My mother nods. 'On my honeymoon, first. Then I've been a few times since . . .' She hesitates, changes course.

'And I'm going again in a few months with my sister. You'll have to meet Breda, Lindsay, you'll like her. We haven't taken a trip together in a long time, probably twenty years.'

'That'll be fun,' I say.

'I hope so,' says my mother. 'But nothing will ever match the time we went over to see Ferdia, will it?'

'Do you think?' I ask, remembering all the problems with the trip. I had eaten something that disagreed with me and had to leave halfway through our tour of the Vatican. My parents had been furious. Then we'd gone for dinner with Brian and Ferdia and Brian had gotten incredibly drunk. And no matter where we went or what we did, Ferdia had been faintly and uncharacteristically irritable, had always seemed to be looking over his shoulder, embarrassed by his awkward Irish family, so out of place, so carefully dressed.

We were due to fly out on the Tuesday afternoon and that morning Ferdia had come to collect us, saying he wanted to show us one last place, that although it was only a block from the Irish College, he'd saved it for our last day. On our bus journey through the city, he explained that, as the pope's seat in his capacity as bishop of Rome, Saint John Lateran is actually the most significant church in the city.

'Everyone thinks it's Saint Peter's, but it's not,' he says. 'In fact, the Lateran is the only archbasilica in the world.'

No one replies. Ferdia is a good guide, but this will be our eleventh church of the trip. We're exhausted, ready to be home.

When we arrive, the archbasilica is quiet, empty but for a group of twenty or so nuns in blue and white habits.

'Sorelli,' says Ferdia, lifting his hand, and they incline their heads as one. Though I know nuns at home, I'm taken aback by these ones, by how young many of them are, and how beautiful. I trail around after two of them, trying not to be obvious, and in front of an enormous statue of Saint Matthew, one of them whispers something to the other and they smile, reach out and squeeze each other's hands. A rush of heat bursts through me like a breaking wave. I turn away, feeling breathless and exposed, and realise that Ferdia is nearby, watching me. How much has he seen? He walks towards me and I try to relax.

'You OK?' he says, and I nod, too quickly. 'Nearly ready to go?'

As we walk slowly to the other side of the church, my body feels tender and slick. The two nuns return to the fold and we rejoin my parents.

'Beautiful,' my mother murmurs to Ferdia.

'And so peaceful,' my father adds.

Ferdia nods and looks up at the enormous vault of the ceiling. 'There's something special about it, isn't there? I come in here all the time.' We follow his gaze. And then he looks at us and smiles, as boyish and shy as I ever remember him. 'Thanks for coming. It's really nice to have you all here.'

My mother beams, my father pats Ferdia's back, we start towards the door. But just as we begin to walk, one of the sisters calls out a clear note, steady and insubstantial as a beam of sunlight. The rest take up the call and then, as though the sound has emerged from empty air rather than the women's bodies, the only archbasilica in the world is shimmering with the sound of an Ave Maria. My mother lifts her hand to her heart. We turn to listen. The sisters sing on for four or five minutes with their eyes lifted to the altar and I can feel my heartbeat, feel every tissue and fibre of my body burning with life. The women's voices rise high and higher and then, just as seamlessly as they started, they stop. Ferdia blesses himself. My father's eyes are red.

'Oh,' my mother says, the sound of her voice coming to me as though from a long way off. My body is so light that I swear I could float. I've hardly recovered when, outside, where it's beginning to drizzle, Ferdia says he'll leave us here, if that's all right, that there's an old man living nearby he's promised to visit. He reaches out a hand to my father, who squeezes it tightly, twitching as though he's tempted to instigate a hug. But he doesn't. Ferdia turns to my mother and kisses her cheek. She rests her hands on his shoulders and whispers something in his ear. He smiles, nods. She clings to him a few moments more and then he extricates himself gently and turns to me.

'It's been so good to see you,' I say, my voice cracking, and he squeezes me tightly, tiny drops of rain starting to gather on his coat. Then he's waving down a taxi for us and holding the door open as my mother and I climb in.

'See you in a few months,' he calls as he steps away. 'God bless.'

The driver pulls away, roaring up the street so fast that I miss my last ever glimpse of my brother, framed in the back window.

We've been quiet a long time. Lindsay is watching me, concerned.

'It was a nice trip,' I say and my mother nods, eyes misty.

'I'll never be that happy again,' she says and I immediately open my mouth to correct her, to break the moment with something upbeat. But then I look at her face, flushed and dreamy, and I see that for her it's true. She won't ever be that happy again. And I realise that eventually the same moment will come for me, for all of us. Maybe my mother is lucky, in her way, that she can call it to mind so easily.

Outside Lancaster Gate, the noise of the rush-hour traffic is starting to build. I look at Lindsay, signalling with a backward nod that it's time to drink up. The bottle is empty and everyone is a little tipsier than I'd like, considering there's a train to catch.

'I hope that we might go back someday,' my mother says. 'You and I.'

'Yeah, that could be nice,' I reply absently, checking the route to the station on my phone.

'Because, you know, when I think of Ferdia being canonised, and please God I'll still be alive to see it, I always picture you there with me, on Saint Peter's Square.'

The words drop like stones. For the first time all afternoon, Lindsay reaches for my hand. And then my mother covers her mouth, suddenly anxious.

'I'm sorry,' she says. 'I shouldn't have said anything. You wouldn't want to do that, would you?'

Lindsay squeezes my hand and I take a deep breath, feeling trapped between them, like I'm navigating an exposed mountain ridge.

'Well, no, to be honest. If it were tomorrow, I wouldn't come.'

My mother swallows. Her shoulders slump.

'But it is probably quite a long time away,' Lindsay says. I look at her quickly and she grimaces and tilts her head. She's taking my mother's side.

'Sorry?' I try to pull my hand away, but Lindsay doesn't let me. She lowers her voice, speaks directly to me as though my mother isn't there.

'I'm just saying, you never know what might change.'

I close my eyes, take a few breaths, and decide to trust her.

'No, I suppose you never do know,' I say very slowly, then turn to look at my mother. 'I guess we'll just have to cross that bridge when we come to it.'

My mother nods and there's light in her face as she looks at me.

'Will we leave it there?' she says.

'Yeah,' I say. 'I think we will.'

# Chapter Twenty-Three

'Well,' says Lindsay, forty minutes later on the main concourse at Marylebone as my mother's train pulls out of the station. 'That did not go how I expected it to.'

I rake my hands through my hair, my shoulders bursting with contained tension. 'No, me neither.'

She leans in to kiss me but I duck away. 'And an unexpected fucking intervention from you at the end,' I say.

'I know, I'm sorry.'

I cross my arms. 'Not a defection to Team Sainthood I would have predicted when I woke up this morning.'

'I can't tell if you're joking or not.'

'I'm not sure myself.'

'It just felt like things had gone so well up to that point ... and it meant so much to her.' Lindsay steps towards me again and this time I let her. She holds me in a hug, kisses my neck. 'Do you want to go home?'

I shake my head. I want to stay out, to cocoon myself in the noise and life of London on a sunny summer Thursday. We leave the station and start walking towards Soho, cutting through the streets at sharp, erratic angles, avoiding the worst of the traffic, the pollution, the tourists. For a long time we walk side by side, not touching or speaking. Lindsay takes out her phone, sends a few messages.

'She's going to Wolverhampton to verify a miracle,' I say after she puts it away. She raises her eyebrows.

'A good one?'

'Disappearing brain tumour, if the rumours are to be believed.'

Lindsay exhales loudly. 'Jay—'

'I like how you do that.'

'What?'

'I like how you use my name when you're about to say something serious.'

She smiles and takes my hand. 'Well, Jay. What I was going to say, and I do feel embarrassed about this, is that I don't think I'd actually understood how intense this all is. I wasn't prepared for it.'

'I don't think there was any way you could have understood, in fairness.'

'Maybe.'

'But thanks.'

We walk on for a bit, looking in the windows of the fancy boutiques and bakeries.

'I mean, what if we have kids?' Lindsay says.

'I know.'

'And they won't even be Catholics.'

'I know.'

'And their uncle is . . .'

'Disembowelled for public veneration? Yeah, I know.'

She shakes her head. 'Fucking hell, mate.'

I laugh. We've reached Oxford Street now and for a few minutes it's too noisy to keep up the conversation.

But no matter how dense the crowd, Lindsay doesn't let go of my hand.

'I don't think you've ever told me about that trip to Rome,' she says when we reach the other side.

'No, probably not.'

'Any reason?'

I take a breath. 'It was the last time I saw him . . .' I manage to say before my voice gives out. I blink, swallow, but the emotion swells high in my chest again and again.

'It was the last time I saw him,' I say finally, hopping on to each word gingerly, using it as a stepping stone to the next. 'And it was the first time I wondered if maybe I didn't like him.'

Lindsay doesn't stop walking, doesn't look at me.

'Why?' she asks and I shrug.

'He was getting to be such a *priest*.'

She sighs. 'You already know what I'm going to tell you, right?'

'Probably,' I smile. 'But give it a go.'

'He was still so young . . .'

'Yeah.'

'. . . and so much could have changed with time.'

'Yeah, I know.'

'I mean you look at . . .'

'At Brian, yeah.'

We're quiet for a minute.

'And, to be fair, you were sixteen. And to a sixteen-year-old everyone is a loser and a dickhead.'

I laugh. 'I hadn't thought of that one, actually.'

'You're welcome.' Lindsay lets go of my hand and wraps her arm around my shoulders instead. 'Always here to remind you of your own flawed subjectivity.'

'But actually . . .' I trail off.

'Yeah, I know. Actually.'

We're well into Soho now, where suits and gays and gays in suits are spilling out of pubs and on to the pavement, roars of laughter bursting sporadically through the hum.

'I just want to be outside and also sitting down,' I say plaintively. 'Is that an impossible dream?'

Lindsay smiles. We round a corner and there, outside the pub we're heading for, with his top four buttons undone and three beers already waiting, sits Clem. He gets up and gives me a squeeze.

'Sounds like you've had quite the day.'

'Where to start?' I ask, looking at Lindsay.

'Your mum's new boyfriend?'

'Oh my God, I'd forgotten! The poet!'

We laugh and clink glasses. I take a long drink, sink lower into my chair and close my eyes.

'Is he hot?' Clem asks Lindsay. 'Jay's new dad?'

'How would we know?'

'You ask to see a picture, obviously.'

'Great, yeah. Not weird at all to be like, "Hello, Mrs Devane, I'm the dyke lover you've heard all about, now can you show me a photo of your boyfriend, please?"'

'If she wanted to tell you about him, she wanted you to ask for a picture.' Clem turns to me. 'Honestly, you should have brought me instead.'

I laugh. 'She didn't do too badly.'

'Though, to be honest, we could bring you next time,' says Lindsay. 'Turns out Jay's mum is very into drinking wine and talking about Italy.'

'Aren't we all?' says Clem and they swerve off into a conversation about the next holiday he has planned: the weather, the climate, the ethics of queer tourism. I don't have to speak much, can just watch them and laugh along. We get another round in – with the cash from my mother – and then a third. No one mentions going for food, or to work the next day, even when the night starts getting cold, and the crowd of drinkers around us begins to thin.

'Anyone fancy one more?' Clem asks just before ten, when one of the bar staff comes to warn us that it's nearly time to go inside, where someone has started playing the piano, and the windows have steamed up with singing. 'Or we could go on somewhere for a dance?'

I shake my head. 'Don't think so. The vibe just now is exactly where I want it.'

'Fair enough.' He smiles and stands to go, pulling his suit jacket over his still-brilliant white shirt. Then he leans across the back of Lindsay's chair, kisses her cheek. I stand up, give him a hug. He holds me very close for a long time then takes off into the street with a backward wave. As I watch him go, Lindsay stands nearby, waiting. I turn and she takes my hand. We begin to walk towards the tube.

'I feel like I'm a lot drunker than you,' she says. 'I was so nervous, I didn't eat any lunch.'

I laugh, ruffle the back of her head. 'You're all right.'

'But I do actually want you to know that I love you. And the more that I know about you the more I love you.'

'That's a lovely thing to say.'

We walk on in silence. I think of my mother, asleep in a cheap hotel somewhere in the Midlands. Of my father, sitting in his big chair, his face in shadow. I wonder if I should have gone on somewhere with Clem and avoided this lull for a little longer. I think of Ferdia. Not as a bright-eyed little boy, a precocious teenager or a man in his twenties so absorbed in his own potential. I think of him as he would be now, in his forties, lonely and overworked and weighed down with other people's worries. Not the saint but the ordinary man he was supposed to live on to be. I take my hand from Lindsay's and stick it into my pocket. My legs feel heavy and I don't want to walk any more or to get on the tube and breathe in the stale dead air.

Then Lindsay nudges me softly with her shoulder. I stagger slightly but ignore her and walk on. She does it again. I stop to look at her and before I can speak she puts her arms around my waist and kisses me. I laugh, surprised, and our teeth clash before I start kissing her back. We wobble, both unsteady on our feet, and she walks me backwards into a doorway, where we stay for five minutes or ten, wearing the faces off each other like teenagers, letting the night catch fire.

# Acknowledgements

Ar scáth a cheile a mhaireann na daoine. This book, and my life, can only exist because of generations of people, particularly women and queers, who have fought and still fight for a freer Ireland and a better world. My first thanks, always, go to them.

Thanks to my agent, Cara Lee Simpson, who saw the potential in this story at a very early stage and helped me to see it too. To Sophie Orme, Clare Kelly, Flora Willis, Zoe Yang, Helen Reith, Vincent Kelleher, Sarah Benton and all the brilliant team at Manilla Press and Bonnier Books UK. Thank you for your care, skill and enthusiasm in bringing this book into the world, and for all your support.

I'm grateful to all the writers and thinkers, far too many to name, who have guided my thinking about this novel. Particular thanks to Professor Kathleen Sprows Cummings. I drew on her work extensively and Kathleen has also been extremely generous with her time. Any errors are, of course, mine.

My heartfelt thanks to the staff, volunteers and taxpayers who sustain the National Library of Scotland, Edinburgh Libraries and Leith Library.

In 2022, I had the privilege of winning the PFD Queer Fiction Prize and being shortlisted for Discoveries, the

Women's Prize development programme. I'm grateful to everyone involved, particularly Claire Shanahan, Lilidh Kendrick and Annabelle Wright. Thanks to the incredible community of writers I've met through Discoveries: Claire O'Connor, Claire Whatley, Emma van Straaten, Jude Reid, Katy Oglethorpe, Nancy Crane, Nikki Logan, Rachel Brown, Rebecca Taylor McKay, Ruth Rosengarten, Sadbh Kellett, Sarah Williams, Sui Annukka, Tara O'Sullivan and Zoe Norridge.

For showing up in all sorts of ways, thanks to Sasha, Claire, Michael, Barra, Sarah, Tom, Orlaith, David, Jac, Niall, Amy, Harry, Ursula, Hamish, Alba and Osian. To Debs, Helen, Fen Allan, Mark, Morag, Zara and all my friends at Portobello running club and Porty Pride.

To those who, in different ways, have been integral to the journey of this book – Eoin O Maoileoin, Gráinne Clear, Muireann O'Dwyer, Sara Ogilvie, James O'Connor, Calum Johnston, Oonagh Prendergast and Rachel Statham. Thank you all.

This is a book about the profound connections that can exist between siblings, inspired in large part by the miraculous good fortune I've had with mine. I am always grateful to and for Aoife Ní Mhaoileoin and Dearbhaile Ní Mhaoileoin.

Finally, this book is dedicated to my mother, Thecla Finnan, who believed in me as a writer from the moment I first picked up a pen. Her belief, faith and goodness are in every page of this story. Her love is with me always.

# Reading group questions

- *Ordinary Saints* opens and closes in London, with the middle set in Jay's family home in Ireland. What do you think the two settings represent, and how is each one portrayed? What impact do they both have on Jay?
- The characters all have very different – and complicated – relationships to their religion; Jay, Lindsay, Clem, Brian, and both of Jay's parents, to name a few. In what ways is religion explored in the book, and how does it impact each character?
- How does Jay's relationship with Lindsay change? Why do you think this is?
- How does Jay learn to open up to those who love her over the course of the novel? Can you think of any particular moments where she does?
- Although he has passed away, Ferdia's presence looms large over the book. How do the people who knew him feel about him, like his parents, Jay, and Brian? And what does Ferdia represent for the wider Catholic community, who leave candles at his grave and pray to him in hope of a miracle?
- How are the novel's religious figures portrayed, such as Father Richter and the priest Jay and her mother meet in Dublin airport?

- The novel depicts different kinds of queer love; from Brian's complicated feelings for Ferdia and Jay's formative crush on Aisling as a teenager and the casual flings she had when she first left Ireland, to Brian's eventual marriage to his husband Tristram, and Jay's committed relationship with Linsday. How are different kinds of queer love important in the novel?
- How are Jay's friendships, particularly those with other queer people like Clem, Cat and her hairdresser, important in the novel?
- Jay's email to Brian as a thirteen-year-old, in which she 'hypothetically' asks him for advice about her feelings for another girl at school, is particularly poignant. How is the fraught relationship between sexuality and religion explored in the novel?
- Jay learns some long-buried family secrets, including what really happened to her father's brother, and her mother's reason for leaving the convent as a young woman. How do these revelations change the way Jay views her family?
- How does grief impact the events of the book? Were there any particular depictions of grief that struck you?
- The novel is, in part, inspired by the media surrounding Carlo Acutis, the first millennial saint. What was your reaction as a reader when you learned that Ferdia might become a saint? What did you think about the process as it unfolded?
- 'I think of him as he would be now, in his forties [. . .] Not the saint but the ordinary man he was supposed

to live on to be'. What kind of person do you think Ferdia would have become if he had lived? What kind of relationship do you think he would have with Jay?
- Jay's relationship with her mother is in a very different place at the end of the novel compared to the beginning. How and why does their relationship shift? In what ways does it stay the same?
- How do you feel about the ending? What do you think the future holds for Jay?